THINGS HE HADN'T TOLD HER

BY VICKY WHEDBEE

This is a work of fiction. The names, characters, and events are either the product of the author's imagination or are used fictitiously.

Designed by Vicky Whedbee
Cover photograph by Vicky Whedbee

ISBN-13: 978-1539302070
ISBN-10: 1539302075

In this book there are words that are spelled incorrectly to show the reader how they were spoken. For example as a child may pronounce certain things, such as the word throw may be spoken as frow. It is also to show the endearing mountain dialect by some of the characters within.

Dedication

This book is dedicated to my brother, Chad Edwards, who we lost to cancer at the tender age of 24. I have had a LOT of support in this endeavor, but he would have been my Number 1 fan, if he were still with us. We miss you Chad, but you live on in our hearts!

I also dedicate this book to my father, Vic Edwards, who is now courageously battling cancer himself. I thank you Dad, for your love and support, for teaching me to never give up, and for believing more than anyone, I think, that I could do this! I love you.

UPDATE: My dear father lost his battle to cancer as well, on November 15th, 2016, about 10 minutes before I arrived to see him. I never got to finish reading him this book. Though he was in Hospice care at home, he was supposed to have several more weeks, so his sudden demise still took us all by surprise. Never lose a chance to spend time with your loved ones. You never know when that opportunity will be gone forever.

TABLE OF CONTENTS

PROLOGUE

"Don't you boys go down near that water," Chad's mom yelled as they ran outside, letting the screen door slam behind them. "*I said*, don't go near the water!" she yelled louder, an unmistakable southern drawl evident in her voice.

"Okay, Mom," Chad hollered back without breaking stride.

"Okay, Mrs. Edwards," Cole echoed over his shoulder, following Chad down the hill.

It was the first sunny day they'd had without rain or snow in over a week. A severe cold front had brought near freezing temperatures and torrential rains to the mountains of East Tennessee causing extreme flooding in the streams and rivers. The hurricane force winds uprooted trees, wrapped them up in power and phone lines, then laid them to rest on several homes and businesses. Area schools had been closed because of the storm and subsequent damage, and Chad and Cole had been cooped up inside since before the weather had gotten really bad. Now they were ready to make up for lost time.

Best friends since the first grade, the boys—now twelve years old and in the sixth grade—headed for the woods down the hill behind Chad's house. Growing up neighbors as well as classmates had— so far—proved to be an adventurous journey. They explored every inch of the woods surrounding their homes and played in Bull Run Creek every summer. But since the storm, Bull Run Creek was well over its banks, the rushing, swollen waters murky with mud and debris. Which was precisely why Chad's mom warned them to stay away from it. Normally the boys pretty much did as they were told, at least to *their* way of thinking, but the excitement of seeing the creek overflowed was more than any red-blooded, twelve year old boy could be expected to ignore. And it was pretty much *impossible* when there were *two* of them.

"Holy cow!" Chad declared, as they broke through the stand of trees at the creeks edge. It was *way* more awesome than they had imagined.

"Man! This is cool!" Cole said with breathless wonder before bending down to grab a stone to skip across the water. As soon as the stone touched the water, it was devoured by its churning depths like a gourmet meal to a starving animal. The creek, about thirty feet across, was generally calm and slow moving, and had once upon a time been used for baptisms back when their parents had been growing up, but the boys had never seen it like this! The embankment going down to the creek had completely disappeared making it at least three or four feet deeper than it normally was.

"Hey! Look at that tree up there!" Cole exclaimed, running up stream. On the opposite bank a massive maple tree had been uprooted by the storm and it's previously underground root system now stood erect, forming an impressive wall. Its gnarled branches had become impossibly tangled in the limbs of the trees that lined the creek on the boy's side. But the most fascinating part was the huge trunk that was extended across the water creating a bridge from one side to the other.

"Cole! Wait up!" Chad yelled, struggling to keep from losing his shoes that were sticking in the thick mud like giant suction cups. By the time he caught up, Cole had disappeared into the branches of the downed tree.

"Where'd you go?" Chad called out, looking around for him.

"Up here!"

Chad looked up to find Cole at least fifteen feet up in the air, camouflaged by the leaves of the toppled maple tree, holding onto the once horizontal branches that were now reaching for the sky. As he watched with trepidation, Cole wound through the limbs, and emerged on the part of the trunk that was suspended over the center of the rushing water below.

"Come on! I think we can make it to the other side!" he shouted, his voice ringing with excitement as he held his arms out like a tightrope walker for balance and began to inch farther across.

"I don't think—" but Chad's warning was suddenly interrupted when Cole's shoes—slippery from the mud—caused him to lose his footing and he fell, plunging into the muddy water below.

"Chaaad!" was all Chad heard before Cole vanished from sight.

"Cole? Cole!" Chad's voice echoed as he rushed blindly into the thick foliage of the tree, fighting his way through. "Cole!" he called again. Nothing. Finally he heard Cole choking and gasping for air, and through the surrounding branches was able to catch sight of him clinging desperately to another limb that was just below the surface of the water. The current was tugging on Cole violently, as if trying to swallow him like the stone he had fed it earlier.

"Hold on!' Chad yelled, looking frantically for something, *anything*, to holdout for Cole to grab onto. Finding nothing and with no time to lose, he realized that he would have to reach Cole himself. Without pause to consider his *own* safety he pushed deeper into the dense foliage. His only thought—to save his friend. When the icy water first began sneaking in through the seams of his sneakers and then over and inside the tops, he knew that Cole wouldn't be able to hang on much longer. If the raging current didn't win *its* battle, the frigid temperature would.

Chad fought back the snake of fear that was coiling tightly around his neck, constricting his throat, threatening to crush his windpipe, and he sucked in a ragged breath. Under him was a submerged, slippery, moss covered limb. Above him was the rough, biting bark of the branches enveloping him. Grasping the nearest one with both hands to stay balanced, he quickly stepped out closer to Cole.

"Hold on, Cole, I'm coming!" he yelled.

Cole's head sank below the surface of the water again, then popped up, before going under once more, like the red and white bobbers they had used on their lines fishing in this very creek so many times before. Chad tightened his grip like a vice around the branch with his left hand, then let go with his right and reached for his friend. But Cole was still too far out.

He could only imagine Cole's agony as he felt the dry fabric of his pants sucking the bone chilling water up his legs like a straw, and in his haste, he nearly stepped right off the limb. He hadn't realized that—under the chocolate water—the slick gnarled branch that was supporting him, bent and curved *away* from Cole instead of closer. Out of options, and with time fast becoming his enemy, he couldn't let another precious second tick by. Teetering, he pulled hard, testing the strength of the branch that had now become his lifeline. Defying his gut wrenching instinct to stay balanced, he leaned over and let gravity pull his body toward the angry torrent, hooking his feet around the limb he had been standing on, in an effort to keep from getting pulled in with Cole. The only thing supporting him now was the lone branch in his hand–which was bending precariously. He stretched with all his might to reach Cole, fighting to keep his toehold on the limb. He was thankful for the coarse canvas and the laces on his sneakers snagging on the bark like Velcro, because he knew if his feet slipped now, it would all be over…for *both* of them.

"Cole! Give me your hand!" he yelled.

With panic threatening to overcome him, Cole let go with one hand in a frantic attempt to grasp Chad's outstretched arm, but the second he did the fierce current very nearly swept him away and he desperately wrapped both arms back around the underwater limb, clinging for his life. For the briefest moment their eyes met then, and though neither of them would give it voice, each could see that they both knew it was hopeless…there was *no* possible way for Chad to reach Cole, and Cole simply could *not* let go.

While the mind numbing realization was taking hold that this creek—that they had so loved, that had been one of their favorite pastimes, that was the center of so many awesome memories—had turned on them like a vicious rabid animal, it seemed, incredibly, to become even *more* violent. As if sensing the sweet taste of victory, it took advantage of Cole's exhaustion, and with one final savage wrench, it ripped his arms loose from their hold.

At the same time, without warning, the branch Chad was holding cracked under the stress of his weight pulling on it, dropping him perilously close to joining Cole, before it abruptly stopped giving. Miraculously Chad was able to hang on and—seeing that he could now reach Cole and silently praying that the limb wouldn't break off completely—he instantly latched onto the back of Cole's coat, just before Cole went under for the last time.

Immediately, without a moment of relief, the watery monster began dragging both of them down, and—with the added encumbrance of Cole's weight—the rough bark began to dig into the soft flesh of Chad's palm. But having thought all was lost just seconds before, Chad refused to give up, and—with the muscles in his arms screaming for mercy—he pulled with every ounce of his strength, until the ferocious wet beast trying to claim his friend reluctantly released its prey.

Trembling with fatigue and weak in the knees, Chad finally managed to drag Cole and himself out of harm's way, and onto dry land. For several minutes they just laid on the ground side by side, gasping for air and shivering from the cold, their arms and hands gouged and bloody from their frightening and nearly tragic ordeal.

After a long while Cole sat up. He was still shaking badly, but he wasn't sure if it was due to the fact that he was freezing, or the lingering effects of sheer terror. He squeezed his eyes shut, yet couldn't seem to block out the harrowing scene replaying over and over in his mind. Giving up, he opened them and stared off in the distance, too embarrassed and even more ashamed to look at his friend. *How could I have been so careless? So reckless? Chad tried to warn me. What if he hadn't been able to save me? Or worse, what if he had fallen in too?*

Chad sat up then, and Cole knew he *had* to say *something*, but as hard as he tried, he couldn't find the words to express his extreme remorse for the senseless danger his actions had put Chad in, *or* his profound gratitude for the selfless danger of *Chad's* actions to save him. All he was able to manage was a paltry—but deeply sincere—"Thank you." Without waiting for the tongue lashing he was expecting and no doubt deserved, he stood up and held his hand out to help Chad to his feet. When their hands touched they each jerked back, stunned.

"Ouch!" they burst out simultaneously. They both looked down then at their scratched and bloody palms, amazed that they hadn't noticed them before now.

Chad figured by the way Cole was acting that he was pretty humiliated, so in an attempt to make light of the situation and maybe salvage some of his friend's pride, he gazed at his hands, and completely deadpan, said, "Well, I guess this makes us *blood* brothers."

Cole, still shamefaced, looked at Chad then, and he saw no blame, or anger, or accusation. Just the reassuring face of an unconditional friend. *That* was pretty cool.

"Yeah" he said thoughtfully, realizing that Chad was the *best* friend that he could ever ask for. Slowly a big grin spread across his face, and with a surge of conviction, he shouted earnestly, "Blood brothers...forever!"

Chad's Journal
June 19, 1995

What if you only got *one* chance?
What if, in life, there *were* no second chances?
Would you try harder to make sure that one chance
was successful, or would you be too afraid to take the chance,
knowing that if you failed, your one chance was gone forever?
Would the world be a better place because people tried harder,
-and succeeded more-
or would it be catastrophic,
because nobody tried at all,
afraid of failing?
What if nobody ever took a chance?
Thank God for *second* chances.

CHAPTER 1

"Cole, I've really got to get back to studying for the finals, and I *know* you need to," Chad said, placing his cue stick back in the rack.

"Oh, come on, just one more game. We'll have plenty of time to study later," Cole stalled.

Reluctantly, Chad picked his cue stick back up. "Okay, one more, and that's it. Then we've gotta get down to business. You've got a lot of catching up to do, and I can't keep saving your butt."

They were at the Old College Inn, located on Cumberland Avenue, Knoxville, Tennessee. The Old College Inn was established in 1939, under the name Brownie's Grill, and at *that* time mainly catered to the nearby railroad workers. However, over the years, as the University of Tennessee campus area expanded and student population grew, it became the hangout of choice for both the students and the faculty. Eventually adopting the name Old College Inn, it was now affectionately dubbed 'OCI' by its loyal patrons.

The plan had been to grab a bite to eat, and have a beer to celebrate Chad's twenty-first birthday. An order of hot wings, a pitcher of beer, and four games of pool later, Chad was still trying to coax Cole back to their apartment to get down to some serious studying. It was the same old story. Chad was and had always been very studious—not to the point that he was considered a *nerd*—just extremely serious about his school work. Cole, on the other hand, was a jock, through and through. He was only interested in sports, or more specifically, football. And he was good at it. So good, in fact, that—after leading his team to the championships every year he had attended Powell High School—his talent & ability had earned him a sports scholarship. But being on the football team meant that in order to play, he also had to maintain his GPA, and accomplishing *that* over the years had been greatly due to Chad. Back when they were in junior high, Cole had come really close to being kicked off the team because his grades on his interim report weren't even close to passing. Without hesitation Chad began a rigorous tutoring schedule with Cole, enabling him to raise his grades just enough to pass by the time report cards were issued. Ever since this incident—which Cole ironically referred to as his "near death experience"—Chad had taken it upon himself to monitor Cole's grades and do any necessary tutoring *before* his friend found himself in that situation again. Cole's teachers secretly worked with Chad by sharing with him any of Coles missed or failed assignments and they were the only ones who ever knew—including Cole himself—the extent that Chad went to keep his grades from dropping too low. However, nearly *everyone* knew that it was Coles lifelong ambition to one day make it to the NFL and Chad was determined to help his friend fulfill his dream.

It had proved to be a bit more difficult when they started college to get the professors and teaching staff to work with him without Cole's knowledge, but they soon came around after getting to know the two of them a little better. They came to trust Chad's heartfelt entreaty that the secrecy was only in an attempt to save any undue injury to Cole's pride. If Cole ever wondered how Chad always seemed to know what assignments he'd had issues with, it was never voiced. And though it was a ritual between them for Cole to complain about studying and for Chad to crack the whip, no words of thanks were needed either. Chad knew Cole was genuinely grateful to him for what he did to help him.

Lately though, Cole had been testing Chad's patience. Chad had been trying to stress to him the importance for him to choose his specialized classes—so that there was at least the possibility of some sort of a career *after* football—but Cole kept putting it off. To him there *was* no other career.

For Chad a career choice had been easy. He had been drawn to medicine for as long as he could remember, and—possibly because of Cole's obsession with football and the fact that Chad had never missed a single one of Cole's games—he had decided to pursue a career in sports medicine. It came as no surprise to anyone when he had graduated top in his class at Powell High School, and earned himself a scholarship as well. There had never really been any question about what college he would attend, because ever since he and Cole had become friends they had dreamed of going to the University of Tennessee together, and even though Cole had colleges from as far away as Washington State vying for his attention, for them, even *considering* any place else just felt wrong.

Chad had never been super athletic—at least not in sports like Cole—but he *was* conscientious about being physically fit. He wasn't a stranger to weights, and would work out with Cole several nights a week. But while he would limit his workouts to about an hour, most of the time Cole would still be going at it, long after Chad had gone back to his studies, and sometimes even after he had gone on to bed. He was an early riser though and ran every morning, returning back to their apartment in time to rouse Cole out of bed for class, so they were in equally good shape.

The two of them were as close as brothers, although it was impossible to mistake them as such. Cole was 6'1", had black hair and brown eyes, a chiseled jaw, and with his broad chest and tapered waist, he could have doubled for Christopher Reeves in *Superman.*

Chad was 5'8", had sandy blonde hair, and a smile that would melt your heart. He was also a born gentleman. Opening a door for a lady, helping an elderly person with their groceries, or assisting someone with a flat tire–it all came as naturally to him as breathing.

Though Cole's heart was in the right place, he just wasn't as aware as Chad of what was going on around him. He was usually so preoccupied with the last game he'd played or the next one coming up, by the time he realized he could have been of assistance, the moment had either passed, or someone else—generally Chad—had already done the good deed.

They both had their share of girlfriends, but nothing serious. Cole's first love had always been football. While the girls he dated—in the beginning—loved the notoriety of "dating the quarterback", after a while, taking a back seat to the game had a funny way of diminishing that air of prestige. In spite of the rapid turnover, there was no shortage of girls lining up to be the next "girlfriend of the quarterback". The rapid turnover wasn't because Cole was a bad guy. He wasn't arrogant or conceited. His priorities were just different than most guys his age. He wasn't even *aware* of the broken hearts that he had inadvertently left in his wake.

Chad, on the other hand, was painfully aware of it. More often than not he found himself trying to do damage control. Part of this was due to his compassion for the girls that took Cole's lack of attention personally and were heartbroken—though, in truth, a few just got really irate—and part of it was for Cole's reputation. He knew Cole wasn't doing it intentionally. So each time, Chad would seek the girl out and explain what happened wasn't really *anyone's* fault. Instead it was simply that Cole's main objective in life right now was football, and even though they probably weren't so sure of it right now, Cole *truly* was a nice guy.

Apparently his sincere rationalization took a lot of the sting out of the dejection. Most of the girls were receptive to giving Cole the benefit of the doubt. Chad vowed he would have a talk with Cole about it soon if it continued.

In spite of all of his experience in dealing with Cole's breakups, he had yet to find himself in the position of dealing with a breakup of his own. He went on dates from time to time, but between his class load, self imposed study ethics, and helping Cole with his grades and reputation, there was precious little time left for anything else. Second dates were usually few and far between. For some reason the girls never took it personally with him. Maybe it was because he made sure that they were aware of his busy schedule beforehand, and he always went out of his way to say "hi" whenever he saw them around. Or maybe it was simply because of his sweet nature in general, but they found it impossible to get upset with him. Overall, the consensus was they thought his commitment to his studies an admirable trait, as was his loyalty to helping his friend with *his* studies. They considered him not only an honorable and sincere guy, but a cherished friend as well.

Chad valued their friendship and found them all interesting and attractive, but he wasn't looking for a steady girlfriend. It never occurred to him that up to this point in his life he had yet to have fallen in love.

He sunk the eight ball. "Okay, that's it! I won! Now it's time to go. No ifs, ands, or buts. We *have* to go!" he yelled over the noise of the jukebox. He glanced around at the crowd that had grown during their game and he noticed a sign on the wall that read 'Maximum Occupancy 80'. He figured they had to be getting real close to maximum occupancy now. It was Friday night—karaoke night—and pretty much standing room only. While he was thinking they couldn't possibly fit any more people in there, the door opened again and a few more filed in. Amazed, he started to wonder how they knew when they reached the limit. Or if anyone ever really checked. Was there some occupancy cop who came around and counted people? And if there was, did they start throwing people out at random, or just shut the place d— , he lost his train of thought when he turned back around abruptly, and barely caught himself before plowing headlong into someone. Reeling from the near collision, he found himself face to face with a girl who he just knew had to be an angel sent straight from heaven above. As he was marveling at the thought, the angel spoke.

"I'm sorry! I was just looking for a seat," she said.

Then she smiled.

And just like that, all thought processes halted. Chad's brain completely lost connection with his mouth. As he tried to untie the knot in his tongue and reestablish a link with his brain, Cole jumped in, pointing to the table they had already occupied *far* longer than they were supposed to, and offered, "We have a table right there, if you don't mind sharing."

"Oh…no, that's okay…" she said, her voice trailing off. She looked back and forth between them doubtfully.

Sensing she was about to leave, Chad opened his mouth in an effort to say something intelligent and with any luck convince her to stay, but all his brain would conjure up was, "Hi pretty lady!"

As soon as the thought entered his head, she turned her attention back to him with an expression on her face that was hard to distinguish between amusement or just plain leery apprehension. That's when it became painfully obvious to him he had actually uttered those words out loud! *Oh man*, he thought, averting his gaze to the ground. Groaning inwardly, he frantically searched the floor for any sign of his runaway brain. A crimson color was creeping up his neck. *Hi pretty lady? Where did that come from*? *That sounds like something a freaking parrot would say!* He had never felt so ridiculous in his life! She was going to think he was some kind of Don Juan or something. Gathering himself, he decided to chance a glance at her in hopes of being able to read her face and maybe determine whether or not she thought he was a fruit loop! He took a deep breath, hesitated... took another deep breath...then went for it, forcing his eyes up, only to find her still watching him with the same indecipherable expression. An interminably long second ticked by.

Then she smiled.

Again.

And without further ado, Chad's brain saddled up and rode off into the sunset without a backward glance.

Damn it! What *is happening to me?* It was though every time he made eye contact with her he seemed to lose all ability to think straight! He wasn't sure what was going on! No one had ever had this kind of effect on him before. Not even Linda Sue, his first crush back in grade school who had secretly danced through his dreams every night for months and then politely refused to acknowledge his existence during the light of day.

"No really," Cole was saying. "We've got room, and look," he swept his arm around to indicate the full house, "there's nowhere else to sit," he stated, flashing his pearly whites. He was confident that if his brilliant observation didn't change her mind, his dazzling smile would. There was no mistake that he meant for her to *join* them, conveniently ignoring Chad's last remark about it being time to go. Without taking his eyes off her, Cole reached to his left and placed his cue stick back in the rack on the wall, while he waited for her to make her decision.

"I don't know..." she said, a little uneasy, looking back and forth again between the two of them, trying to decide what she should do. She was familiar with Cole because *everybody* knew who Cole was, so even though she had never personally met him, she didn't consider him a potential threat. But she didn't know the one who was acting a little strange. Despite the fact that he was very cute and *seemed harmless*, "cute" and "seemed harmless" were just latent observations and didn't mean anything. And they certainly weren't on her mental list of acceptable factors to make a sound judgment call. Trying to make her mind up quickly, she flip flopped, debating whether or not it would be wise for her to accept their invitation. She looked around the room thinking *it* should *be okay... with so many people in here... and I really need to enter the karaoke contest...*

The contest was the only reason she was there. She was hoping for a shot at the $250 prize money because she'd run a little short on cash this month. She knew all she had to do was ask and her parents would have gladly given her whatever she needed, but while they were more than financially stable, they were not, by any stretch of the imagination, what she would consider *wealthy,* and they had worked very hard for everything they had. They'd always been the most wonderful parents and exceptionally generous—though not foolishly so—when it came to her and her older brother. She couldn't remember a single time in her life when she had ever wanted for anything. Because of that she didn't take asking them for more, lightly. *I really don't want to ask Mama and Daddy for money*, she thought, *besides I need to be responsible and stand on my own two feet*. That was the deciding factor.

"Okay," she finally said. "You've got a deal."

She pulled out a chair and sat down at their table, and Cole immediately plopped down in the chair to her left. Chad watched as they took their seats and then realized he was still standing there with his cue stick in his hand like an idiot. Anxious now to get rid of it, he was halfway to the rack to put it away, when a guy who had been waiting patiently for them to finish playing, took it off his hands. On his way back to their table the *pretty lady* remark crept unbidden into his mind and he cringed again. He was unsure as to whether he wanted to sit across from her or beside her. Opting to be closer to her, he chose the chair to her right, and sat down.

"My name's Cole," Cole was saying.

"Yeah, I know," she said, smiling. "Number 7!"

Cole grinned, obviously pleased that she knew who he was. Continuing with the introductions, he gestured to Chad, "This is—"

"My names Chad. Chad Edwards," Chad interjected quickly. She reached over to shake his hand and he said a silent prayer of thanks that he had gotten his name right.

"Nice to meet you Chad-Chad Edwards," she said, teasing him. Then extending her hand to Cole, she added, "And you too, Number 7."

Cole gave her hand a confident squeeze and bestowed her with his most manly smile. Picking up his mug, he leaned back in his chair and took a big swig of his brew.

"And *my* name is Maggie Thompson," she offered in return. "So, are you guys here to enter the karaoke contest?" she asked.

Cole choked mid swallow, but Maggie politely looked away giving him a chance to recover without compounding his embarrassment.

As Cole wiped the beer from his chin, Chad waited apprehensively for the snide remark that was sure to come about the karaoke contest and the snowballs chance there was of them singing in it. Realizing that Maggie was waiting for an answer, he tore his eyes from Cole, effectively ending what he hoped was his best warning glare. He casually replied, "Umm, no... no, we just came to grab a bite to eat. We're *supposed* to be studying." He glanced at Cole who had recovered enough now to quickly avert his eyes. "But we've got some time," Chad added. "Are *you* going to sing?" he asked, hoping that she was. He could see Cole's perplexed expression in his peripheral vision.

"Well, I was going to give it a shot. Which reminds me, I'd better go put my name in!" She got up and hurried to the little stage in the back of the room where Big Rod was setting up the microphones and karaoke machine. Chad and Cole watched her as she made her way through the crowd. She was petite, only about 5 feet tall and couldn't weigh a hundred pounds soaking wet, with long straight blonde hair. It had already crossed both of their minds that she had the most gorgeous blue eyes either of them had ever seen. Cole was thinking that she was so pretty she'd make one heck of a cheerleader. That smile of hers could drive a man insane. He began to wonder if maybe that explained *Chad's* peculiar behavior. He didn't say anything though. In fact, absolutely *nothing* was said between the two of them while she was gone, because neither one of them took their eyes off of her until she made it back to the table. Just as she did, the waitress stopped by to check on them.

"Can I get you guys anything?" she asked. "More beer?" Her name was Karen. She'd worked at the OCI for several years and in her thirties, was like everyone's big sister. She was pretty and only stood about 5'2", but she was broad shouldered and solid as a rock. Despite her short stature and friendly personality, her no nonsense reputation preceded her. Everyone knew and respected her, and none of them—even when they'd had too much to drink—ever gave her any flack.

"Uh, I'll have a Coke," Chad said, feeling a bit dazed.

"You mean Pepsi?" Karen corrected, casting him a puzzled look. She'd been serving him Pepsi for a couple of years now, and knew he was fully aware that they didn't serve *Coke*. When Chad just nodded his head absently in response, she shrugged it off, amused, figuring he was a little tipsy from the beer. At the same time she was a bit impressed—proud of him in a weird sort of way—that he wasn't getting totally inebriated just because he was legal now. She'd witnessed countless other students celebrating coming of age in this place over the years and they usually didn't know when to stop.

"Yeah, me too," Cole said, staring at Chad curiously, trying to figure out what happened to him being in such an all fire hurry to get back home to study.

In the ensuing silence, Maggie was wondering why both the waitress and Cole were looking at Chad like he'd suddenly sprouted horns, until all eyes turned to her.

"Oh, I'll have a Mountain Dew, please."

"Just put it on our bill," Cole added.

"You got it," Karen answered as she hurried off.

"No, that's okay, I'll..." Maggie tried to tell her, but Karen was already gone.

∾⌘⌘⌘∾

Almost two hours later, after several pathetic renditions of *Old Time Rock and Roll,* and *Crazy*, it was Maggie's turn. While they had been waiting, Cole and Chad learned that Maggie was attending UT to get her degree in teaching, she loved kids, and she was also from Tennessee like them. Most of her family was scattered around east Tennessee, and her parents still lived in the small town of Parrottsville—located between Newport and Greenville—where she was born and raised.

When the conversation inevitably got around to Cole asking Maggie what she thought about football, Chad knew Cole was prepared for the whole song and dance about 'how much she loved it', and 'what a great quarterback he was', and so on, but she shrugged and told them, "It's okay I guess. I don't really know that much about it. I've never been to a game," she admitted innocently.

Ouch! Chad winced, sneaking a peak at Cole. The look on his friends face was comical. He would have paid good money to have a picture of Cole's bewildered expression.

It took a few seconds for Cole to bounce back from her unexpected answer. When he did, he stated matter of fact, "But you've watched it on T.V." Though it wasn't a question, he waited for her confirmation. He was sure she'd misunderstood, because, well jeez, everybody that couldn't attend a game in person *at least* watched it on T.V.

With an apologetic smile on her face that said "I hate to rain on your parade", Maggie hesitantly shook her head.

"*Never*?" Cole asked, incredulous. As she continued to shake her head, he was trying his best to comprehend how she could have gone her *whole* life without ever watching football. He wasn't stupid. He realized that probably not *everyone* felt about football the way he did, but they at least *pretended* to around him! He had never encountered someone who actually admitted—to his face—to having made a conscious decision *not* to attend a hometown game in person! Even if they couldn't make it to a game for some reason—like they were deathly ill or something—they would at least watch it on T.V.!

Noticing his pained expression and how he seemed to be struggling with her admission, Maggie tried to ease the impact a little, realizing too late how personally he'd taken it. "It's not that I *don't like* football," she explained. "It's just that I've never really thought much about it, one way or the other." She searched his eyes expecting to see enlightenment, but he looked even *more* confounded.

Cole couldn't wrap his mind around her cavalier stance regarding football. He gave up trying to. It was insanity. Deciding on a course of action, he set about to save this girl.

Maggie could almost see the proverbial light bulb go on over his head. His eyes lit up, and a big grin spread across his face.

He said, "Spring training starts Monday after next. You want to come watch?"

Surprised by how much it seemed to mean to him, she figured, *What the heck? I might actually like it!* "Sure," she said "It sounds like fun!"

"You promise?" he urged.

Laughter bubbled out of her at his persistence, "Yes! I promise!" she answered. Studying him for a moment, she got the feeling that this invitation wasn't just about some jock jumping at the opportunity to show off. Oddly enough, it was almost as if he was doing this more for *her,* somehow.

When Maggie agreed, Chad couldn't help but be excited at the prospect of seeing her again. He was a student assistant in Athletic Training and had just been interviewed and re-hired for the following academic year. Since he was always at Cole's practices and games anyway, becoming an assistant was a bonus with all the 'hands on' experience he was gaining. Not to mention being a 'return' student this year, he would actually get paid a small salary as well. The possibility that Maggie would be there was icing on the cake.

As they continued getting to know each other, Chad gradually relaxed enough to join in on the conversation, and soon there was an easy banter between them, as if they were old friends. They talked mostly about where they grew up and all the places they had visited throughout their lives.

The topic of waterfalls eventually came up and Maggie became visibly animated. She professed her love for them and her desire to seek them out. "It just thrills me to find a new waterfall! And the absolute *best* thing is finding an undiscovered one, you know? That no one else has found? Or that at least the *general public* hasn't found... hidden somewhere off the beaten path..." her voice took on a dreamy quality as it trailed off on a soft sigh. She pulled herself from her reverie when she thought of one waterfall in particular. "There's one right on Highway 321! I'll bet you guys didn't know that!" she challenged.

Their brows knit together trying to place it.

"You'd be surprised how many people don't! I can't tell you how many times my parents and I drove right by and not noticed it. But just by chance I happened to be looking in the right place at the right time, and there it was! My daddy about had a heart attack when I shouted out," she said, giggling at the memory, "but he turned around and went back and pulled over to the side of the road so we could get out. Oh it was just gorgeous! It was just roaring, and rushing so fast the water was white. I think that's the only reason I noticed it that time. It had snowed a *lot* that winter and so when all the snow started melting..." she stopped suddenly, mid-explanation, realizing she was preaching to the choir. Blushing, she said, "Yeah, you guys know all about how that works, huh?" But her enthusiasm couldn't be tempered for long, before either of the guys could ask where the fall was, she was off again. "But get this! While we were pulled over, a *bunch* of other people stopped to see what we were looking at, and this one woman said that she had lived there all her life and never knew it was there either! Everyone was taking pictures and everything! It was so neat!"

She paused for effect, and Cole jumped at the opportunity. "Where on 321 is it?" he asked, perplexed.

"Yeah," Chad intoned. "I've never heard anyone mention one *right on* Highway 321."

"Okay, do you know where Pittman Center is?" she asked them.

"Yeah," they answered in unison, nodding their heads.

Chad added, "Our parents rented a cabin near there for a weekend one summer," he explained, canting his head in Cole's direction, "and we all went together. But I don't remember a waterfall."

"Me either," Cole said, searching his memory.

"Well, there's a big wooden sign for Pittman Center, and right near that there's a little bridge with guard rails, but you don't even really realize it's a bridge since there's guard rails all over the place because of the ravines. Anyway, on the south side of Highway 321, just east of that sign, it's *right* there! There's huge boulders, and it goes up kind of high, and me and Daddy climbed up the bank on one side, and when we got to the top you could see the stream went way on back in the woods. Ooh! And there's this tree up there that's bent and leans way out over the waterfall, then curves back up," she mimicked the shape of the tree with her hands, "and Daddy walked way out on that tree over the water!"

Chad and Cole both had flashbacks to a similar incident long ago with a tree over the water, but neither of them said anything.

"Momma got a picture of him, but it didn't turn out, because it was so dark up under all of those trees," Maggie was saying, her voice filled with nostalgia. "You'll have to see it sometime, and hopefully it will be like it was the first time I saw it. The water goes right under the road and down through the woods on the other side, and even though the waterfall's pretty wide, it *is* kind of hidden because it sits back off the road and the trees all around it hide it. I guess since most people are usually looking up ahead when they're going down the road, that's how they miss it. You've got to be right on it and looking directly to the side to see it before you've passed it. Now the *last* time I saw it, it wasn't nearly as impressive because of the drought. There was barely a trickle of water, but still, once you see it you'll wonder how you never noticed it before!" She stopped then, realizing she had been talking for a while, pink staining her cheeks again. "Oh my goodness," she said, embarrassed. She squeezed her eyes shut and murmured reproachfully, "Listen to me going on and on..." She was sure that she had bored them to tears.

But they were anything but bored. Chad found himself caught up in her excitement and the cute way she began talking faster and faster as if she could take them there with her words. That, coupled with the rosy glow on her face, had him deciding then and there to be on a mission to find every single waterfall within a 100 mile radius! Hell, the *whole* state and every bordering state too!

Cole was thinking that with all that enthusiasm, she'd sure make one heck of a cheerleader for the team!

Maggie was a little self conscious after getting so carried away and monopolizing the conversation, so she encouraged Cole and Chad to talk about some of the things that they liked to do—determined to just listen—but as they shared stories of white water rafting expeditions they had been on, she couldn't help but join in again when she realized that three of them had been rafting the previous summer on the same day, with the same rafting outfitter on the same river! They'd just had different guides. They were all amazed! What were the odds?

Chad wondered how many times their paths had come so closely to crossing in the past, and if possibly—without them even realizing it—they actually *had* crossed before! His stomach clinched at the thought of how many times they could have simply missed each other.

∾⌘⌘⌘∾

Maggie was on stage now. When she first started to sing they were having a hard time hearing her. Her voice was so soft, and the noise in the room was really loud, but as she continued the noise level slowly diminished, until the only sound that could be heard was her beautiful voice.

She was singing a new song by Sarah McLachlin, about being in a hotel room and flying away from fears in the arms of angels.

Chad wasn't familiar with the song, but was sure he would never forget it.

She continued, coming to the last line of the song about some wreckage, reveries, and finding comfort.

You could have heard a pin drop when she finished. Then without warning the whole room erupted with applause. There were shouts and whistles from everyone present, male and female alike, including Cole and Chad. But when Chad glanced around at the *overly* boisterous display of appreciation from most every guy in the room, he found himself swallowing back a feeling he couldn't quite put his finger on.

Maggie was smiling modestly, clearly shocked by the crowd's reaction.

"Well, I guess this contest has a winner!" Big Rod announced, and everyone cheered and applauded again.

CHAPTER 2

Chad had an assignment in the tenth grade at Powell High School to keep a journal for a whole semester. It was an assignment that stuck with him. He'd continued with it, jotting down his thoughts and feelings, finding it kind of relaxing, a sort of release. He didn't write every day, but he'd still accumulated several journals over the past four years that he kept in a box tucked safely away in the back of his closet. For the past few days though, writing in his journal had failed to deliver the desired effect.

Unable to sleep, he kicked off the covers and rolled out of bed, deciding to go for a run, thinking maybe it would help to clear his head. It was Sunday morning, and he hadn't gotten a good night's sleep since last Thursday night–the night before they'd met Maggie at the OCI. Ever since then he hadn't been able to stop thinking about her. Those big blue eyes, her soft voice with that country twang, and the song she had sung kept echoing in his head. Every waking moment, she'd been in his thoughts. It was the strangest thing. He felt as though he'd known her all his life. But there was something *more* to it than that. It was a little disconcerting, and he was having a hard time figuring out what to make of it. When he finished getting dressed, he slipped out of the room, closing the door quietly, careful not to wake Cole.

Their apartment was a 15 X 25 foot efficiency they had rented off campus. Their landlord rented exclusively to college students, and the rooms were much like the dorms at Hess Hall on campus, down to the cook top, mini fridge, and microwave that every college student familiar with dormitory life considered their basic survival equipment. The one exception with their rental from the dorm rooms was the tiny space that housed an actual cabinet with a sink, and a small round dinette set that wobbled because the legs were uneven. The apartment was on the ground floor with the front door on the west side of the building. Upon entering said door, to the right was the makeshift "kitchen and dining area", and on the immediate left was a wall, behind which was a bathroom and shower that was so small when you turned around you bumped into yourself.

When they first moved in, the room beyond this section looked like a mirror image, separated by an invisible line down the middle. On each side there was a built out closet, if you used the term *closet* loosely; they were more like the lockers they'd had in high school. Then, snuggled up beside the closets, they each had a chest of drawers. Next, hugging opposite walls, were twin beds with no headboards, allowing them the added luxury of deciding which direction they wanted to sleep. Finally, on the far east wall sat two desks, side by side, under two windows with blinds that were presently closed to block out the morning sun.

Now however, the mirror image more closely resembled a before and after picture. Chad's side of the room—on the south wall—was neat and orderly, his books and papers stacked squarely on top of the desk, pens and pencils gathered in a mason jar, the seat of his desk chair pushed evenly beneath the desk top. The only thing not in order, was his unmade bed, the twisted covers evidence of his restless night.

Cole's side of the room was a sharp contrast. Clothes hung from his desk chair, some had fallen to the floor. Books were scattered across his desk, a jumble of papers stuck in between the pages, and there wasn't a pen, pencil *or* mason jar in sight. And, unlike Chad, Cole was tangled *amongst* his twisted covers, sleeping soundly.

Chad made his way down to the street, and started his usual route from their apartment on Laurel Avenue, running east to Twelfth Street, then headed north up Twelfth to Forest Avenue. He turned west on Forest and ran to Sixteenth Street, where he usually headed south back to Laurel, but he continued past Sixteenth to Seventeenth. Up ahead, he noticed several people making their way inside Fort Sanders Baptist Church. For a moment he considered turning around, feeling guilty that he was running instead of attending church like them, assuming that everyone who saw him would be thinking the exact same thing. But then he decided, *if anything, they'd probably just invite me inside.* It was then that he spotted a girl up ahead with long blonde hair. His heart started pounding–not from his run, but from the possibility of it being Maggie. He slowed his pace, then came to a complete stop. He wasn't sure if it was her, but if it was, did he really want her to see him like this? All hot and sweaty? For a moment it seemed the decision was about to be taken out of his hands when she glanced over her shoulder and looked directly at him, but she looked back ahead and continued walking up the walkway to the church. It was definitely Maggie, and she didn't even acknowledge him!

Deflated—with all concern over his appearance forgotten—he was about to call her name, when she looked back again.

"Chad?" She turned, and cutting across the grass, she walked back to him, smiling. "Hey! How are you?"she asked. He thought she sounded surprised—and looked happy?—to see him. She was wearing a pastel floral print dress, white strappy sandals with heels, and a dainty little white purse was suspended from her shoulder by a long strap. He swallowed, drinking in the vision headed toward him, but the closer she got, the more he focused on her little purse. Wondering what in the world she could fit in that little thing, he realized she'd asked him how he was, and just like before his brain went on hiatus. His mouth absolutely refused to work. *Say something!* he thought to himself nearing panic. Stammering, he finally managed, "G...Good. I'm good...*You* look great!"

"Thank you!" she said sincerely. Still smiling, she looked around. "Isn't it beautiful out today?!" her voice rang with a whimsical exuberance. She closed her eyes and inhaled deeply, breathing in the warm spring air.

"Yes," he agreed, totally entranced by the sight of her. "Beautiful," he added, though it wasn't the *weather* he was referring to.

It was unusually warm for this time of year. Just two weeks prior the town had been coated in a few inches of snow, which was equally unusual for Knoxville. The warm weather was a pleasant welcome after the long cold winter.

Glancing down at his running shoes, she said, "I see you're a runner." She looked intrigued.

"Every morning. Weather permitting" he answered. *All right,* he thought, *you can do this! Let's go for more than two words at a time now.* It was happening again! His legs felt like they were made of Jell-O! His brain seemed to shut down. He just didn't understand it!

"That's so neat! I wish I had the discipline to do that," she said earnestly.

Chad knew he had to overcome this complexity he was feeling real quick or run the risk of her thinking he was loony tunes forever more, so he made a split second decision to ask her if maybe she'd like to try running with him sometime, when she said, "Well, I really need to get inside. I'm going to be late. See you tonight?"

"Tonight?" he asked, puzzled.

"Yeah! I ran into Cole yesterday, and he invited me to have Chinese tonight," she explained. "Sorry, but I've gotta run!" she apologized, reaching out to touch his arm briefly. "See you later!" she called over her shoulder as she was turning to hurry inside.

Frozen in place, he watched her go, wondering why Cole hadn't mentioned running into her.

Or that he had invited her to have dinner with him.

On Sunday night.

Chinese night.

Sunday night Chinese had been a ritual of theirs since moving into the apartment last year. Time they reserved for just the two of them to chill out and catch up. No studying, no talking about school, just two best buddies hanging out.

After a moment and seemingly of their own volition, his feet began to carry him back to his apartment, slowly at first, one step at a time, until eventually reaching his normal running pace. He was a bit surprised when he found himself at their front door, and after opening it, he could see that Cole was still sleeping. Not bothering to be quiet, he shut the door loudly and went over to his desk, pulling open the blinds on the window above, flooding the room with sunlight. The sudden brightness finally roused Cole from his slumber. "What's up, man?" he mumbled irritably, pulling the covers up over his head.

Chad didn't answer. He sat down at his desk and opened a book, but he couldn't focus on the page. He and Cole had had their share of getting on each other's nerves before and sure, there had been minor disagreements or differences of opinion, but the air always cleared quickly. And yeah, lately he had been frustrated with Cole for procrastinating about his major and the girlfriend thing, but they'd never had what could be called a real argument before. This was the first time he could ever remember feeling so…what? mad? hurt? jealous? Confused, he tried to determine if he was upset because Cole had asked someone else to go with him for Chinese, or if it was because it was *Maggie* he'd asked. Truth be told, he didn't even like Chinese all that much! In the beginning, he'd only gone because he knew it was Cole's favorite, then it just sort of became what they 'did' on Sunday night. A guy thing. Now Cole was going with Maggie. Maggie! Of all the girls he could have asked, it had to be Maggie.

He'd thought Maggie was different. Not because she seemed so sweet and down to earth, but mostly because she hadn't appeared to be the type to be 'star struck' by Cole! He shook his head in exasperation. Well, he'd obviously been wrong about *that*, hadn't he! Exhaling with a huff, he dragged his hand down his face, and tried to tune in on the book in front of him, resigned to just forgetting about Maggie and Chinese night! All of it! But damn it—he slammed the book shut—that didn't mean she deserved to have her heart broken like all those other girls! Cole Rivers was his best friend, but he'd be damned if he would just sit by and watch him break her heart like he'd done with all the others.

The loud slap of the book had Cole pulling the covers down just below his eyes. He raised his head a little, squinting from the light. With the covers still over his nose and mouth he muttered a muffled, "Hey! You think I could get some sleep here?"

But Chad had other things on his mind and letting Cole sleep wasn't one of them. Uncharacteristically letting his annoyance and confusion get the better of him, he jumped in with both feet, answering Cole's plea with a question of his own.

"When were you going to tell me you were taking Maggie for Chinese tonight?" he asked, his voice loud and tense.

Cole threw the covers back and rose up on his elbow. "Is *that* what this is all about? What's the big deal? Yeah, I asked her to join us. I didn't think you'd mind."

After a beat of deafening silence, Chad said sheepishly, "Us?" realizing now he must have had it all wrong.

"Yes, *us*. What? Did you think I was going to tell you to stay home? Look, if you don't want her to come, I'll—"

"No!" Chad burst out, then added more calmly, "I mean, no...it's fine. Sorry! I was just a little surprised you didn't mention it, that's all," he said contritely with a chuckle and half grin.

"*Okay,* then! Can I *please* get some sleep now?" Cole asked. He collapsed back down and pulled the covers over his head again.

Pangs of a guilty conscience for his misconstrued assumptions racked Chad as he twisted back around in his chair, but by the time he was facing his desk again he had moved on to more pressing matters...*They wouldn't want* me *along if they were interested in each other!* he thought triumphantly, mentally high fiving himself. *Right*? he immediately floundered

∾⌘⌘⌘∾

Later, after Cole got up and showered, Chad learned they were meeting Maggie at the restaurant at seven. Cole told him he had offered to pick her up, but she'd said she was familiar with the place and would just meet them there.

At seven o'clock sharp Cole and Chad pulled into the parking lot. Maggie was already there, standing outside the front door, waiting. This time she was wearing a blue and tan print shirt tucked into flare legged jeans with a brown leather belt. On her feet, she wore brown open toed platform heels, which Chad noticed because her pink painted toenails were peeking out from under the hem of her jeans. He thought she looked just as beautiful now in blue jeans, as she had dressed up for church that morning.

"Hey, you two!" she said in greeting as they approached.

"Hey, yourself," Cole teased, ambling up to her.

"Hi," Chad answered with a smile. "Been here long?"

"Nope, I just got here," she replied cheerfully. "You're right on time!"

When they reached Maggie, Chad restrained the crazy urge he had to hug her and instead concentrated his efforts on opening the door for her, taking advantage of the opportunity to admire her reflection in the glass.

They stepped inside and were immediately seated at a table by Ling Chao who owned the restaurant with her husband. She was a petite Asian woman dressed in a traditional red silk Cheongsam blouse with a plum blossom pattern and black silk pants. Her long black hair was pulled back in a sleek braid that hung well below her waist. She looked as if she had just stepped off the pages of a vintage Mandarin fashion magazine.

In addition to running the restaurant in general, Ling did her share of the cooking, and more often than not, was the waitress as well. Despite the fact the restaurant was normally pretty busy, it was on the small side and after years of experience, the husband and wife team had fine tuned their business to a point of precision that didn't necessitate the use of outside help. Though they *had* been known, from time to time, to hire a desperate student looking for some work to make ends meet, simply because they didn't have the heart to turn them away. After all, it was the college students that comprised at least fifty percent of their customer base.

Maggie took a seat, Chad sat down across from her, and Cole sat to her right.

After taking their drink orders, Ling left them with menus and went to get their refreshments.

"So, what do you recommend?" Maggie asked, perusing the menu with interest.

"The Moo Goo Gai Pan is really good, and the Kung Po Chicken is *excellent*," Cole offered.

"All I can vouch for is the *Vegetable* Lo Mein and fried rice," Chad said, putting emphasis on the word vegetable. "And the egg rolls," he quickly added, "they're really good."

Maggie looked up from her menu at Chad. "Why did you say "*Vegetable* Lo Mein" like that? Are you a vegetarian?" she asked, curious.

Chad glanced over both shoulders then leaned closer and whispered, "No, I've just heard the stories...*you* know."

After a moment's hesitation, she realized what he was insinuating. She laughed out loud and said, "Oh! Come on! That stuff's not true."

Cole and Chad didn't crack a smile. They sat with looks on their faces that clearly said 'I wouldn't be so sure if I were you'.

Her smile slowly transformed into a look of concern, as she looked back and forth between them. "*Is* it?" she asked naively, suddenly worried.

They finally burst out laughing and she rolled her eyes. "Oh, ha, ha. You guys are *sooo* funny," she replied dryly, acting put off.

Neither one of them knew Maggie well enough yet to know whether or not she could take a joke, but only time would tell. They went back to checking out their menus. Innocently enough, as Chad and Cole began to bravely toss around some of the more exotic options, one thing led to another and it somehow morphed into a game of dare between them. Maggie joined in, playing along, sure that they were only joking around, each one coming up with a more outrageous selection. Some of the items she couldn't believe were even on the menu, unaware until then, that anyone *could* eat, never mind *would* eat these things, at least not willingly. As the game of dare progressed however, she couldn't help but begin to wonder if the guys were seriously going to go through with their choices. She'd be really impressed if they did, although admittedly, a little surprised at the lengths it seemed they were prepared to go to outdo each other. She wondered if they were this competitive all the time or if her presence had something to do with it.

Ling came back to take their orders and Maggie cleverly deferred by asking the guys if they would go first. They agreed, and Cole started by ordering duck tongue with chive flower, and braised shark's fin with bamboo fungus soup, then with a glance at Chad, he threw in some squid jerky for good measure. Chad, undaunted, ordered blood sausage, sea cucumber, and bird's nest soup. Maggie kept her eyes averted, concentrating hard on keeping a poker face until it was her turn. Feeling their eyes on her, no doubt curious as to what she was going to order, she looked up at Ling, smiled sweetly and said, "And *I* will have the *Vegetable* Lo Mein."

She almost lost her composure when she risked a glance at Chad and Cole, and would have loved to have known what was going on in their heads because judging by the looks on their faces they had already eaten what they had just ordered, but she quickly excused herself to go to the ladies room.

Walking away, she was thinking it would serve them right to have to eat that stuff they ordered for getting so carried away, but she just didn't have the heart to make them do it—or the stomach to watch them either, for that matter—so as soon as she was out of their sight, she rushed to catch up with Ling and asked her to change the guys meals to something that they normally ordered. Ling agreed without question and smiled knowingly.

∾⌘⌘⌘∾

Their food arrived quickly and when it was placed in front of them, Maggie watched with veiled eyes as looks of confusion flashed briefly across their faces, followed almost instantaneously by ones of pure relief. In perfect synchronization—as if it had been practiced for weeks—they looked up at Maggie and their gratitude was palpable.

They were met with an expression of total innocence from Maggie. "What?" she asked demurely, taking a sip of her drink.

Chad and Cole glanced at each other with unspoken understanding, both thinking, *"Oh yeah, this girl is good!"* With wide grins they grabbed their forks, anxious now to dig in. They stopped short when they eyed Maggie unwrapping and snapping apart her chopsticks. Without missing a beat they each quietly laid aside their forks and nonchalantly unwrapped their chopsticks too.

The mood was considerably lighter after Maggie's merciful rescue, saving them from the embarrassment of a potentially disastrous bout with their sudden case of machismo. They were able to relax and enjoy their dinner and each others' company. While they ate they talked about their classes, their upcoming finals, and how they would be spending the summer. Chad and Cole told Maggie they were going to stay near campus for summer break because Cole had training starting shortly after the semester ended. Since they knew they weren't going to be free for the summer, they'd spent spring break with their families.

"So, what about you, Chad? Why do you have to stay too?"she asked.

"Well, a couple of reasons actually," and he went on to explain to her about being a student assistant and how that meant he'd also be taking part in the training. "I've gotta learn how to patch up my buddy here, in case he scrapes his knee," he joked. "I also enrolled in a few summer classes that were available.

"Wow! That's ambitious! It sounds like you're going to have a full plate. I'm impressed!" she remarked.

Chad felt himself melt inside just a little, and canting his head, he shrugged his shoulders as if it were nothing. It was a classic "awe shucks, ma'am" moment.

During this entire exchange, Cole was preoccupied with picking up more than two grains of rice at a time with his chopsticks.

"Well, I'm going back home for about a month," Maggie said. "To help my parents on the farm. I'm really excited! I mean, I love being at school and all, but I miss being able to help out my parents and my brother–just being with them in general, you know?" Her face radiated warmth and affection as she spoke about her family.

"What about all those boyfriends you're going to have to make time for?" Cole teased playfully.

Chad witnessed the tenderness reflected in her eyes doused by a wave of pain when the conversation innocently turned to her private life. The question obviously caught her off guard, and a raw wound was momentarily exposed. She recovered quickly though, and this glimmer of unmasked emotion was tamped down as quickly as it had surfaced, replaced by her captivating smile and light hearted personality, leaving Chad to wonder if he'd just imagined it.

As casually as if she were merely commenting on the weather, she went on to acquaint him and Cole with that facet of her life. "I haven't been in a relationship for several months. The last one ended very badly. I discovered "he who shall remain nameless" had not one but two other girlfriends, one of which was four months pregnant."

Chad and Cole glanced at each other, then turned their attention back to Maggie and continued to listen quietly.

"I happened to be in Wally-world picking up baby wipes..." she stopped mid sentence, seeing the look on their faces. It was a cross between polite awkwardness and shock. "I keep them in my car for emergencies and to be able to clean my hands." She couldn't help but giggle when they both visibly sighed in relief.

"Anyway, where was I?," she asked, shaking her head to clear it. With her eyes focused intently on the bottle of soy sauce in the center of the table, she picked up where she'd left off, and it was apparent that she was visualizing the scene in her mind again. "I was walking down the aisle to get the wipes, and I couldn't help but notice this adorable couple with their backs to me, lovingly picking out baby items. They were so affectionate. It was sweet. I was really touched." With that said, she looked up and made an attempt at a smile that didn't quite make it to her eyes. She swallowed hard. "Then *he* turned around. Looking right at me was my boyfriend of seven months." She paused to take a sip of her drink.

Chad tried to imagine how distraught she must have been when she had been struck with the sudden realization that this heartwarming scene was being played out by, none other, than her *own* boyfriend!

Cole glanced up—halting his attempt to spear a piece of chicken with his chop stick—and noticed the sympathetic look on Chad's face. Realizing the gravity of what she had just told them, he pasted what he hoped was an appropriate amount of concern on *his* face. He felt bad for her. Really, he did. But he was hungry! Keeping his eyes on her to let her know he was listening, he pushed the chopsticks under his napkin, picked up his fork and scooped up a heaping bite of fried rice.

Maggie didn't tell them how she forgot her wipes and blindly made her way out of the store and back to the privacy of her room before succumbing to the humiliation and heartbreak of her revelation. Shrugging her shoulders she said, "It was just as well. I found out about girl number two from a friend of a friend. To this day he's made no effort to contact me, no explanation, no goodbye, nothing. I *do* feel fortunate *now* though, that I caught him red handed. There's no telling how long I'd have been in the dark if I hadn't." She summed up by admitting that, in regard to the pregnant girl, she had struggled for a while with indecision as to whether or not she should tell the girl that her baby's father was a low life jerk, but ultimately decided to stay out of it and instead pray that he would change his ways and everything would work out. "The last I heard, they were still together and had a beautiful baby, so I hope," she said, holding up crossed fingers, "that for the sake of the mother and child, I made the right decision."

"All right, enough drama!" she said. Then her eyes lit up. "My Aunt Sylvia always has an apple stack cake waiting for me every time I come home, and you've never had apple stack cake until you've had my Aunt Sylvia's!" she said, changing the subject.

Chad was still caught up wondering what kind of idiot her last boyfriend was, and his heart sank when Maggie started talking about the apple stack cake because he remembered she'd told them she would be gone for a month.

"Hey! You said you'd come to watch when we start training," Cole accused, pretending to pout.

"And I will, as soon as I get back," she assured him.

∾⌘⌘⌘∾

After they had finished eating, Ling returned with the check on a little black tray with three fortune cookies on top.

"You like?" she inquired about their dinner, as she stacked their empty plates.

The three of them replied that everything was great. With her hands full of dishes, Ling left them to their fortunes, but not before sending Maggie a sidelong glance with a sly smile and wink. The guys were oblivious to the exchange between Maggie and Ling, their attention now on the cookies Ling left behind and the goofy fortunes that they held.

They graciously waited for Maggie to choose the one she wanted and they each grabbed one of the two left.

"Read yours first," she urged Cole.

She didn't have to ask twice. He already had the cellophane wrapper removed. He broke open his cookie, popped a piece of it in his mouth, pulled out the fortune and read aloud, "PRESSURE: turns coal into a diamond."

"Hey!" Maggie exclaimed. "How cool is that?!" She spelled it out. "C-O-A-L…C-O-L-E. Awe, are you gonna be a diamond someday, Cole?" she teased in a singsong voice.

Chad laughed, and Cole, feigning offence, said charmingly, "For your information, I already *am* a diamond."

"Oh, really?" she asked dubiously. She looked at Chad for confirmation. "Is that right, Chad?"

"Oh, without a doubt," Chad validated, laughing good naturedly. Cole beamed proudly.

They both prompted Maggie, "Read yours!"

"Okay!" She anxiously broke open her cookie, dropping the pieces on a napkin and pulled her fortune out. "Let's see..." she said. Pausing, she turned it right side up, then slowly read out loud, "It says, "A Fortune *Foresees* Your Future...In Your Future, *Four C,S* Are Your Fortune." She looked a little puzzled, then chuckled. "Huh, there's a typo in this," she murmured almost to herself.

"What kind of typo?" Cole asked. "And what the heck does four sea's mean anyway? Like the 'Red Sea'? 'Chicken of the Sea'? What?"

"Not sea, s-e-a, you goof. 'C' as in the *letter* c," Maggie spelled it out for him.

"What's the typo?" Chad asked.

"Well, it's got a comma instead of an apostrophe where it has four c's. The *letter* c," she emphasized again for Cole's benefit, casting a glance in his direction. In an attempt to explain it better, she said, "It's got the c, but instead of an apostrophe, there's a comma and then the s, but the s is capitalized. So instead of capital C, apostrophe, little s, it's got capital C, comma, capital S. Here, look. That would be easier," she said, handing it to Chad. "I mean, it's no big deal. I just have this *thing* about stuff like that," she added as Chad reached for it.

Temporarily forgetting the fortune she'd just handed him, he asked, "Stuff like what?" He was eager to learn all about her and *any* stuff she a *thing* with.

She leaned forward to answer his question. "Okay, say you're watching a movie and on screen two people are alone in a bedroom..." She instantly had Cole's full attention. Continuing, she said, "and they're having an argument..." She lost Cole again. "...and the camera is going back and forth between them and behind the first one there's an unmade bed, then the camera cuts briefly to the second person and when it cuts back to the first one, suddenly the bed's made up behind them! And then maybe in the next shot, it's unmade again! Stuff like that. It drives me crazy that I notice it. Most people don't."

Chad was nodding his head in agreement, thrilled that he had this in common with her. "Yeah! I've noticed stuff like that a bunch of times!"

"Really? Does it make whoever you're watching the movie with nuts when you point out the mistakes?"

Before Chad could answer, Cole interrupted, snapping his finger. "I've got it! I know what your fortune means!" he declared, as if it were still the topic of conversation.

Chad and Maggie looked at him, then back at each other shaking their heads at his childlike exuberance and the fact he was still stuck on making sense out of her crazy fortune.

Deciding to play along Maggie leaned back in her chair and gave him her full attention. "Okay, so what does it mean?" she challenged, crossing her arms over her chest. When he wasn't looking she glanced at Chad and winked, inviting him in on the charade.

Chad smiled discreetly in return, accepting her invitation. At least that's what anyone watching Chad saw on the *outside.* On the *inside* his heart was turning cartwheels, his stomach was doing flip flops, and there was a full blown party going on complete with chips and dip, courtesy of one little wink!

Unaware of Chad's party and eager to share his brainstorm, Cole sat up a little straighter and cleared his throat. "Okay, four c's in your future, right?"and without waiting for her to answer, he began. "Well, there's College," he stated and held up his left hand with his index finger extended. He paused to look at each of them in turn to make sure they were following him. Confident that they were, he continued. "Cash," he revealed next, adding his middle finger to his index finger as if he were holding an invisible cigarette. He was clearly pleased with himself and his eyebrows inched up a notch for dramatic effect before his big reveal. "And Cole!" he announced, splaying his arms wide like a magician after pulling the rabbit out of the hat.

Maggie and Chad exchanged a glance and it was all they could do to keep straight faces.

"College, cash, and Cole, huh?" Maggie struggled to say without laughing.

"Um…that's possible, I guess," she said, thinking he was just too cute! She didn't want to burst his bubble, but she just had to know. Clearing her throat she hesitantly asked, "But…just out of curiosity, what happened to the *fourth* c?"

Cole's look of triumph turned to a blank stare. He was silent for a moment. You could almost see the wheels turning. Suddenly he slapped his palms on the table and stated matter of fact, "*Duh… Camaro…?*"—like it was a no brainer—referring to his car, a '68 Camaro that he and Chad had restored. It was so absolutely ridiculous that for a second Maggie and Chad were taken aback, wondering who was kidding who. He looked totally serious! For the life of them they could not keep from cracking up.

Maggie finally caught her breath and giggling in between every few words, she managed, "Well…I don't know about all that...Why Cole? Why not Chad? He's a 'c' too! Where's his part in this?"

"Yeah, what about me?" Chad chimed in. He tried his best to look hurt but was unable to pull it off with his face contorted from struggling to not to burst out laughing again. It reminded him of the time back when he and Cole were about eleven or twelve years old. They were in church one Sunday morning and old Mr. Waddell, sitting in the pew in front of them passed gas. Startled, at first they watched for everyone else's reaction, but apparently they had been the only ones to hear it because no one else so much as flinched. One glance at each other was all it took for the giggles to start, so—afraid to look at each other without losing it—they both took a deep breath and held it with their cheeks puffed out like chipmunks, until their snickers and snorts and quaking shoulders brought them a warning glare from Chad's dad. They were barely able to keep from laughing out loud, but the harder they'd tried *not* to laugh, the harder they had. Just about the time Chad's unsuspecting father turned his attention back to what the preacher was saying, the smell crept up and over the pew, and when he caught a whiff of it his face wrinkled up like a prune! It was hilarious and despite their best attempts, a muffled cackle escaped Chad. Cole blew raspberries before clamping his hand over his mouth, earning them several turned heads from various members of the congregation in front of them. Which, brought a withering look from Chad's mom, who had no clue as to what had transpired. At this point Chad and Cole knew they had no other option but to high step it out of the sanctuary. In the freedom of the outdoors they doubled over laughing as soon as the door shut behind them. Their laughter died on their lips though when they looked up to find Mr. Edwards hot on their heels. They stood soldier straight, sure that they were in for it *but* good, because he looked like he was about to explode. They glanced at each other as if trying to decide whether or not to run, but Chad's dad no sooner made it out the door before he let out a howl and collapsed in stitches. Going weak in the knees they sank to the ground too. Before long the funny part caught up to them again. Chad was pretty sure he'd wet his pants a little, but wasn't sure if it was from laughing so hard or seeing his dad come out the door. Thankfully, trying not to laugh now wasn't quite as bad as that time in church—and the consequences not nearly as dire with his mom not there to answer to this time!

Cole was openly flirting with Maggie but Chad wasn't concerned. He'd already jumped to one wrong conclusion that morning when he found out Cole had invited Maggie, and this was the Cole he knew and expected. This was Cole just being himself.

Cole amended his answer again, not ready to give up. "Okay then, college," he began, thinking it over carefully, beginning with his thumb this time to count it off. "Cash," he added slowly, concentrating, and raising his index finger. Then, in rapid succession, he spouted, "Cole, Camaro, and Chad!" adding a finger with each count. Finished, he sat beaming and holding up *five* fingers.

It was clear that, for some reason tonight, math was not Cole's strong subject! Chad and Maggie just looked at each other for a moment poker faced.

Realization dawned. "Football," Chad said. "It wasn't about football..." That was the only logical explanation.

Enlightened, Maggie nodded. "Gotcha."

Again, Chad felt as though the clock had been turned back to that day in church, except that *this* time *Maggie* was his accomplice. They couldn't contain it anymore. They lost it. The situation was compounded tenfold by Cole laughing uproariously with them, having absolutely no idea that they were laughing *because* of him! And had they known that he was saying under his breath, "*what the* hell *has football got to do with the sea?"* they would have been rolling on the floor!

Every glance at each other had them laughing harder. Physically beginning to hurt, they had to force themselves not to look at each other.

"Think about something else! School or something!" Chad begged, tears running down his face.

They each tried concentrating on something serious, just so they could catch their breath. They were finally getting it under control when Maggie realized Chad hadn't read *his* fortune yet.

"You still need to read your fortune!" she reminded him, noticing as she said it her cheeks were tender from laughing so hard!

Chad picked up his cookie. "I'm almost scared to, after yours and Coles! They were *way* too profound for me! My sides are killing me!" he said, shaking his head. "I laughed so hard it was borderline agony!"

He and Cole always enjoyed the fortune cookies, but they'd never had this much fun with them before. Getting psyched up to try to decipher something cryptically philosophical, he broke the cookie in two and pulled the slip out, dropping the cookie pieces on his napkin. Cole and Maggie leaned forward, prepared to decipher.

Chad took a deep breath and read, "Help! I'm being held prisoner in a Chinese bakery!" Feeling gypped, he looked up. "Really?" he said dryly. They burst into another episode of sidesplitting laughter—Cole actually knew what they were laughing about this time—and they officially crossed over the borderline!

∾⌘⌘⌘∾

Long after the three of them had departed and the restaurant had closed, the Chaos' were making a final round, double checking that everything had been cleaned and all of the fryers and stoves were shut down for the night. Satisfied everything was in order, Mr. Chao grabbed the last of the bags of trash to be disposed of, and on their way out, as Ling locked the back door, he tossed them onto the heap of a nearby overfilled Dumpster. Upon impact one of the bags split open and some of the contents spilled out, sliding into any available crevices surrounding it. A gentle breeze caressed the now exposed sections of Chad's discarded fortune cookie and dislodged a *second* little slip of paper that had been stuck in the folds and overlooked. Unconfined now, it fluttered away on the wings of another gust of air. It read: Three can keep a secret...if you get rid of two.

CHAPTER 3

The next few weeks passed in a blur of activity. First came the stress of finals and then the frenzy of relieved students rushing to go home for a few earned weeks of fun and relaxation. Chad felt that he had done well on his tests, and was glad for the chance to just let go and unwind for a few days.

Cole wasn't as sure that he had passed his exams, but Chad didn't think he seemed to be too concerned about it. He never did. It was all just a means to an end to him. To play football.

∾⌘⌘⌘∾

They'd had such a good time when Maggie joined them for Chinese they'd invited her to come again the next week. She told them she'd had a wonderful time, but that she and a couple of her roommates had already planned to help each other prep for their exams. She asked for a rain check, which they were only too happy to extend. So the past Sunday it had been just the two of them, and though neither would admit it, they both missed Maggie's company. They talked about school—a forbidden subject on Chinese night—but Chad was hoping to nudge Cole in the direction of deciding what path he was going to take career wise. Until now, all he'd been taking were core classes, the ones everyone were required to take. He hadn't chosen any specialized classes, because he wasn't able to make up his mind about what he wanted to do with his life, other than football anyway. But he couldn't play football forever, and Chad was concerned about what would happen *after.*

The evening hadn't gone well.

"Cole, you do realize that because I've been taking on extra classes, and with my summer sessions, I should be ready to graduate next year?" he reminded him. "You haven't even *started* any goal oriented classes. You need to make a decision and sign up for those classes now, before they're all filled up or it's too late." When Cole didn't respond, Chad continued, "I'm worried about you, man. Once I graduate, who's gonna be around to pull you out of the hole?" he joked.

That finally elicited a response from Cole, but not what Chad was looking for. Cole hadn't considered being there without Chad around, and the thought of it unnerved him. He pounded his fist on the table, causing the glasses to jump. "Don't you get it, Chad?" he said leaning forward, his voice raised. "Football. That's all I want to do. I'm good at it. It *is* my life. None of that other stuff matters!" He hesitated, then emphasizing each word, he slowly said, "I – just – want – to – play – football," and with that he got up and walked out. Chad was momentarily taken aback by Cole's unexpected reaction and abrupt departure. He sat there a while trying to figure out what happened, then he paid the bill and went out to find Cole, but he was nowhere around. Assuming he had started walking, Chad figured he'd pick him up on the way home but didn't see him anywhere. It was totally out of character for Cole to blow his top like that. He always made a joke out of everything. Chad didn't know what to expect when he got back to their apartment, but Cole wasn't there either. He thought about going back to look for him but decided he probably needed some time alone, so he went to bed early—having a test at 8 a.m. the next morning—hoping Cole would sort things out, and maybe finally, make a decision about school.

He didn't know when Cole had finally gotten in, but was glad to see he was there when he woke up the next morning, and judging by the snoring, asleep—or doing a really good job of faking it—so he got dressed and headed off to class. That evening when he returned, Cole was at home and acting like nothing had happened, so Chad decided to just let it go.

∾⌘⌘⌘∾

Finally it was Friday, and all of their finals were behind them. After they both got in from classes, Cole said, "Hey man, what do you say we go down to the OCI for a game of pool and some wings?"

"That sounds good," Chad sighed heavily. "It's been long week."

"You can say that again," Cole agreed.

The OCI wasn't as crowded that night, as most of the students had either already left for wherever they were going, or were packing to head out soon. With plenty of tables and booths to choose from, they selected a booth, ordered wings and a pitcher of beer, and claimed a pool table.

Cole had just won his second game out of three when Big Rod announced it was time for the karaoke contest. The prize tonight was only $150, probably because so many students had left for the summer.

"Guess that's our *cue* to go," Cole joked, holding up his cue stick.

"What? You don't want to hang around and join the contest this time?" Chad jested.

"Are you kidding me? You know I don't sing, and these jokers had better be glad Maggie's not here, or *they* wouldn't stand a chance either," he scoffed.

"Yeah, that's for sure," Chad agreed. Then almost as an afterthought he added, "I haven't seen Maggie around. I guess she already left for home."

As Cole was putting his cue stick back in the rack, he said "I guess so. I haven't seen her either."

For some reason, Chad was relieved to hear that.

Chad's Journal
April 25, 1998

I can't wait to see her again.

CHAPTER 4

Several weeks later Cole was out on the field warming up for another rigorous day of training and Chad was on the sidelines, when he glanced around and saw Maggie in the stands, watching. He was surprised to see her, and his stomach did a little flip flop. He smiled and waved, then headed over toward her. He couldn't get into the stands from where he was, but she was sitting down on the front row.

Feeling bold, he called out, "Hey pretty lady!"

"Hi Chad!" she answered. "How are you?"

"Great! When did you get back?" he asked.

"Yesterday. I had to get back to help my sisters with a fundraiser."

"Sisters?" Chad asked, a confused look on his face.

"Oh! I can't believe I didn't tell you! I'm a Kappa Delta! We do all sorts of things to raise money…for orthopedic research, the girl scouts, Children's Hospital in Virginia. This time it's a spaghetti dinner, to raise money to help with the prevention of child abuse."

"Wow! I thought being in a sorority was just like one big party. So where's this spaghetti dinner? At your house?"

"Yeah, right," she laughed. "No silly. It's going to be on campus in the Grand Room over at the International House. You should come! And bring Cole! Bring *all* your friends."

"I will!" he said quickly, then realizing he sounded too eager, added, "I mean, being it's for such a good cause and all. So, do you live in a sorority house?"

"Well kind of. There aren't any sorority houses on campus, so after our freshman year a bunch of "my sisters"," she made quotation marks with her hands, "got together, and rented a huge old house over on South Seventeenth. It's not far from the church where you saw me that Sunday. I've been there going on three years now. Don't you and Cole live on campus?"

"Not anymore. We spent our freshman year in Hess Hall and luckily we got our applications in early enough to be roommates, but you never know for sure if you're going to be roommates from year to year, so we rented a place too. Nothing as nice as a whole house though. We just have an efficiency over on Laurel Avenue, but it works for us," he shrugged.

"You guys are pretty good friends, huh?"

"Since first grade," he confirmed, a hint of pride ringing in his voice.

Impressed, she said, "That's pretty amazing."

"Yeah, Cole's a good guy." He glanced over his shoulder at the team hard at work training on the field. "Look," he said reluctantly, hating to end the conversation. "I've got to get back over there, so...when's this spaghetti dinner?"

∾⌘⌘⌘∾

Chad felt good! No. He felt freaking awesome! She had invited him to dinner! Sure, it was a fundraiser, but who cares! She asked *him!* And, yeah, she had said "bring Cole", but it was a fundraiser! Of *course* she would say that!

Flying high, he spent the rest of the day telling everyone he ran into about the important fundraiser taking place right on campus. It started out as an inane attempt to impress Maggie—like she would really know who invited who—but somewhere in the midst of invitations the importance of the cause hit home and soon he truly was advocating for the kids. It was humbling yet gratifying, and he was glad to be a part of it. He figured he'd have a hard time talking Cole into going but, surprisingly he was more than agreeable. Chad suspected that Cole's enthusiasm was because there was food involved, spaghetti being one of his favorites, but whatever the reason, the kids would benefit, so it was all good!

CHAPTER 5

The Fourth of July fell on a Saturday, and so far the day was looking great. There wasn't a cloud in the sky and the temperature was forecast to get up to the mid nineties. A few weeks earlier at the spaghetti dinner, Maggie and some of her friends told Chad and Cole they were planning on going tubing on the fourth and asked if they would like to join them. The guys readily agreed.

Because it was the girls' specialty to organize events, they assigned everyone certain things to bring, ranging from tubes, chairs, and blankets, to bread, lunchmeat, and chips, with more than one person assigned to certain crucial items in case there were 'no shows'. What good was a cooler full of lunch meat if no one showed up with bread? Once the guys accepted the invitation they were dutifully relegated to bring a large bag of chips and a couple of bottles of soda.

Chad and Cole had never been to Maggie's house but realized they couldn't have missed it when they turned onto her street and saw the activity going on. As they were parking they recognized a couple of guys they knew from school throwing a Frisbee back and forth, and saw a few others they knew milling around and talking to friends. Their attention was drawn to a stream of girls—some of which they recognized from the fundraiser—carrying things out of the house, presumably for the picnic, to a table that was set up in the yard, but there was no sign of Maggie.

They were about to go say hi to some of the people they knew when they heard Maggie call out to them. They looked over to see her getting out of the passenger side of a little pick-up truck.

"Hey you guys! Can you give us a hand with this?" she called to them, pointing to a very large cooler in the bed of the truck. She, and her best friend Maresa, had gotten the cooler filled with ice on campus. Maresa—"pronounced like Theresa but with an m" she'd told them while serving them a plate of spaghetti at the fundraiser—was blonde like Maggie, but a little taller, around 5'3", and to quote some of the guys they'd overheard that night, "real easy on the eyes!" She'd been Maggie's closest friend since they'd met their freshman year and became sorority sisters.

They hurried over and each grabbed one side of the large ice chest, following Maggie and Maresa to the table where some girls were waiting to divide the ice into several smaller coolers loaded with food and drinks.

"Thanks, you two." Maggie said to them sweetly, giving them both a quick hug. "It's good to see you! Glad you made it!" she said. "Everybody, this is Cole and Chad," she said, gesturing to each of them respectively, while she helped divvy up the ice.

The girls chorused, "Hi Cole! Hi Chad!"

Maggie indicated each girl as she called out their names, and when she came to Maresa she said, "And of course you've already met Maresa! I'll introduce you to the guys as soon as we get this finished!"

After introductions were made everyone began to load things up. Maggie and one of her other sorority sisters and close friend, Stephanie, planned to ride together. They grabbed the bags with their personal things, and some of the picnic supplies and headed toward Maggie's Volkswagen bug. On the way Maggie noticed Chad opening the back of his Jeep Wrangler. She was surprised. She'd expected them to be in Cole's prized Camaro. After checking with Stephanie, she called out to them. "Hey! Would you guys mind if we rode with you since you've got all that room?"

"Sure," Chad agreed, shrugging his shoulders nonchalantly. He had no idea where everything he had in his hands landed, but it was somewhere in the back of his Jeep and that was all that mattered. Before Maggie could blink, he'd taken what she had and put it in the back, and by the time Cole finished placing the supplies he was carrying inside, Chad had Stephanie's armload of things loaded as well. He was ushering them to the door of his Jeep, to seal the deal, before anyone could change their mind.

Climbing in the back seat, Maggie couldn't resist the temptation to tease Cole. "I thought for sure you'd be driving your baby! Are you lost without her?" His response surprised her even more.

"Nah. There's not much room for parking at our apartment, and since we're so close to school anyway we just trade back and forth and only keep one vehicle here at a time."

It was a logical solution, but she hadn't expected Cole and his ego to be so sensible as to agree to this arrangement, especially when it came to his C*amaro,* which she was under the impression he viewed as an extension of his manliness. Her amazement continued to mount when they told her that Cole liked cycling, and rode his bike around campus to classes as much as possible. She formed the image of Cole actually riding a bike around campus while she was trying to digest all of this information and it occurred to her that maybe there was more to him than what met the eye. It was certainly food for thought.

The group ended up in six cars between them, with a few cars carrying more than the maximum allowable number of passengers, some of the girls sitting on their boyfriends' laps. They started a caravan heading toward Pigeon Forge.

The idea for the outing originally came about when a couple of the guys, Josh and Zack, had been exploring the mountains looking for good places to go hiking, and in their search found a really great spot for tubing on the Little Pigeon River. Barring any heavy traffic it was only about a 45 minute drive from campus, but since it was off the main drag and only Josh and Zack knew exactly where they were going, everyone followed behind them. Being the Fourth of July, they did get slowed down going through Pigeon Forge, where throngs of people were already gathering for all of the festivities going on, but soon their caravan was headed into Gatlinburg. Shortly after reaching the city limit they turned onto Hwy. 321, which took them away from the hustle and bustle of the holiday traffic before they got into the heart of it. They only went a short distance out of town before they turned onto SR 416. In just those few miles they had been transported from the overcrowded tourist attractions in town, to the quiet winding roads in the foothills of the Smoky Mountains, where time—it seemed—slowed its pace. They were surrounded now by lush green mountains, the beautiful scenery alive with hearty summer growth, and massive areas blanketed with thick kudzu. As they drove along everyone watched for and pointed out little waterfalls hiding in crevasses between rocks and trees, and though they had all seen it before, they still marveled at the huge boulders jutting from the mountainsides that looked as if they could fall at any moment. They had, in fact, already passed several signs that read 'Watch for Falling Rock'. Cole tried his best to convince Stephanie and Maggie that "Falling Rock" was the name of a lost Indian, but they didn't give him the satisfaction of falling for it.

SR 416 was known by the locals as Pittman Center Road, and was a serene, winding, two lane road with a few houses scattered here and there until the Little Pigeon River emerged and became visible down a steep drop off alongside the left side of the road. The right side turned into nearly vertical rocky embankments up the mountainside, with not much room for error on either side. Just when everyone was beginning to have their doubts as to Josh and Zack's idea of a perfect spot, the shoulder on the side of the road next to the river widened, and as if by design there was just enough room for them to pull off and park their cars.

As Chad and Cole were helping Maggie and Stephanie out of the back seat, their attention was drawn to the mounting excitement and activity around one of the other vehicles and they began to watch—shaking their heads in disbelief—as a seemingly unending number of people, one by one, untangled their bodies and extricated themselves from the vehicle. Once out, they immediately launched into a spirited but comical dance of hopping and stretching, in an effort to get the circulation flowing back to their numbed limbs. A loud cheer rang out when, at last, the final person disembarked in one piece, bringing the staggering total to 14 people in a two door sedan!!

"I can't believe they did that!" Maggie exclaimed. She'd figured some of the cars were overcrowded, but didn't know to what extent.

"They may have broken a record! And they were lucky they didn't get pulled over on the way here!"

"I know!" Chad agreed, chuckling in amazement. "I bet they won't be going back the same way!

Someone who had been crammed in the car laughed when he overheard Chad and said, "You got that right! It ain't happening!"

Maggie was glad. She was all for everybody having a good time but not to the point of recklessness! Ever the sensible one, she was thinking she would hate for someone get hurt, when Cole called out to them.

"Come on! Let's check this place out!" he yelled, gesturing to them with a wave of his arm, turning to follow everyone else.

The group spread out, quickly giving the area the once over. It was unanimously deemed worthy, and they all congratulated Josh and Zack with high fives and pats on their backs for finding and sharing the perfect spot!

After that everyone was anxious to get down to the water and have some fun! The food and supplies were unpacked and a few of the guys made their way down the incline to the bank by the water to catch tubes, towels, and whatever else that could be tossed down to them, while the rest grabbed something to carry down with them as they went. Before long everyone had a chosen spot, clothes and shoes were shed, and it was time to brave the icy cold river. A few simply jumped right in choosing to get the shock over all at once, others crept in slowly letting their bodies acclimate to the water, and a few—after several aborted attempts—got a little help from some of their friends by getting pushed in. One way or another, everyone was christened by the frigid water.

A few of the other more adventurous souls, including two guys named Blaize and Xaine, grabbed some tubes and made their way upstream. There the river narrowed and was a torrent of white water rushing over and around the big rocks, and they rode the tubes back through the rapids. Maggie was content to wait and join the group that were tying their tubes together to take a relaxing peaceful ride *down*stream where the water was calmer and slow moving.

When Xaine and Blaize made it back in one piece and told everyone how much fun it was, Chad and Cole were able to convince her to give it a try with them. She'd been tubing many times throughout her childhood and teenage years growing up in the mountains, but she'd never been one for having the need of an adrenalin rush by doing risky or dangerous things—much to her mother's relief—so this was going to be something new and adventurous for her. And she was fully prepared not to like it much.

Determined not to show her skepticism, and okay, maybe a little bit of fear, she graciously accepted their help getting down to the water. She quickly settled into her tube directly behind Cole, after Chad politely gestured for her to go before him. They had barely gotten started downstream when she found herself wondering why she had never tried this before. A minute or two later she was kicking herself for all the chances she'd missed! There was no denying that it was a blast. When they got back she admitted that she'd loved every minute of it and was ready to go again, but now there was a line. Apparently there was a shortage of tubes compared to able and willing bodies.

"Do you guys want to do it again after they've had a chance?" she asked, gesturing to the line.

"No! We were scared!" Cole whimpered. Then he laughed, and said, "You bet! We'll go as many times as you want to!"

He and Chad passed their tubes on to Matt and Kyle, first in the line, who took them and hurried down the road. Maggie handed her tube to Logan, who was next, but he'd been waiting to try the white water with his girlfriend, Michelle, so they still needed another tube. Since most of the others were still pretty far upstream and it would be a while before they made it back, he started to hand the tube off to the next guy behind them, but Michelle stopped him.

"You can go ahead and go. I'll wait and we'll go together later. I don't want you to miss your turn! I know you're dying to go!" she said.

"I am! But I don't want you to miss your turn either." He lit up. "You know, we could go together…" he said grinning, "…if you're game."

"What do you mean?" she asked intrigued.

Much to her delight he said, "Well I'm so tall and thin and you're so little, I bet both of us together don't weigh as much as either Cole or Kyle. I think you could just sit on my lap!"

"I like your idea a lot better than mine! Let's do it!"

Logan took her hand and they ran to catch up with Kyle and Matt, but they were already in the water and on their way, so Logan dropped the tube and settled down into it with his arms and legs draped over the sides, then grabbed Michelle and pulled her down on his lap before the current swept him away. She wrapped her arms around his neck and clung to him, liking his idea even more now. Their combined weight on the tube gave the rushing water more to grab onto and it took off with them, promising them the ride of their lives. Michelle was a little surprised at first by how fast they were being propelled downstream until Logan tightened his hold on her reassuringly, and she relaxed until the adrenaline overtook them. It was so exhilarating! All they could do was laugh hysterically and hold on to each other as they were expertly maneuvered over and around the huge boulders. Each time they thought they were sure to crash into one, they would be whipped away at the last second to travel the path of least resistance. They were about two thirds of the way through the whitewater section, before they had their first sign of trouble. Or at least Logan did when the tube and his back side dragged over the top of a boulder. It didn't hurt, just surprised him since it was the first contact they had made with any of the rocks so far, but he didn't particularly want to do it again. It happened so fast that, before he could even say anything to Michelle, they found themselves underwater. In a matter of seconds the tube had lost so much air, it all but disappeared beneath them. Suddenly they were struggling to right themselves. They didn't know what happened to the tube and it didn't really matter. The end result was the same. They had no choice but to try to navigate over and around the boulders without it. The current was so swift that it kept pushing them along. There was absolutely no chance of stopping until they were through the white water.

Logan was worried about Michelle and called out to her. "Chelle, hold your arms out in front of you and try to keep from colliding with any boulders, and try to hold your body up as high as you can in the water!"

"I'll try!" she sputtered, gasping for a breath.

In reality there really wasn't much either of them could do but hope to keep their heads above water. At this point they had everyone's undivided attention, but Logan and Michelle couldn't hear any of their useless shouts of advice or the words of encouragement. Some of them could only stand and watch breathless, biting their nails, and still others were preparing to pull their unconscious bodies out of the water.

After what seemed like an eternity, Logan and Michelle made it through the whitewater to where the river widened and the current abated and everyone was waiting to make sure they were okay. There was a collective sigh of relief from the group when Logan and Michelle stood up, and applause rang out when they confirmed that they were unharmed. Battered, bruised, and a little weak kneed, but otherwise okay. Logan rushed over to check for himself that Michelle was, in fact, all right and when he was satisfied that she was, he pulled her into his arms.

Then all the questions started. "What in the world were you thinking?" "Why didn't you guys use rafts?" "Didn't you know you could have been hurt?" "What happened?" "Was it scary?"

What happened to the tube was a mystery so they answered what they did know. When everyone was satisfied all was well, the mood turned lighter and good natured nick names started getting tossed around making everyone laugh. "Aqua man and Aqua woman", "Mark and Michelle Spitz", "Neptune and Salacia", "Poseidon and Amphririte".

Cole chuckled. "Poseidon! That's funny!" He looked at Chad. "Who's Ann Frito?"

Chad just shook his head. "Poseidon's wife," he answered, without going into detail. He'd explain it later.

Slowly the crowd dispersed as people went back to swimming, eating, or lying on the boulders soaking up the sun. Whatever they were doing before the suspense filled interruption. Even the tubing resumed without another incident. The rest of the day progressed with everyone having a good time enjoying each other's company, and in spite of the mishap with Logan and Michelle's inner tube, Maggie made several more runs through the whitewater with Cole & Chad. On one of them, Chad could have sworn he heard Cole call Maggie "Ann Frito".

It was hours later before the food ran out, but the sun was setting and the air was starting to turn a little cool, so they began gathering everything up. They all planned to go to Patriot Park in Pigeon Forge where there was going to be a huge fireworks display. Maggie noticed that several people from the overloaded car from that morning had begged rides with others for the drive back.

It was a little before 8:00 p.m. when they got to the park. The fireworks didn't start until 9:00 p.m., but there had been concerts going on since about one o'clock that afternoon, so it was already pretty crowded, and the caravan had to split up to find parking spaces.

Chad found a spot and parked, and the four of them maneuvered through the crowd, dodging kids with sparklers, until they found a place they could spread out the blanket that Maggie brought. While she and Stephanie got settled, Chad and Cole offered to go get everyone a soda from one of the vendors that were set up.

When they returned, the girls were sitting on the end of the blanket nearest where the fireworks were set to go off. Cole handed Maggie her soda then dropped down on the blanket behind her, where he proceeded to stretch out on his back with a relaxed sigh. Chad handed Stephanie her drink and sat down behind her on the only available spot left on the blanket, wishing he'd been able to sit where

Cole was, closer to Maggie. But looking across at her, it only took a moment for him to realize that he had the best seat in the park after all. She was turned slightly on the blanket talking to Stephanie animatedly and occasionally glancing up at the sky as if willing the fireworks to start, and it occurred to him that his vantage point allowed him the opportunity to sneak glances at her completely unobserved. Yes, he definitely had the best view in the park.

Maggie was glowing. It was no secret that she loved fireworks. Anyone that had been around her for more than a few minutes at a time that day heard her make some sort of reference to the show that night, whether it was to make sure that they *knew* about it, or to see if they were *going* to it, or just to say how long she'd been looking *forward* to it. More often than not, it was all of the above! Somebody that didn't know her may have found it annoying, but since everyone there adored her, they all thought it was cute how excited she was and knew she just didn't want them to miss out on the fun! Now that the time was drawing near, Chad noticed she was growing more anxious with each passing minute waiting for the show to begin. Between 8:59 and 9:00 she must have looked at her watch at least fifteen times.

She'd just glanced down again when the sky directly overhead suddenly erupted into a kaleidoscope of colors. She looked up and a smile spread across her face. With each explosion above, he watched a myriad of emotions transform her face, from excitement and clapping with joy like a little girl, to almost mesmerized in a quiet wondrous awe. He had to admit, the fireworks *were* pretty amazing, but they were nothing compared to what he saw when he looked at her.

Chad's Journal

July 4, 1998

I've never met anyone like her

CHAPTER 6

The next day was Sunday and Chad and Cole went to see their parents for a couple of hours, switched vehicles, then headed back to campus to shower and get ready for Chinese that night. After the fireworks the night before they asked Maggie to join them again and she accepted and even agreed to let them pick her up this time.

During dinner they learned more about each other's families, and told stories about their childhoods, ranging from before grade school to beyond high school, yet despite all the crazy stories that Cole and Chad shared, neither one of them so much as even *mentioned* Bull Run Creek *or* the secrets that it held of the incident so long ago. In fact, as if by unspoken agreement, neither one of them had breathed a word about that day since it happened—to each other or to anyone else. Instead, they stayed on neutral ground, bringing up safe topics like learning how to drive, old movies they liked, and eventually to their shared hobby of restoring old cars, including the vehicles they drove now.

When talk turned to their futures, Maggie expressed her desire to teach grade school children, and with just one look at her face Chad could actually *feel* how much it meant to her as she talked about wanting the opportunity to work with kids and be a part of their education. She told them she couldn't wait to share her love of music and hopefully inspire kids to appreciate the *art* of music, whether it be intricate classical compositions or simple rock-n-roll ditties. He had no doubt that if she taught with *half* as much conviction as she had talking to them now, she would be wildly successful. Just hearing the passion in her voice made him wish he'd paid more attention to *his* music teacher, Mrs. King, back in the fourth grade when she was trying to teach his class to play the recorder. Somehow though, he didn't think Maggie would have any trouble capturing and keeping, not only all of the little boy's attentions, but the little girls as well.

After dinner, Maggie asked them if they would like to accompany her to the OCI on Friday night for karaoke. They both agreed to go with her. "Maybe I can get you guys to sing," she added, teasing.

"Yeah, that'll be the day," Cole replied, laughing.

∾⌘⌘⌘∾

Their dinner that night proved to be as fun as the first time, including the fortune cookies. None of them knew it then, but from that point on, Maggie would never miss another Chinese night dinner, and Cole and Chad would never miss another Friday night karaoke with Maggie.

∾⌘⌘⌘∾

Several weeks later they were at OCI looking over the list of songs Maggie could choose from to sing in the contest. They put in an order for some wings and a round of sodas. Cole had to forego his usual beer because he had his first game of the season coming up, Maggie *never* drank and Chad just wasn't in the mood for it.

After ordering, Cole slipped off to go to the bathroom. While he was gone, Chad and Maggie noticed a girl they had never seen before sitting at a nearby table, trying but failing to hide the fact that she was crying.

"I feel so bad for her. I hope she's going to be okay," Maggie whispered sympathetically.

They turned their attention back to the list of songs but Maggie's eyes kept drifting over to the girl, who was crying even harder now. Chad was touched by the amount of concern and compassion he saw on Maggie's face for this girl that she clearly didn't know and it melted his heart. Then apparently Maggie couldn't take it anymore because she said, "I'll be right back." She went over to the girls table, approaching her from the front so as not to startle her. When the girl looked up and Maggie was confident that she had been seen, she made her way around the table and gently placed her hand on the girls shoulder, then bent over and said something in her ear. The girl nodded, so Maggie pulled a chair over closer to her and sat down.

Chad tried not to stare but he was so moved by Maggie's selfless act of kindness that he found it hard to tear his eyes away. He couldn't hear what was being said, but the girl was talking and Maggie was listening intently. They talked back and forth, and after a few minutes the girl looked as if she was feeling a little better. When Maggie got up, the girl was smiling as she reached out and took Maggie's hand giving it a squeeze. She looked up at Maggie gratefully. Chad could read her lips as her mouth formed the words "Thank you". Maggie leaned down and hugged her, then headed back to their table, where Chad sat watching her, mesmerized. Her eyes were shining and there was a glow on her face. Then her eyes met his, and at that moment, Chad fell in love with Maggie.

∾⌘⌘⌘∾

He sat numbly letting this realization wash over him as Cole returned and they continued their quest to find a song for Maggie to sing. But Chad was only pretending to help, lost in his own little world. Cole was saying something about judging by everyone else's singing, she could choose the alphabet song and have no competition, but before her turn came, Big Rod called *Cole's* name. Hearing Cole's name announced brought Chad crashing back down to earth. Cole grinned at them as he got up and headed toward the karaoke stage, leaving Maggie and Chad looking at each other, stunned.

They were wondering what was going on as they watched him go straight up on stage to Big Rod. They both knew there was no way he was going to sing. He would *never* do that. But looking pretty confident, he *did* take the microphone and as Rod Stewart's *Maggie Mae* began to play, Cole started to sing. He was looking directly at Maggie, leaving no question as to who the song was intended for.

Unable to believe it, she stood up, her eyes locked on his, amazed that he was doing this. He was out of key and probably couldn't have sounded worse to everyone else there, but incredibly, no one made a sound. It was as though they knew it had taken an incredible amount of courage for him to get up there in front of everyone and sing. Maggie knew it too, and to her it sounded beautiful! It was at that moment Maggie fell in love with Cole.

Chad's Journal
August 28, 1998

I love her.
I may have lost her.

CHAPTER 7

Chad threw himself into his classes with a renewed vigor trying to keep his mind occupied and off of Maggie and Cole and what transpired when Cole shocked everyone by serenading her at karaoke. But no matter what he did, that night kept playing over and over in his head like a video tape stuck on replay. It started at the point that Maggie and Cole made eye contact while he was on stage and she realized that he was singing to her. She got to her feet slowly, and stood in surprise. As Cole continued to sing it was as if they were the only two people in the room. By the time he finished singing, the cheeky grin he usually wore was gone, his face now utterly devoid of *any* emotion. With his eyes still locked on Maggie, he stepped off stage and began to wind his way through the crowd toward her. It was agonizingly quiet as everyone began to part making way for him to pass, and turn to watch the scene unfolding before them. Cole came to a halt in front of Maggie, but neither of them said a word, they just continued to gaze into each other's eyes. After a moment Maggie placed a hand on each side of Cole's face, stood up on her tip toes and gave him a very soft kiss on the mouth that lasted for several seconds. Then someone in the room, who evidently knew who Cole was, shouted "SCORE!" and broke the spell. It was then Chad realized he had been holding his breath. He exhaled slowly, then swallowed, trying to get his mind to comprehend what his heart had just witnessed. When everyone started cheering, he noticed Maggie blushing—she hadn't realized everyone was watching until then—and she sat down quickly, pulling Cole down into the chair next to her.

The rest of the night was spent as though nothing had changed between them *except* for the fact that Cole and Maggie stayed hand in hand, and *that*, in and of itself, was a glaring reminder to Chad that *everything* had changed.

Maggie had initially chosen the song *Imagine,* by John Lennon, to sing in the contest, but when she got on stage after Cole's performance, she switched her choice to the Chiffon's, *He's So Fine,* and it was pretty obvious at this point as to who she was referring to. She won hands down.

Later that night, as they were leaving to go home, she asked them if she could fix dinner for the three of them the next night, but Chad politely declined, saying he'd already made plans, hoping she wouldn't press the issue. He told Cole that *he* should go though, so Cole accepted her invitation and went on to say something about them all having Chinese together on Sunday.

Chad wasn't exactly sure what was said after that. His mind was in turmoil. He told himself he just needed some time to sort everything out.

∾⌘⌘⌘∾

After practice on Saturday, Chad went straight to the library, giving Cole time to shower and leave for Maggie's, before he went back to their apartment. He spent the evening thinking over the past few months since he'd met Maggie. He tried to look for signs, something, *anything* he could have missed that would have cushioned the blow of what had blossomed between Cole and Maggie. Why hadn't he seen it coming? Would he have done anything different if he *had* seen it coming? Cole was his best friend. Maggie was the most incredible girl he had ever known. Would anything more come of it? A short while later he got his answer.

He was at his desk, trying to study, when Cole came home around ten-thirty. He had never seen Cole so excited, not even about football, and he knew then that his chance was lost. He swung around in his chair to listen, as Cole paced back and forth unable to stop talking about Maggie. He raved about how great she was, and what a good cook she was. He told him about the steak and gravy that was so tender you could cut it with a fork, and the mashed potatoes that melted in your mouth. He said she'd made the best strawberry shortcake from scratch he'd ever had in his life. He went on and on about the evening, and about how they just talked about everything under the sun. He said they didn't waste any time watching T.V. or anything like that, but instead they'd gone for a long walk after dinner. Then he announced that she'd told him the most amazing thing.

He stopped pacing and looked at Chad. "You are never going to believe this, Chad!" he said, shaking his head as if he was still having a hard time believing it himself. "She told me that there was something I needed to know about her...that we couldn't go forward in our relationship until I knew. I gotta tell ya, she had me really worried there for a while. And then, when she finally told me what it was, at first I didn't know what to say, but when she explained it to me I just thought it was so awesome!" He paused and his face became serious. "Now this has got to stay between the two of us Chad. You can't tell anybody."

When Chad nodded that he understood, Cole went on.

"Oh man," he said with a chuckle, "this is really going to blow you're your mind!" Then in a voice a little more subdued, he said, "She told me that she's never slept with anyone, Chad! Can you believe it? She's a *virgin*!" he exclaimed. There was no ridicule in his tone, just complete awe. "And she's really proud of it! She said it was the most precious gift a girl could give her husband and that she wanted to save herself for *her* future husband. Isn't that something? I mean, I've never really thought much about it before, and I haven't been with a *lot* of girls, but none of them were virgins! I just didn't think anybody really did that anymore, you know? Or I guess I should say *didn't* do it," he said as an afterthought, but wasn't trying to be funny. "Look, I know I shouldn't be telling you this, Chad," he admitted apologetically, "but I know you won't say anything to anyone." Pausing, he raked his fingers through his hair, contemplating the significance of what Maggie had told him. He shook his head, bewildered that he just couldn't seem to find the words to express the extent of his admiration. Then, with intense conviction through nearly clenched teeth, he blurted, "Man! I'm just so proud of her! Do you how important this must be to her to put up with some of the stuff she's had to put up with? And the strength and integrity that it's taken for her to stand firm to her principles?" he asked, looking at Chad.

Chad had never seen Cole this impassioned before, but he knew Cole wasn't really expecting an answer, so with a sinking heart he waited quietly for him to go on.

After a moment Cole took a deep breath and his whole body visibly relaxed. "I've never met anyone like her, Chad," he uttered wondrously.

He sat down on his bed and kept talking, but Chad's thoughts were elsewhere now. He'd grown to know Maggie well enough to know that her interest in Cole had nothing to do with him being the quarterback, and he knew Cole well enough to know that this relationship was going to be different than any he'd had in the past. And Chad wasn't surprised about Maggie's news. He'd *already known* she was special. He'd *already known* she was amazing. He'd *already known* there was no one else like her. And yeah, now he *knew* that he'd *already* lost her.

And then the video tape in his head started over at the beginning.

Chad's Journal
September 10, 1998

My best friend is in love with a very special girl.

CHAPTER 8

Maggie woke up the next morning with a smile on her face. Her first thought was of Cole and she immediately got butterflies in her stomach. He had completely swept her off her feet just like in the fairy tales, and she could honestly say she hadn't seen it coming. It was such a wonderful feeling to be in love again, and it seemed so right!

She turned over on her side, fluffed up the pillow under her head and sighed in contentment. Her thoughts drifted to the evening they'd shared the night before and she knew it couldn't have been more perfect! When her sisters had discovered that Chad wasn't going to be joining her and Cole for dinner they had suspiciously disappeared giving the two of them some unexpected but welcomed privacy, which changed the tone and set the mood for the evening. The dinner she cooked had turned out flawless and Cole really seemed to enjoy it, asking politely for seconds of everything and secretly thrilling her in doing so. The conversation flowed effortlessly and he was funny at times, but not silly, confident, but not arrogant, and most of all, every second of every minute he was an absolute gentleman. She fell more in love with him as the night progressed. She guessed there really was something to the old adage about being friends before becoming lovers. Even though technically they weren't lovers, falling in love with your best friend was incredible.

After dinner they went for a walk and talked. They were completely comfortable with each other, yet it was still so exciting! He was the easiest person to talk to. And he listened, *really* listened to her, and cared about what she had to say.

She hadn't seen this side of him before. There was no joking around or being silly. They spent hours sharing their innermost thoughts and aspirations.

She never dreamed at the beginning of their evening that they would end up having the personal conversation they'd had, but it had been so easy, so natural. He was the only boyfriend she had ever told about her virginity that hadn't either laughed or acted like she was demented afterward. He not only understood, he was impressed! He'd told her he was proud of her, for crying out loud!

She just couldn't believe it! She was so happy! She rolled onto her back and stretched, humming to herself. Everything was just so perfect! Reveling in the feeling, it occurred to her that she didn't have any idea what the tune was she was humming. She hummed it over and over and didn't recognize it as anything she'd ever heard before, but she really liked it! Inspired, she grabbed a pen and her spiral notebook she wrote her ideas for songs in, and began putting the tune to paper. She'd toyed at writing songs before, but rarely was it as clear to her as this was.

A while later—after a few alterations—she had the tune down, and went to work putting words to the music. Finally, happy with the finished product, she sang what she'd composed to herself, testing the feel of the words.

"When we first met
I had this feeling deep inside
It's growing stronger
Too much to be denied
I'm so afraid
Never felt this way before
My head is spinning
And my footing is unsure
Should I confess now?
Should I tell him how I feel?
Lost in confusion
How am I to know it's real?
It's getting harder to decide
Where's all this going
Should I try to run and hide?
Without him knowing
Of this feeling deep inside
Why can't I tell him?

Is it fear or foolish pride?
How can I tell him?
Of this feeling deep inside
How can I tell him?
Of this feeling deep inside"

"Oh my gosh" she said under her breath, not quite able to believe that after so many attempts over the years to write a song this had come so easily to her. She sang it again with more confidence this time. "I did it!" she cried when she finished, bouncing up and down on her bed, ecstatic. She had actually just written her first song! And it sounded so pretty! She loved it! It made her think of one of her favorite songs, *That's all I ask of you*, from *Phantom Of The Opera*. Her modesty immediately kicked in. "Not that I would ever presume to be so talented!" she said to herself. "It just sounds like something you would *hear* in an opera like that," she clarified.

Thoroughly pleased with the finished composition—and with herself for her accomplishment—she gently tore the pages out of her notebook. Sliding off the bed, she went to the chest her dad made for her before she went off to college. She unlocked it and tucked the pages safely inside, taking care to lock it back when she was through. Her dad crafted it with a secret lock and she was the only other person who knew how to open it. It was where she kept all of her special keepsakes and other things that were important to her. It had a curved top, like the treasure chests the pirates always had in the movies, and the wood was from a black walnut tree off their farm. Besides being a conversation piece and—because no one could figure out how to unlock it—an enigma to her friends, more importantly, it was her most prized possession. Now it held what she felt was one of her finest achievements. How fitting, she thought with a smile.

CHAPTER 9

The Volunteers were gearing up for their first home game of the season, and having beat Syracuse at the Carrier Dome in New York, 34-33, the excitement level was high, both on campus and around town. Everywhere you looked there were orange and white UT banners, UT flags on houses and cars, as well as UT tags and bumper stickers. The citizens of Knoxville took their college football seriously, rallying behind their team, showing their support. Even Maggie was caught up in the excitement of the upcoming game, having a vested interest now. She'd been to the stadium many times before but always on the outside, because, like today she was participating in a fundraiser that went on before the game. It was the annual War of Wings, where fraternities and local businesses donated everything, and competed for the best wings. For five dollars tailgaters got wings, chips and a soda, and the proceeds went to Children's Hospital. This game would be the first one she would actually be attending after the fundraiser.

Chad was going be working on the sideline the first half of the game, but Maggie made him promise to come find her at halftime so he could explain some of the rules and regulations of football to her. And in spite of the fact that Cole and Maggie were an item now, Chad was actually looking forward to it. Just being around her filled him with a peacefulness that even 100,000 screaming football fans couldn't penetrate.

She told him, "You'll be able to spot me, I'll be wearing an orange and white number 7 jersey!" as she disappeared into a sea of orange and white jerseys.

He smiled at her sense of humor. He knew that she knew exactly where she would be since she was sitting with his and Cole's parents. She'd met Mr. and Mrs. Rivers that morning, along with his older brother Chris, Chris's wife Savannah, and Cole's younger sister, Cheyenne.

The group of them had gotten together at a little restaurant near the stadium, for a late breakfast. Maggie hadn't been the least bit nervous at the prospect of meeting Cole's family without him, and she liked them instantly. His mom—anxious to meet the girl who had finally managed to compete with football and capture her son's heart—recognized Maggie the moment she came in the door. She rushed over from the table where they were waiting and met Maggie halfway. With a huge smile she asked, "Maggie?" barely waiting for affirmation before embracing her. Somehow she just knew; call it a mother's intuition, that she was holding someone that would become very dear to her.

She released Maggie and stepped back. "Well my goodness, I probably scared you half to death, but I just knew it was you! You *are* beautiful, just like Cole described!"

Maggie blushed. "Thank you, that's so sweet of you to say," she said humbly. She decided Cole had to have inherited his brown eyes from his mom. They were identical. Mrs. Rivers was a few inches taller than her, maybe about 5'4", slender, with jet black hair. Another trait passed on to Cole, Maggie imagined. His mother's complexion looked very much as though she were of Native American descent. Maggie would learn later that Mrs. River's grandmother was a full blooded Cherokee Indian. Cole's mother was very attractive, with a thin, delicate nose, and full lips that looked as though they were painted with a deep, berry colored lipstick, but Maggie could clearly see that she wore no makeup at all.

Cheyenne joined the two of them then, and she and Maggie exchanged a hug. Cheyenne was beautiful, with long silky black hair like her mothers' and brown eye's like her brothers. And although Maggie loved Cole's brown eyes, she thought Cheyenne's looked as though you could get lost in them. Enhanced by shadow and mascara, it made them appear luminous. Maggie had no doubt though that even without an ounce of makeup; Cheyenne would be just as striking.

They led her to the table where the others were waiting, who stood when they approached.

Mrs. Rivers introduced Cole's dad who was on the far side of the table, and reaching across, the two of them shook hands. He was evidently where Cole got his stature from, being so tall and broad shouldered. Unlike his wife and children, he had light brown hair, and although there was nothing notably remarkable about his facial features, Maggie thought he was a very handsome man. She was surprised to see that his eyes weren't brown, but a bright sky blue, almost the same color as hers, and when he smiled, two little dimples appeared on each side of his face. She simply couldn't imagine anyone not liking him at first sight.

Next, she met Chad's brother, Chris, who wasn't at all what she had expected. He stood several inches taller than Chad, she guessed around 5'11", and had strawberry blonde hair, with a slightly freckled complexion that made her think he would burn easily out in the sun. He seemed physically fit, and his weight was complimentary to his height. In spite of the fact that he looked nothing like his brother, Maggie thought he was a very nice looking guy, too.

Chris's wife, Savannah, had long, curly, auburn colored hair, that Maggie commented on, before even saying hello. "Your hair is gorgeous!"

"Oh, thank you," Savannah replied with a smile, reaching up to push a handful back away from her face. "You might not think so, if you had to fight with it every day!" They both laughed.

Maggie thought Savannah's hair was the perfect frame for her pretty oval face and emerald green eyes. Most people with auburn hair and green eyes had a pale freckled complexion similar to her husband Chris, but Savannah's skin tone was an olive brown, which made her look healthy and vibrant.

When they were taking their seats Maggie glanced around at everyone and couldn't help thinking what nice looking people they were. They enjoyed a nice brunch and were told by the staff that they could stay and visit for as long as they liked, so they took advantage of the extra time to get to know each other. When Maggie had to leave for the War of the Wings fundraiser, they made plans to meet her there later to do their part by buying wings before the game started at 8:00 that evening.

∞⌘⌘⌘∞

The consensus was unanimous. All of them adored Maggie, and she felt the same way about them. Especially Cheyenne, whom she'd, bonded with instantly, despite the age difference and the fact that Cheyenne was only a senior in high school.

While they were at the restaurant Cheyenne, her father and Chris had gotten wrapped up in a discussion about the game that night. Hearing Chad's name mentioned and thinking that Cheyenne wasn't paying attention to them, her mother and Savannah whispered speculations to Maggie that one day Chad and Cheyenne would become a couple. Maggie had glanced at Cheyenne and thought she couldn't believe they weren't a couple already! Cheyenne was gorgeous!

What they weren't aware of at the time, was that Cheyenne *had* heard them, and out of the corner of her eye had seen Maggie look in her direction. She'd had to suppress a shudder at the thought. Her and Chad? A couple? As in boyfriend and girlfriend? *Where* had that come from, and how long had they been thinking *that*? No, she was going to have to squash that crazy idea like a bug! Bring any thoughts they had of matchmaking to a screeching halt! Sure, she loved Chad, very much, and he loved her too, but a couple? Eww! They were like brother and sister! As soon as she could, she was going to have a talk with all of them and set the record straight. Tell them in no uncertain terms that there was *no* chance of her and Chad being anything more than they were now!

And she did. After they all made plans to meet later, the second Maggie was out the door, Cheyenne told everyone she'd overheard what her mom and Savannah told Maggie earlier. "I just want to make it clear how I feel about Chad. We are *very* close and always will be."

Thinking they knew where this conversation was going they all glanced at each other, smiling.

"BUT, he's like my *brother,* like *family.* That's all we'll *ever* be and there's *no* chance of it growing into *anything* more." She paused for a moment, and everyone was silent. "Nothing. Nada." She drove her point home and let it sink in, looking each one of them in the eye. "So are you crystal clear on the subject?"

Everyone assured her that they were.

Everyone except Maggie.

∾⌘⌘⌘∾

The Volunteers were playing the Florida Gators—who had beaten them in their previous five games against each other—so they were going to fight hard for a win. Cole had a little extra incentive, not only because it was Maggie's first game, but because it was her first chance to see *him* play the game.

At halftime the score was tied 10-10. By the time Chad joined them, Maggie was pretty much up to speed with the rules of the game—having so many helpful tutors—but she did ask Chad to explain to her the difference between being off sides and a false start.

In the second half of the game, both teams scored a touchdown in the third quarter, and held each other off with no scores in the fourth, resulting in a tied game of 17-17, and overtime. Since Chad had joined them at halftime, he'd been witness to a side of Maggie that was, though unfamiliar to him, equally as heartwarming as everything else he knew about her. Usually soft spoken and reserved, she hadn't held back, cheering for Cole and the team during the game with all the excitement and passion as a seasoned football fan. He thought it was a beautiful sight.

The Vols ended up winning in overtime with a field goal. It was a huge victory, and couldn't have gone better for everyone involved. Except maybe the Gators.

Chad's Journal
September 19, 1998

What's a man to say,
What's a man to do,
When he has not the right
To say,
Pretty Lady I Love You

CHAPTER 10

On Sunday, the day after the big win, Maggie took Cole and Chad to Parrottsville to meet her parents, Clarence and Stella Thompson. Chad felt a little awkward, like a third wheel and tried to decline, but Maggie insisted, saying her parents *had* to meet the 'Dynamic Duo'. So he relented without putting up too much of a fight, and at the end of the day they all had a great time.

Any reservations he'd initially had were short lived after meeting the Thompsons. Maggie's mother, Stella, was petite, with blonde hair that was infused with silver. It was easy to see where Maggie got her beauty and tiny physique from. Had he envisioned what her mom would look like beforehand, he would have imagined the heavy lines and wrinkles typical on many of the faces of women who have spent their lives working in the sun on their farms, but Stella's skin was smooth and almost opalescent, like that of a porcelain doll. She greeted them warmly, hugging the boys as though she'd known them all their lives, then set about fussing over them and getting them refreshments. She was a sweetheart, and he and Cole instantly felt comfortable and at ease.

Maggie's father, Clarence, came closer to fulfilling ones mental image of a Tennessee farmer. He was stocky, about 5'8", with rugged features and weathered skin that portrayed the evidence of hard work out in the unforgiving elements nature presented. But—as if in defiance to these conditions and time—he had a head full of dark wavy hair that would make most men green with envy. In his T-shirt and overalls, he was the very depiction of a figure from the Saturday Evening Post.

After visiting for a while, Maggie and her Dad took the guys on a tour of the farm, where the Thompsons grew hay and raised cattle. Once the tour was complete, Maggie thought it would be fun to teach them a little about farm life.

They got their first lesson on how to drive the big tractors, something they had never done before being "city boys". Chad's lesson was uneventful, but after Cole almost took out the side of the barn when he was caught off guard by a temperamental and territorial bull that charged up to the almost nonexistent fence and he forgot how to stop the tractor until seconds before impact, Mr. Thompson decided it was time they had their next potentially less destructive lesson. Horseback riding. So they helped Maggie saddle up three horses and set off to explore her family's property. They rode on a well used trail that went up the mountainside, and since it was the guys first time riding, Maggie chose horses for them that were gentle and knew the trail forward and backward. There was little room for error. In fact, it was questionable that this could even be considered a riding lesson, because the rider didn't really have to do anything but stay on the horse. And being their first time, she'd picked one of the shortest trails, so she was a little surprised when they asked to take a break about halfway through because their backsides were numb. She felt bad because she had been worried that the trail was going to be too easy for them, forgetting that even though they were both very physically fit, horseback riding for the first time could get a little uncomfortable. Knowing they still had to make the ride back, she didn't have the heart to tell them that later they would probably be *wishing* for numbness! She just hoped it didn't affect Cole with his football practice. They made it back with no complaining at all, but Maggie did notice them squirming in their saddles from time to time.

After they tended to the horses and got the tack put away, they made the decision to skip their Chinese ritual that night and stay on for dinner with Maggie's family. Partly because they were having such a good time, and partly because Mrs. Thompson had pretty much insisted earlier. She wanted the boys—as she so sweetly referred to them—to meet Maggie's older brother Vic and his family, who'd already agreed to join them for dinner. Their house was just over the hill. Maggie had pointed it out to the guys during their horseback ride.

They went in the house to find Maggie's dad sitting on a stool at the counter in the kitchen sipping iced tea and keeping her mom company while she prepared dinner. There were three glasses of tea ready and waiting for them. Maggie took hers and gestured for the guys to have a seat on the other stools next to her dad, while she went to work helping her mom put the finishing touches on dinner.

"Have you told the boys anything about your brother or Ann?" Stella asked Maggie.

"A little," she answered. "I showed them their house while we were riding, and they know he works here on the farm full time." Turning to address Chad and Cole she added, "Besides working here with Momma and Daddy during the week, my brother teaches adult education classes in Newport two nights a week."

Stella added, "Well you can only talk so much to us and the cows! He needed *something* that would get him off this farm and around some other human beings besides family once in a while!" They all laughed.

"Yeah, we bout had to run him off, thought maybe he could coach little league or somethin, but he decided he wanted to teach these classes, so whatever so long as he gets away ever now and then," Clarence said.

Chad said, "It's ironic that he chose to teach, and that's what Maggie wants to do too. It must run in the family."

"Huh, you're right! I hadn't thought about it like that!" Maggie realized.

"Well what about his wife? Does she work here on the farm?" Cole asked.

Maggie answered, "She used to, full time, until Gabrielle turned six and started school."

"Oh, just wait till you meet Gaby!" Stella said with a big smile.

Clarence chuckled, "Yeah, Gaby's somethin now. She'll steal yer heart in no time."

"They're not kidding!" Maggie confirmed. "She's a cutie! And Ann, her mother is a sweetheart too. She went to work in the pharmacy at the Walgreens in town, when Gaby started school. We grew up with the manager, and he schedules Ann's hours around Gaby's school, so she's home when Gaby's home. One of the perks of growing up and living in a small town."

Cole said, "That's good. I think the mom should be home with the kids, like our mom's were." He looked over at Chad, who nodded in agreement.

"And if Gaby can't go to school, she gets to stay here with me!" Stella explained with a wink at the boys.

Chad and Cole both said, "We'd pretend to be sick all the time!"

"She *has* been known to pull one over a time or two!" Maggie admitted.

By the time Vic, Ann and Gaby arrived, Cole and Chad felt like they already knew them. In just a short while they could tell how close they were, especially Maggie and Gaby. And they were right. Gaby was a doll, and the spitting image of a picture on the mantle of Maggie at about the same age that Gaby was now.

Cole had figured that Maggie had learned to cook from her mother and when dinner was served his suspicions were confirmed. It was delicious. They had roast beef, mashed potatoes, and green beans from her mom's garden, along with mouth watering rolls her mom made from scratch. During dinner they talked about everything from running the farm, to school, to the highlights of the exciting football game the day before. Maggie's dad and brother had watched the game on television, and Maggie told them about how much fun it had been to actually be at the game, admitting that now she wished she had gone to one before.

For dessert they got to have Maggie's Aunt Sylvia's apple stack cake that she dropped off that morning on her way to church. She had been disappointed that Maggie and her friends weren't there yet, but she couldn't stay, having been asked to play the organ at the wedding of the daughter of a close friend. She would be at the church all day and into the evening for the Sunday night service. She asked Clarence and Stella to tell the kids she was looking forward to seeing Maggie and meeting the boys the next time they got to come visit. Maggie hadn't exaggerated though. The apple stack cake was to die for.

While they were having desert, Vic asked Chad and Cole how they liked their first horseback ride. They both said that they really enjoyed it and looked forward to doing it again, when they recovered. No explanations were needed. Everyone chuckled.

When the horses were brought up, Gaby asked if Maggie had told them her 'horse story'. Maggie blushed and looked at her Dad in disbelief, surprised that now *Gaby* was bringing it up. She didn't know why they got such a kick out of it, it was no big deal. Clarence had loved telling the story over the years because he was so proud of Maggie's ingenuity and thoughtfulness, he just couldn't help it, and when he realized that the boys hadn't heard it yet, he jumped at the chance to tell it again, and Gaby urged him on. Maggie didn't want to disappoint them, so she let them tell it again.

"Well we had us some company visitin', my cousin Clyatt and his wife Thelma. Now they was from the city. New York, wasn't it Mama?" he asked Stella, knowing perfectly well it was New York, having told the story so many times, and Stella just nodded her head, like she did every time he told it. Gaby nodded her head as well, knowing the story by heart, delighted to be hearing it again.

"Well now, they done seen the horses out in the pasture, and Thelma took a notion that she wanted to go horseback ridin'. Now ordinarily that wouldn't be no problem, but ya' see, Thelma weighed about 350 pounds." He threw his hands up in defense, "Now don't get me wrong, I ain't got nothin' against big women. Thelma was a fine lady. As good as they come. The problem was we didn't have no horse that could've carried her and another 50 or 60 pounds of tack and saddle." He shook his head regretfully. "I shore was hatin' to have to tell her that, and spent most of the evenin' trying to figure out what I could say without hurtin' her feelin's, but Maggie here saved me havin' to tell her no," he said, cocking his head toward Maggie, beaming with pride. Maggie blushed again.

"Tell 'em what she did, Papaw!" Gaby said, anxious to get on with the story.

"Well, the next mornin' Thelma brought it up again," he went on, "and just when I thought I didn't have no other choice but to tell her she couldn't go ridin', Maggie comes in and says it won't be no problem. I thought she'd done went and lost her mind, but she just looked at me and winked. Come to find out, Maggie had got up before everbody, and rode on over to Mr. Huckaby's place down the road, and told him about Thelma. You see, Mr. Huckaby was a purty good size fella himself, and he had a twenty year old Belgian Draft horse, that stood at about sixteen hands and weighed about seventeen hunnert pounds. Now, let me tell you, this horse was the gentlest horse I ever did see, and carried old man Huckaby around all day like it was nothin', so Thelma, for an hour or so, wouldn't be no problem a'tall. Maggie had brought that horse back with her and Thelma got to go ridin', and never even knew that horse wasn't one of ours! Now don't that beat all? Maggie wasn't but eleven years old, but she come up with that all by herself and made Thelma's day! Mine too cause it saved me from embarrassin' Thelma!"

Gaby clapped when he finished telling the story, like it was the very first time she'd ever heard it. Cole and Chad liked it too! It sounded exactly like the Maggie they knew.

After desert Chad and Cole spotted the piano in the family room, and were told it was the same piano Maggie learned to play on as a child, so they asked Maggie if she would play something. Glad for the opportunity to get off the subject of her 'horse story', she readily agreed.

They all moved from the dining room into the family room and Maggie took a seat at the piano. She motioned Gaby over to sit beside her and she began to play the first song she had learned as a child, *Amazing Grace*, and sang, accompanied by Gaby. They sounded beautiful together. It was a tender moment between them, and they shared a hug at the end. To liven things up, Maggie played *Crocodile Rock* and got everyone to join in. No one was bashful about singing along and then making requests for Maggie to play and they continued until it started getting late.

They didn't want to call it a night, but Maggie and "the boys" needed to get back to Knoxville because the three of them had early morning classes, so they said their goodbyes and headed back.

CHAPTER 11

The Vols continued their season unbeaten, and Maggie made up for lost time by attending every single home game. She was thrilled that she got to go with Cole's family and Chad to Athens when they played Georgia—where she shared a room with Cheyenne and heard more about Coles childhood—and she watched three of the other four *away* games with Cole's parents at their house. Chad's parent's always joined them at the Rivers' house, and Chris and Savannah usually did as well. It truly was a family affair.

The third of October was Cole's twenty second birthday, but fell on a Saturday when he had a game at Auburn, so much to Maggie's relief, they celebrated it the day before. She had been dying to give him her gift. Everyone knew that Cole's dream was to play for the Indianapolis Colts one day, and that his all time hero was Johnny Unitas, so she'd begun searching months earlier for the perfect gift. She eventually found an original photograph of Johnny Unitas that he had autographed, complete with a Certificate of Authenticity. She would never forget the look on his face when he opened it. It was the first time she'd ever seen him speechless. He loved it.

They each spent Thanksgiving with their own families, and for the final game of the season the following Saturday at Vanderbilt, all three families got together and watched the game at the Rivers' home. The Volunteers won, 41-0. To celebrate the team going to the SEC Championships at the Georgia Dome in Atlanta, the families met again to watch the game together. A central point for all of them was a sports themed family restaurant in Sevierville that had more big screen T.V's than you could count. Again, the Vols won against Mississippi State, 24-14.

∾ℋℋℋ∾

On Friday, December 18th, at the OCI, Cole asked Maggie if he could take her out for a while Saturday afternoon. He said he had something he needed to talk to her about. There was something about his expression and the tone of his voice that was so serious, she got a little worried. She gave Chad a questioning look, but he shook his head looking clueless, indicating he didn't know anything.

"Sure," Maggie said hesitantly. "Can you give me a hint what we need to talk about? Is everything okay?

"Everything's fine. Don't worry," he assured her. "I just need to talk to you."

"Okay. What time?"

"Is three o'clock okay?"

"That's fine. Can you at least tell me where we're going, so I'll know what to wear?"

He debated a second, then said, "Mmmm...no, sorry, I can't. Just wear something comfortable and warm."

"Comfortable and warm," she repeated, even more unsure now about what to think, despite his assurance that everything was fine. "Okay." She swallowed hard past the lump in her throat, and looked at Chad again, but if he knew anything, he wasn't talking. It occurred to her then that he had been a little quiet all evening, which didn't exactly help her overactive imagination. Now she was really concerned there was something wrong.

∾⌘⌘⌘∾

Cole had asked Maggie's best friend Maresa earlier in the week to see if she could make sure there weren't any fundraisers or events Maggie was committed to on Saturday, then asked her to promise not to tell Maggie he had inquired. Sensing a surprise in the making, she agreed to check and was able to confirm to Cole that Maggie was indeed free on Saturday. Cole thanked her for her help and again swore her to secrecy.

Chad's Journal
December 18, 1998

Such an enormous price to pay,
for the things I can never say.

CHAPTER 12

Saturday, Maggie spent all morning trying to figure out what to wear that afternoon, packing to go home for Christmas, and worrying about what Cole had to tell her. When she thought back over the past week, she admitted to herself that both Chad *and* Cole had been acting a little strange, but Chad really didn't appear to know what was going on either. By the time Cole arrived to pick her up, she was a nervous wreck. She was watching for him and stepped out onto the porch when he drove up. She was wearing a bulky cream colored cable knit sweater, blue jeans tucked into brown suede, flat heeled boots with a fluffy wool trim around the top, that also lined the insides, and carrying a brown suede jacket. When Cole got out of the car, she noticed he was wearing jeans, hiking boots, and a heavy sweater, still giving her no clue as to where they were headed. She tried to read his expression, getting nowhere.

"Hey,' Cole said, as he approached the steps. He smiled slightly and to Maggie it looked forced. "You all set?" he asked.

"I am," she said, hoping that she was. He gave her a quick kiss, lifted the jacket from her arm, took her hand and led her to the car, opening the door for her. She slid in and watched him as he walked around the front of the car, got in and started the engine. They drove in silence for a few miles and every time Cole glanced at Maggie she hoped he would say something, but he just had that same half smile on his face and offered nothing in the way of letting her know what was going on. He drove to Interstate 40 and headed east.

Maggie couldn't stand the silence any more. She had to ask. "You still won't tell me where we're going?"

"Can't. So…how are we going to work out seeing each other on Christmas?"

Relieved to hear he was making plans for Christmas—which meant he wasn't breaking up with her—she decided to play along since he was trying valiantly to change the subject. For the next several miles they made plans for Christmas, talked about gifts they had already purchased, and the shopping they still had to do. Before she realized it they were in Gatlinburg, turning north on Hwy 321. If she hadn't known better, she would have thought he was taking the long way to her parents home, but a few miles out of Gatlinburg he turned off onto a side road and was soon pulling up to a covered bridge. Maggie lit up when she saw it.

"Oh my gosh! It's so beautiful! How did you find this?" she asked, getting out of the car as soon as Cole parked and turned off the engine.

Grinning, Cole got out and joined her. Looking a bit smug he said, "I've got connections." He took her hand and led her down to a grassy area beside the creek. Up in the distance Maggie could see a small fire with what appeared to be a blanket and woven basket on the ground beside it. She glanced around nervously, thinking that they were intruding on someone's picnic, but didn't see anyone else around. Then she searched for posted signs saying it was private property. She looked questioningly at Cole but he just continued to lead her up to the fire, stopping at the edge of the blanket. He looked down at her and smiled and Maggie could tell that this smile was genuine.

"Would you care to join me?" he asked.

She looked at him astonished. "This is for us? How in the world did you *do* this?" she asked, looking around again for somebody else.

"Like I said, I've got connections," he answered cryptically, not yet ready to reveal his accomplices. He motioned for her to have a seat on the blanket, which she did, and he sat down beside her. He reached for another blanket that was folded up next to the picnic basket, pulling it over their laps.

"Comfy?" he asked her.

"Yes. It's awesome" she sighed, breathless with wonder.

From where they were sitting they could see the stream. The sight and sound of the water flowing over the rocks was so peaceful and serene. Maggie felt herself relax for the first time that day. She leaned into Cole and they cuddled and talked about their surroundings for a little while, enjoying the fire. Then Cole announced quietly, "I've been invited to participate in the NFL Scouting Combine."

Excited by the news she turned to face him. "Cole! That's fantastic! When is it? Where do you have to go?"

"It's in February, in Indianapolis."

"I'm so proud of you! What did your parents say? And Chad?" she asked, noticing that he didn't appear to be very enthused. Something seemed to be bothering him.

"They're happy. Worried about school though."

"Oh." The realization that Cole wouldn't be graduating that year suddenly sunk in. Concerned herself now, she asked, "What are you going to do?"

With an earnestness that startled Maggie, he said, "Maggie, it's what I've always wanted. It's in my blood. I've *got* to go for it. I can finish school later. I can't pass this up! That's why I wanted to talk to you. If I make it to the draft, I don't know where I may end up. I'll have to move, and I know you're graduating soon, but your teaching license will be for Tennessee." He looked at her, his eyes pleading, "How do you feel about long distance relationships?"

She was quiet for a moment, trying to process everything, then she said, "We'll work it out, Cole. Whatever it takes. Let's see how things go at the combine. Maybe you won't have to move *too* far away and we can still figure out a way for you to earn your degree, too," she assured him.

Visibly relieved, he stood and reached for her hand to help her up. "I love you," he said, pulling her to him.

"I love you, too."

He kissed her, then took her hand and they strolled down by the water. Maggie was glad to know now what had been on Cole's mind. She'd been so worried.

He stopped walking suddenly and turned to face her. He took her free hand in his, and she stood, stunned, as he knelt down on one knee.

Her heart started beating frantically as he looked up into her eyes.

"Maggie, you are the first thing I think of in the morning and the last thing I think of at night. Will you marry me?" he asked softly.

"Will I?...Cole! Yes! Yes, I'll marry you!"

He rose, pulling her in his arms and kissed her. After the kiss he leaned back and cupped her face in his hands. "Thank you! I love you with all my heart." Then he took her hand and slipped a diamond solitaire engagement ring on her finger.

Maggie's eyes widened when she saw the ring. The diamond was much larger than she would have been happy with and more than she thought that he could comfortably afford. She looked up to tell him she didn't need a ring like that but he looked so happy she decided not to spoil the moment. They could talk about it later. She pulled his face down to hers and kissed him instead.

Coming up from the kiss, he smiled. "Happy?" he asked.

She nodded her head emphatically, not trusting herself to speak.

He grinned bigger. "Hungry?"

She realized she was famished. She hadn't eaten all day because she had been so worried. "Yes!" she answered.

Still reeling from the unexpected proposal, as they made their way back to their fire, Maggie told Cole she couldn't have been more surprised or happy. They settled back down on the blanket and Cole unpacked their picnic dinner. She watched as he pulled out a bottle of wine, two glasses, and a corkscrew. After he removed the cork, he poured a bit into each wine glass, handing one to Maggie.

"To us," he saluted and they clinked glasses and took a sip. Then he pulled two shrimp cocktails from the basket and un-wrapped them.

In awe, Maggie asked, "How did you arrange all this?" as she took the cocktail Cole offered her.

"Well, first of all, I went to see your mom and dad last week—"

"What?!" she interrupted.

"Well I couldn't ask you to marry me without asking your dad first, could I?"

"You mean they know about this? What did they say?"

"Yes, they know. They're the ones who told me about this place, and they gave me their blessing."

"*I* didn't even know this was here. I wonder how *they* knew? Wait! They gave you their blessing?"

Cole laughed. "You say that like you're surprised! Yes, they gave me their blessing. They were excited and they didn't say how they knew about this place, but I told them I wanted to find someplace peaceful and private, and beautiful. After they told me about it, I came by and talked to the people who live over there," he said, pointing to a house down the lane. "They gave me permission to bring you here, and have a fire and all. Sometimes people go on the other side, over there, for picnics and stuff, but I wanted to make sure we wouldn't be interrupted, and they said okay."

"I just can't believe this," she said, holding her hand up to admire her ring. "So how did you get all this stuff here, and who got the fire going?"

"We have to thank Chad and Cheyenne for that. Chad went with me, after I talked to your parents, to pick out your ring. Do you like it?"

"Of course I do! It's beautiful!" she exclaimed, looking at it again.

"Anyway, Cheyenne and Chad put together our dinner, picked out the wine, borrowed the glasses from my mom, along with the blankets and basket, then came over earlier and set everything up. They left when they saw us coming. That's why I was driving real slow, so you wouldn't see them."

"You are amazing," she said, shaking her head in disbelief. "What does *your* family think about all this?"

"You know they love you, Maggie. They told me I'd better not let you get away!"

She smiled bashfully. "I'm so happy, Cole. I love you, I love your family. And Chad and Cheyenne...That was so sweet of them to do this!"

Cole chuckled. "There was no way Cheyenne was going to let anyone else do it. She was all excited about it."

"That's because she's a sweetheart, just like you. I didn't know you were so romantic!" She leaned over and kissed him. They finished eating and put everything back in the basket, then cuddled up together under the blanket and talked about their future until the fire went out.

CHAPTER 13

Everyone was thrilled about Cole and Maggie's engagement! It was followed with a wonderful Christmas and New Year. Classes had resumed and everyone got back down to business, especially Maggie and Chad, who were preparing to graduate in the spring. Cole and his father flew to Indianapolis for the Combine in February. Cole was at his best, and had interviews with several different NFL teams.

∾⌘⌘⌘∾

Maggie's birthday was February twenty-seventh and Cole had a special surprise for her. He got together with his family and Maggie's, and of course Chad, and they all pitched in and bought Maggie a shiny new Gibson acoustic guitar. She didn't know what to do when she opened it. It was something she had always wanted, and it was all the more special, because Cole and everyone she loved had gotten it for her. As tears pooled in her eyes and spilled over, a hush came over the room. Glances of uncertainty circulated as everyone held their breath. Cole and Chad had never seen Maggie cry before, and the scene before them was more than a little unsettling. Then she looked up, her eyes shimmering, as she flashed an elated smile, relieving everyone.

"This will be a cherished part of my life for as long as I live," she said, her voice breaking.

∾⌘⌘⌘∾

In March, Cole submitted a written application to the NFL renouncing his remaining college football eligibility, and on Pro Day at UT several NFL coaches attended to watch Cole and some of the other NFL hopefuls.

As the NFL Draft approached in April, the reality that their lives were about to change drastically was setting in for the three of them. No one knew what was in store for Cole with football, or where the careers for Maggie and Chad would take *them,* and it was nerve wracking. While Cole prepared for the draft, Maggie and Chad began researching positions available and acquiring applications, wanting to be prepared and aware of their options after they graduated.

∾⌘⌘⌘∾

The weekend of the draft was only days away. It was being held in New York City and Cole and his father had tickets to fly there on Friday, April sixteenth. As it happened, that was also Chad's birthday, so the trio celebrated the day before.

With everyone's schedules so full and hectic, Maggie and Cole thought it would be a welcome change to take Chad someplace nice for a relaxing dinner. They asked around for recommendations, and after considering their options decided on 'Calhoun's on the River' when they saw that it was #5 on the Tennessee Restaurant Review. They had never been there before, in spite of the fact it was right next to the campus overlooking the Tennessee River.

On Thursday evening, Cole made a big deal about him and Chad getting dressed up—which for them meant jeans and an oxford shirt rather than shorts and tee shirts—and they went to pick up Maggie, who was wearing a pretty dress. They got in the car and buckled up, prepared for the ride to the restaurant. All two blocks of it. Chad got a kick out of the unexpectedly short drive and was pleasantly surprised that they were finally getting the chance to go to Calhoun's. And as luck would have it, during dinner he had the pleasure of a second unexpected surprise.

They had just finished ordering when Chad heard someone calling his name.

"Chad? How the heck is ya?" someone called in a heavy southern drawl.

He looked around to see a pretty young lady approaching their table. She was carrying an adorable little girl on her hip. He was puzzled, not recognizing her for a moment. Then it hit him.

"Linda Sue?" he asked in disbelief, his mind rewinding all the way back to grade school.

"Yes! How the heck are ya?" she asked again.

"Good," he nodded his head. "Is this your little girl?" he asked.

"Yes, it is! This is Amanda. She'll be two years old next month! Can you say "Hi" Mandy?" she prompted her daughter, bouncing her gently. The little girl hid her face in her mother's hair. Linda Sue said, "She's being bashful now," looking back at Chad. "Why, if I had known how good lookin' you was gonna to turn out, I'd have kept that Valentine you gave me!"She teased.

Chad's face turned several shades of red and though he was thinking *just kill me now,* he managed a smile, and before he could think of how to reply, she, thankfully, changed the subject.

"So whatcha doing with yore self nowadays?" she asked him.

He told her about going to school to be a sports therapist, and then he realized that she and Cole evidently didn't remember each other, and Maggie had never met her, so he took the opportunity to introduce her to them.

After the introduction, Linda Sue said, "Well, it was shore good seein' you. You take care of yore self now, ya hear? Say Bye-Bye, Mandy," she added, raising her daughter's hand to wave. "Nice to meet ya'll," she waved to Maggie and Cole, who smiled and waved in return.

As she walked away, Chad sat back down and looked at Maggie and Cole who were waiting with raised brows for him to spill the beans. When he didn't offer any explanation, Cole asked, "So, what was all that 'Valentine' business about?"

"Oh. That was nothing," Chad tried to side step.

"Uh uh." Cole shook his head, grinning. "Spill it."

Reluctantly, Chad explained. "Back in the fourth grade, I gave her a Valentine, that's all," he shrugged.

"That's all, huh? Why did she say she *would* have kept it?" Cole pressed, not cutting Chad any slack at all.

"Because…" he cleared his throat, stalling. "I gave her the Valentine with a stick of gum and a nickel," he said, glancing up at them. They were waiting for the rest of the story. Lowering his voice, he admitted in a rush, "And she kept the gum and the nickel, and gave the Valentine back."

"Oh Chad!" Maggie said sympathetically, reaching over to touch his hand.

But Cole cackled loudly. Catching himself, he glanced around to see if anyone was looking. Then he resumed laughing. Uncontrollably. Just quieter.

Chad looked back to Maggie, expecting an ally. She was trying desperately to maintain her look of sympathy. A slow smile crept across his face as he realized that, in hindsight, it *was* pretty funny, even though he was sure that he'd never hear the end of it.

Chad's Journal
April 15, 1999

I celebrated my birthday tonight
with two of the people
I love most in this world.

CHAPTER 14

Everyone waited anxiously to hear from Cole, and as it turned out, they didn't have to wait too long. He called early Saturday afternoon with the news. He was the first round draft pick quarterback for the Tennessee Titans in Nashville, formerly known as the Tennessee Oilers. He was ecstatic, in spite of the fact that it wasn't the Indianapolis Colts. It was Tennessee! He wouldn't be far from his family, and most of all Maggie! It was all he could have asked for.

When he called Maggie to tell her the news, she was so happy for him and so relieved he would be that close to home, she burst into tears. She hadn't realized how nervous she had been till now that it was over. She was glad it was behind them.

∾⌘⌘⌘∾

Back home from New York, Cole and his dad filled everyone in on the details and the excitement of the draft, then Cole went directly to Maggie's. He pulled in the driveway and saw her sitting on the porch, studying.

She looked up when she heard his car. Taking the steps two at a time, he was barely out of the car before she hopped into his arms, wrapping her legs around his waist. "I missed you!" she cried out.

"Oh, Baby, I missed you, too," he said, holding her tight.

She unwrapped her legs and put her feet back on the ground. Looking up at him, she asked, "Are you happy?"

He grinned. "Very," he said, and kissed her. Then he kissed her again.

Pulling out of his embrace, she grabbed his hand and headed back up on the porch, "Come tell me everything!"

He hung on to her hand and followed her up the steps. There was a gentle breeze rustling through the huge, billowy maple trees that towered above and shaded the house and lawn. They sat down on the porch swing, and Maggie turned sideways to face Cole. He was looking out over the sun dappled yard, thoughtful for a moment. Seeming a little nervous, he asked, "How would you feel about coming to Nashville with me?" He turned to face her then.

"When?" she asked, meeting his gaze.

Encouraged by her response, he became visibly enthused. He told her about signing a six year contract with the Titans and receiving a sizable signing bonus, enabling them to get married, move to Nashville, buy a home and get settled before he had to report to training camp at the end of July.

Overwhelmed, Maggie was trying to digest everything. The money! Getting married! Nashville! Buying a house! Moving! She had mistakenly thought when he asked her to go to Nashville that he had meant to just take a trip! Wow! She was *way* off!

Cole was saying, "...and you won't even have to work if you don't want to," but he stopped talking when he looked back at Maggie. She was looking down and shaking her head. She was saying no. His heart sank.

Maggie wasn't aware she was shaking her head, or that Cole had seen it. She couldn't think straight. It was all happening too fast. It was too much. Suddenly the silence became deafening. Wondering how long he had been waiting for her answer, she looked up, her face a combination of emotions. After what seemed like an eternity, she finally spoke. "I think...I think that maybe we can make that work," she said, looking as surprised to hear herself saying the words as Cole did.

He jumped up off the swing, his arms held high in victory, "Yes!" he shouted. "I love you!" he said forcefully, as he turned and picked her up off the swing and spun her around. "I love you! I love you! I love you!"

Clinging to him, she managed to say between the giggles, "I love you, too!"

"Let's go tell Chad!" he said, sitting her down and taking her hand.

Chad's Journal
April 16, 1999

Tonight I celebrated the anniversary
of her coming into my life,
and Cole celebrated his future.

Chad's Journal
May 15, 1999

I fight these feelings
that can never be.
I can't
hurt the two I love so.

CHAPTER 15

It was going to be a picture perfect day for a wedding. Maggie and Cole were getting married at the Thompsons' family church; the one Maggie had attended her whole life, before moving to Knoxville for school. The reception was being held at her parent's home, where a huge white tent had been set up by "Tiffani's Bridal", a well known establishment that provided everything for weddings, from Maggie's gown, to the band and catering at the reception. It was a beautiful setting with the majestic mountains highlighting the background. Everything was in place, the tables were decorated, and garlands of pink and yellow roses—Maggie's favorite—adorned the tent and the stage set up for the band. A rented dance floor lay in wait for the bride and grooms first dance.

As a special surprise, Maggie's parents arranged for a horse drawn carriage and liveried driver to pick the newlyweds up after the ceremony and take them for a scenic ride on the back roads, giving guests time to make their way to the reception site.

The wedding was to take place at 1:00 p.m. Maggie and her mom, along with Maresa, her maid of honor, and Cheyenne, her bridesmaid, had been at the church since around 11:30 that morning doing each other's hair and makeup, and anxiously tending to Maggie's every need.

The men in the wedding party arrived around 12:00, dressed and ready to begin seating the guests that began arriving at about 12:30. At precisely 1:00, the Pastor, Cole, Chad, the best man, and Cole's football buddy, Dave, the groomsman, were in place for the ceremony. The music began, played by Maggie's Aunt Sylvia, and through the double doors in the back of the sanctuary, Cheyenne, who looked beautiful in a pastel yellow gown, carrying a small bouquet of pink tea roses with baby's breath, began the procession. She was followed by Maresa, who looked quite beautiful as well—her dress and roses the opposite of Cheyenne's—in a pastel *pink* gown, carrying *yellow* tea roses with baby's breath. After Maresa, Gaby began making her way down the aisle, dropping pink and yellow rose petals that matched her pastel rose print gown, looking adorable and extremely pleased to be the center of attention for the moment.

Once Gaby was in place, the Wedding March began, and everyone turned their attention once again to the back of the church to get their first glimpse of the bride. There were audible intakes of breath when Maggie emerged on the arm of her father, who was hardly recognizable without his overalls. Though he was extremely handsome in his tuxedo, he was barely noticeable beside Maggie. She was stunning. Her hair was pulled back from her radiant face, swept up high and curled, so that ringlets cascaded down in back. Her white satin gown had lace appliqués from the floor length hem, up to the empire waist. Lace covered the satin bodice, where just above her breasts the satin ended, and the sheer lace continued, tapering up to her neck, ending at a crystal encrusted band around her slender throat. As they made their way down the aisle you were able to see that the back of her gown had two thin jeweled straps that traveled from the center back of the band around her neck, down to where they met the high waist of the skirt on the dress, forming an inverted vee, leaving the smooth, golden skin of her upper back and shoulders exposed. Together, she and the dress were exquisite. No one could take their eyes off her, as her father escorted her on her final walk as a single woman. When they passed the front and final pew, Cole stepped forward to exchange places with her father.

The Pastor asked who was giving Maggie for marriage, and her father replied, "Her Mother and I do".

Maggie was beaming as she took Cole's arm, and side by side they approached the Pastor, while her father took a seat next to her mother, who already had tears streaming down her face. The Pastor spoke for a moment about the sanctity of marriage, then said a prayer asking God to bless their union, after which he asked Cole if he had the ring. Chad, who had been clutching the ring tightly in his hand, handed it to Cole. Cole then glanced at the Pastor, who gave him a slight nod to continue.

He took Maggie's hand, began to slip the ring on her finger, and looking into her eyes, he said, "I, Cole Rivers, take you, Maggie Thompson, to be my wife, my partner in life, and my one true love. I will cherish our union, and love you more each day than I did the day before. I will trust you, and respect you, laugh with you, and cry with you, loving you faithfully, through good times and bad, regardless of the obstacles we may face together. I give you my hand, my heart, and my love, from this day forward, as long as we both shall live," then he slid the ring firmly in place.

Maggie handed Maresa her bouquet and took Cole's ring, then turning to Cole, she began to place the ring on his finger. Looking up at him, she said, "I, Maggie Thompson, take you, Cole Rivers, to be my husband, my constant friend, my faithful partner, and my love from this day forward. In the presence of God and our family and friends, I offer you my solemn vow to be your faithful partner in sickness and in health, in good times and bad, and in joy as well as sorrow. I promise to love you unconditionally, to support you in your goals, to honor and respect you, to laugh with you, and cry with you, and to cherish you for as long as we both shall live." Then she slid the ring on his finger.

They turned back to the Pastor then and he said, "By the power vested in me, I now pronounce you husband and wife. You may kiss your bride."

Taking Maggie's face in his hands, Cole leaned down and kissed her softly for several seconds. As he pulled back he told her he loved her.

"I love you, too," she said softly, her eyes shimmering.

The Pastor announced, "I now present to you, Mr. and Mrs. Cole Rivers."

There was applause from everyone who wasn't too busy wiping the tears from their eyes.

∾⌘⌘⌘∾

In the carriage, Cole wrapped his arm around Maggie's shoulders and she snuggled close, as the liveried driver pulled away from the church. The horses pulling the carriage were identical in color, a chestnut brown with blonde flowing manes that shone in the sunlight. They were magnificent. A portrait of fierce strength and yet a serene, graceful beauty simultaneously. The carriage rolled forward with ease, a testament to their power, their muscles rippling as they moved.

While the driver guided the horses and carriage smoothly along the winding mountain lane, under the canopy, shielded from the brilliant sun, Cole and Maggie were oblivious to their surroundings. They couldn't take their eyes off each other. As they rolled alongside and then over a clear sparkling creek, Cole pulled Maggie closer still, and with a slight tremor in his voice, whispered in her ear, "I am so blessed".

CHAPTER 16

It could have been a scene from a movie, Cole and Maggie approaching in the carriage. Everyone scrambled to get a picture, along with the hired photographer.

Maggie had requested that not so many 'still' photos be taken, where everyone lined up like a firing squad, but rather, she wanted candid photo's of everyone enjoying themselves. This was a shot the photographer didn't want to miss!

When the carriage rolled to a stop, Cole stepped down and turned to assist Maggie. Placing his hands around her slender waist, he lifted her as if she were light as a feather, and placed her gently on the ground. They made their way to their places of honor at the table, accepting compliments and well wishes along the way.

Champagne or sparkling apple juice was being served as everyone took their seats, and when everyone had a glass for the toast, Chad stood, and a hush fell over the guests. Raising his glass, he said, "Cole, it is an honor to stand here as your best man, to be a part of your fairy tale wedding to your gorgeous bride. You are my best friend and a true gentleman…and one darned lucky guy." Laughter rippled through the crowd. "Maggie you are truly beautiful. You possess a beauty that goes deeper than the eye can see. You have an amazing spirit, a kind and generous heart, and are a blessing to everyone you meet. The two of you are beginning what I'm sure will be a wonderful journey together, and I couldn't wish it for two better people." Raising his glass in salute, he concluded, "I love you guys, God Bless."

Amid the tinkle of glasses meeting in toast, Cole stood and shook hands with Chad, pulling him into an embrace. "Thank you, Chad," he said sincerely.

"You're welcome, buddy." Chad replied. Standing back, he gave him a squeeze on his shoulder.

Maggie was waiting and hugged Chad warmly. “Thank you so much.” She kissed his cheek, then gently wiped away the traces of her lipstick.

“You’re welcome, Pretty Lady,” he managed. Swallowing back a lump in his throat, he picked the microphone back up and said, “Everybody can eat now!”

∾⌘⌘⌘∾

After everyone had eaten, the dancing began with Cole and Maggie waltzing to *Wedding Day*, the band and singer doing the Bee Gee’s credit, followed by Maggie and her father pleasing the guests with the traditional father/daughter dance, to Bob Carlisle’s rendition of *Butterfly Kisses*. Chad was next in line to dance with Maggie while Cole danced with Maresa, and the band called their parents and the rest of the wedding party to the floor. It was several dances later before Maggie got to dance with Cole again—more because he stole her back than for lack of willing partners—when the band played Eric Clapton’s *Wonderful Tonight.* Chad was dancing with Cheyenne now and murmurs of what handsome couples they both made, spread between the guests.

Later, when the band took a short break, Maggie took center stage. “I have a little surprise for Cole,” she announced.

While everyone found their seats, someone took a chair to the center of the dance floor and seated Cole, and a member of the band carefully brought Maggie her cherished Gibson guitar. Showing it off, she said, “This was my birthday present! Isn’t it beautiful?” Cheers and applause resounded. Getting situated, she looked at Cole. “I wrote this for you,” she said softly. Strumming her guitar, she began the slow melody…

“As a girl I often dreamed how true love would be,
Would my heart sing out, for all the world to see,
Would he ride in on a white horse,
Would he fight to set me free,

Now a thousand dreams combined, is standing next to me."

She smiled at Cole, singing volumes with her eyes, then continued, her voice breaking softly...

"You're the compass in my heart, to guide me every day,
I promise to be faithful, in each and every way,
You're the answer to my prayers,
From the good Lord up above,
He sent you to me, made you for me to love,
And now my hearts singing,
For all the world to see,
Cause the man that I love,
Is standing next to me,
You're the compass in my heart, to guide me every day,
I promise to be faithful, in each and every way,
Cause you're the answer to my prayers
From the good Lord up above."

As the final note faded, Cole stood and went to Maggie. With her up on the stage, he now had to look up to her. His voice was filled with awe as he asked, "How did I ever deserve you?" He wrapped his arms around her waist, and laid his head on her chest, holding her close. It was so touching, tears were flowing once again–even from some of the men this time, though they were trying unsuccessfully to hide it.

ᔓ⌘⌘⌘ᔓ

After Stephanie caught the bouquet, and Dave got hit in the head with the garter, the celebration began to wind down and Maggie and Cole prepared to leave. Everyone called on Chad to say something in closing, to send the couple off. Once more, Chad took the floor. Taking the microphone, he cleared his throat and shrugged his shoulders.

"What do you say to your two best friends at a moment such as this? Well for Cole, I'll put it in terms he understands. Cole, you just scored a touchdown!"

Everyone cheered in agreement. Cole and Maggie looked at each other, laughing, and Cole signaled a thumbs up.

Chad continued, "But the game has just begun. Be extra careful not to run out of bounds, because I'll be on the sideline watching you. And on the field of life, if you're ever faced with a third and long, be sure to go to the best receiver any man could hope for. I know in my heart, my friend, you will win the game."

More cheers and applause.

"And Maggie, I know through my own personal experiences that this man can be hard to keep up with, but I think you will find it's worth every effort." He placed his hand over his heart in sincerity, and concluded, "May all your dreams come true." Trying hard to maintain his composure, he hugged them both and quickly moved away to allow the other guests and family the opportunity to say their goodbyes.

While they were busy doing that, the sorority sisters passed out little fabric wrapped bundles of birdseed that Maresa and Stephanie had prepared earlier that week. After everyone hugged and kissed and wished them well, Maggie and Cole made a run for their car under a rain of birdseed. But Maggie wasn't aware she had a surprise wedding gift waiting from Cole, so she was a little confused when she didn't see the Camaro right away. She knew that it was supposed to be there waiting for them, because they had packed their luggage in it the night before. Scanning the parked cars, she stopped short when she saw that the car Cole was leading her up to had "Just Married" carefully written in shoe polish on the back window.

"It's yours," he told her with a big smile.

"Oh. My. Gosh." Maggie managed to utter slowly. It was the dream car that she had always admired but didn't remember ever mentioning to Cole! A silvery blue 1986 Jaguar XJ-S.

Cole would have gladly bought her a new Jaguar, but he'd understood completely when Maggie told him that she only liked that particular year, before the style changed, and only in that color. So instead, he searched relentlessly until he found one in mint condition. It would be a classic soon, just like his Camaro.

"Cole! You didn't!" she exclaimed, slowly inching closer as if it were a mirage and could disappear at any moment. "Oh my gosh!" she sighed breathlessly, while walking around to the front of the car. "It's the exact one! I can't believe you did this!" she cried, and ran back to hop into his arms planting kisses all over his face. "It's perfect! I love you!"

Everyone had been silent watching and waiting for her reaction to the car, and when they applauded, she remembered that she and Cole had an audience. She had a tendency to forget such things when her emotions overtook her. Pulling from his arms and grinning from ear to ear, she called out to them, "Do you see how lucky I am?!" but it was more a statement than a question and without waiting for anyone to answer, she opened the passenger door and climbed in, carefully tucking her dress in around her.

Cole got in the driver's seat and started the car. The engine purred like a kitten, and Maggie grinned even bigger. As they pulled away, he blew the horn in farewell, and drove off, leaving their families and guests marveling about their unforgettable wedding.

Maggie and Cole were headed to a rented cabin, at nearby Meadow Creek Mountain Resort, where they would spend the night, before heading to Nashville in the morning. They planned to spend their honeymoon in search of the new house, where they would build their lives together.

Chad's Journal
May 29, 1999

How does one live around the love of his life,
when the love of his life becomes his best friend's wife?

CHAPTER 17

The month of May brought about more than one life changing event for Chad. He graduated Summa Cum Laude, with a BS Degree in Biology, bringing his time at the University of Tennessee to an end. Cole and Maggie's wedding brought an end to having his best friend for a roommate. Then came the phone call from Cole, toward the end of their week in Nashville.

"Hi Buddy! You miss me?" asked Cole.

"Hey! What are you doing calling me on your honeymoon? I *know* you don't miss *me*. If you do, you aren't doing something right!"

"Well, smart guy, I think you'll agree I'm doing everything right."

"How's that?" Chad asked.

"Our realtor knows of a couple of real nice townhouses that are available to lease!"

"Okay..." Confused, Chad asked, "But I thought you guys were looking for a house? To Buy?"

"We found a house, and man it's a beauty, but you're gonna be needin' someplace to sleep. I love you man, and no offence, but I've lived with you long enough," he laughed.

"Cole, what are you talking about?"

"Well, Doc, I took Maggie to the Coliseum to show her around, you know, maybe meet some of the coaches and staff, or whatever, and do you know who we ran into?" Not giving Chad time to answer, he blurted, "Jeff Fisher and Brad Brown!"

Chad knew this was the Head Coach and Head Athletic Trainer, but couldn't fathom what that would have to do with him. "Yeah, and?" he asked.

"Well, we got to talking, and I kind of mentioned you, and how you're gonna be this big shot physical therapist and all, and well, let's just say it's payback time, that's all."

"Cole, what *are* you talking about?"

"I'm talking about, you need to get your butt over here and pick out one of these townhouses, and bring your resume, then get enrolled at Belmont University, because you've gotta be goin to an accredited University in order to complete this internship with the Titan's."

Chad was silent for a moment. "Cole, I can't—"

"There's no "*can't*" to it, Chad. It's all settled. They just need your resume and enrollment papers, and you're in business, my man!"

"Cole, there's—" Chad started, but then it sounded like Cole dropped the phone.

"Chad?" It was Maggie's voice.

"Hey, Pretty Lady."

"Hi! Listen, Cole's put a lot into this Chad. He really wants..., we *both* really want you here. Everything's worked out Chad, all you have to do is get here, like Cole said. Isn't it what you've been working for? We'll all still be together. Please don't say no," she pleaded.

Thoughts were running through his head like a whirlwind. Could he do it? *How* could he possibly do it? How could he tell her no? It was *exactly* what he'd been working for, only a lot easier and quicker than he'd ever imagined. But could his heart take it? Before he could analyze it too much, he relented. "Okay!"

He could hear Maggie's squeal as she handed the phone back to Cole. "He said "Okay"!!"

They made plans for him to drive over that afternoon, Cole promising to get him a room where they were staying, and setting up a meeting with Brad the next day. They would stay a few days longer than planned to help Chad get everything in order.

Chad hung up wondering if he'd done the right thing. It felt bittersweet.

CHAPTER 18

It had been a little over a year since that phone call. The move went smoothly, and everyone settled into their new routines. Maggie spent the first two months having a ball decorating their two story, four bedroom, three bath home, making it ready for the family to visit for the games. She loved that the first thing you saw when you opened the front door was a gorgeous mahogany staircase that curved around to the second floor. It was a beautiful focal point. Decorating their home had been one of the most enjoyable things she had ever done. While shopping for furniture, draperies, linens, and of course, all of the knick knacks and pictures, she realized if she ever wanted to change careers, interior decorating would be a real close second to teaching. She loved searching out all the little Mom & Pop shops, and finding treasures. The furnishings Maggie chose were tasteful and unpretentious, with just a few antique pieces she had gotten a bargain on, that she hadn't been able to resist. The overall effect was picture perfect. It was a dream home, and Maggie couldn't believe it was theirs.

∾⌘⌘⌘∾

Cole and the Titans had a stellar year, winning every game before a sold out stadium known as LP Field. It was the best season in franchise history, finishing at 13-3. Then they won the first round playoff game against the Buffalo Bills, who Cole's groomsman, Dave, now played for. Dave was also now happily married to Stephanie, Maggie's sorority sister, whom he'd met at Cole's wedding. The winning play against the Bills, now known as the "Home Run Throwback" in the Titan playbook, was where tight end Frank Wyecheck made a lateral pass to Kevin Dyson—who was only on the field because another player was injured—on a kickoff return with sixteen seconds left in regulation. The Titans were trailing by one point. Dyson ran the pass back seventy-five yards, for a touchdown. The Titans then defeated the Indianapolis Colts in Indianapolis, and went on to defeat the Jacksonville Jaguars in Jacksonville, in the AFC Championship game, taking them to Super Bowl XXXIV, at the Georgia Dome, in Atlanta.

There they played the St. Louis Rams, and the Titans were stopped one yard short of the end zone, when time ran out. The score – Rams 23, Titans 16. It was a heartbreaking loss.

∾⌘⌘⌘∾

Chad was devoting every minute to school, when he wasn't working with the team, trying to get his masters in record time, and making good headway. Maggie enthusiastically helped Chad get his townhouse "livable", as she put it. He had been content with the bed, dresser and desk he'd bought, spending the majority of his time on campus or at the stadium. At least Maggie made his place comfortable for his family when they visited, which was pretty often, for the games.

Maggie and Cole had planned to take a real honeymoon in Hawaii after the season ended, but due to unforeseen circumstances in Maggie's condition, they had to postpone again.

Chad was on his way to the hospital now, after receiving a frantic message from Cole that morning, saying he had been there with Maggie all night. At the nurses' station they told Chad what room she was in and that it was okay for her to have visitors.

After knocking, he pushed open the door and the first thing he saw was;

IT'S A BOY!

Chad Alan Rivers

6 lbs. 7 oz.

"Car? You named him Car?" he kidded, knowing full well Cole's initials were C.A.R., and assuming that the "C" was for "Cole". "Congratulations, you two!" he said as he sat down a stuffed animal with balloons attached for the baby, and a beautiful bouquet of pink and yellow roses for Maggie. When his hands were free, he turned and gave Cole a big bear hug, patting him heartily on the back. Then he turned to Maggie, who was propped up in bed, beaming as she held her baby boy.

"Hey Pretty Lady," Chad said, leaning over to kiss her on the forehead. "That's a handsome little guy you've got there. So that's Cole Jr., huh?"

Maggie looked over at Cole, who said, "Why don't you take another look," pointing at the clear plastic baby bassinet the nurses use to take the babies to the nursery.

Chad stepped back around the baby cart to take another look at the card with the baby's name printed on it. He saw then, the small letters he had missed before.

Chad Alan Rivers

He blinked a couple of times as if to clear his eyes, then swallowed and looked up at Cole, then Maggie, then back at Cole. They were smiling at him expectantly, waiting for his reaction. He opened his mouth to speak, but nothing came out. Still speechless, he raised his open palmed hand to the name tag, then dropped his hand down to his side, and he looked back at Cole and Maggie.

"I don't know what to say," he said in disbelief, and his eyes welled with tears. He never dreamed of such an honor, and the magnitude of this gesture was overwhelming.

"You don't have to say anything," Cole said, smiling.

Chad went back over to Maggie, and with his index finger, gently touched little Chad's fist. The baby reacted by wrapping his tiny fingers around Chad's finger. Amazed, Chad grinned proudly, as if the baby had just done something miraculous. Still grinning, he softly said, "Hey, little Car."

Chad's Journal

August 6, 2000

How can anyone look at a baby and not believe in God?
What little miracles they are!
And this little miracle bears my name.

CHAPTER 19

Maggie's parents came to visit first, so her mom could give her a hand with the baby, since Cole was busy preparing for his second season with the Titans, the first game only a few weeks away. It turned out Maggie hadn't needed any help at all. She was a natural, though she was glad to see her parents and show off little Chad.

Cole's parents were desperate to see their first grandbaby, but knew there was going to be a bunch of visitors right away, so they were trying to be patient and not go until the trip they had previously planned for Cole's first home game. That, of course, was subject to change. Cheyenne, however had classes starting at UT in September, and wasn't sure when she would be able to get away again, so she made the trip after being assured she wasn't intruding. Maggie made sure that Chad came over every night he could, while Cheyenne was there. She knew how close they were and everyone was waiting for an announcement that they were a couple and enough was enough! It was time for them to get on with it already! She still didn't know that it was the farthest thing from either of their minds.

Maggie's brother, Vic, and sister-in-law, Ann, came for a short weekend, because school was in and Gaby had just started second grade. She was fascinated with little Chad, and kept asking if she could take him for a walk, like she did her new puppy at home. She settled for sitting on the couch with pillows propped all around, and holding him on her lap. She doted on him all weekend, like a proud little mommy.

Mr. and Mrs. Edwards came to see Chad the same week Cole's parents came, so they could see the new baby and take in the first home game of the season, too. Cole was like a son to them, and they, like Chad, were humbled and honored that the baby had been named after him.

Everyone loves babies and little Chad was no exception. They all said the same thing after seeing him. He was perfect! Maggie would have no shortage of babysitters if she needed one, especially if Gaby had anything to do with it.

One day during Cheyenne's visit, the baby was taking a nap and they were relaxing with a cup of coffee, when Cheyenne had surprised Maggie by asking her if she would teach her to play the guitar. Thrilled to be asked, Maggie eagerly gave Cheyenne her first lesson right then.

That started the wheels turning. Now, with all the company gone, Maggie began to consider her idea. She was licensed to teach and still wanted to have her own classroom one day, but now that she had little Chad, and Cole's career made it possible, she wanted to stay home and take care of their son. After giving Cheyenne her lessons, Maggie realized there was a chance she could do both. She could give lessons from home. She wondered what Cole would think about it, then remembered a conversation that had taken place the day that Cole and Chad met her parents for the first time. Cole had said he thought a mother should be home with the children. That night she discussed her thoughts with him, and he agreed it was a great idea. He loved having her home with their son.

Four days later, Maggie answered the door to find three deliverymen. After a brief exchange, with Maggie insisting they had to be at the wrong address, they convinced her they were, indeed, at the right place. Wondering what Cole had ordered, and why he hadn't told her about it so she would be expecting the delivery, she watched in stunned silence, while a beautiful, new, baby grand piano, was placed in their formal living room.

∾⌘⌘⌘∾

She began giving guitar and piano lessons four days a week to a few of the kids in the neighborhood. She loved it, and the kids were doing great. It seemed like it was really going to work out, and she was grateful to Cheyenne for helping it to come about. She still volunteered occasionally with the Kappa Delta's in Nashville too. Once a Kappa Delta, always a Kappa Delta. She also began visiting churches on Sunday morning, while the guys were at the stadium during the season, trying to find the right one for their family. She was in search of one that reminded her of the church she grew up in. It was proving to be quite the task.

∾⌘⌘⌘∾

After finding it next to impossible to negotiate the baby and all the accouterments that entailed into the backseat of the two door Jaguar, Maggie waylaid Cole one evening after practice, and found the nearest car dealership. She loved the Jaguar and no intentions of ever letting it go, so the only alternative was to buy an additional vehicle that was more practical. They ended up picking out a Chevy Tahoe. The salesman called the color 'sandalwood', but it was just a fancy name for sage green, a color they both really liked, and it had brown leather seats that would be easy to keep wiped down and clean with a baby on board. There was ample space for the three of them, including all of little Chad's necessities, with room to spare for guests. Best of all, it was much safer for their precious cargo, who was an absolute blessing.

Maggie thought he just had to be the best baby in the world. He rarely cried or fussed and was always so happy, smiling about everything. He was also growing incredibly fast, and she found herself at times wishing she could somehow slow the process down.

Her life was wonderful. She was in love with a wonderful man, she had an adorable baby boy, a beautiful home, her students and the sorority. After a lengthy search, she'd finally found a great church. Yet, with all that, and possibly *because* of all that, she found herself, at times, worrying about Chad. He deserved all that and more. She was concerned that he spent too much time either at school, at home studying, or at the stadium. She had hoped something would have transpired with Cheyenne, but if there was any possibility of it, they were both blind to it.

Frustrated that they couldn't see how perfect they were for each other, she began mentally sorting out girls she'd met since moving to Nashville, that could be a good match for Chad. When she came up with a few she thought he might like, she decided she was going to throw a dinner party so he would have the opportunity to meet them. She would invite a few married couples too, and maybe a single guy or two from Cole's team so it wouldn't be so obvious. She checked the game calendar. The Titans had a Monday night game against Jacksonville, so a Saturday was free. Then she began making some calls.

Thoroughly satisfied with her plan, with all the invitations made, she went to work on the details for the party. Finally, after two weeks of scheming, the time had arrived. Everyone she'd invited showed up and it was such a good blend of people, she was confident no one would figure out the underlying motive. Her plan was off to a good start. She circulated for a while, introducing those who hadn't met, making sure everyone felt comfortable enough to mingle on their own. Cole livened things up with some music, and soon the party was in full swing. Maggie, ever the consummate hostess, was careful to keep a watchful eye on Chad, whispering a silent prayer when she saw him talking to one of her 'special' guests. But Chad being Chad, he was intent on lending Maggie a helping hand and kept gravitating to her, so she had to keep assuring him she had everything under control and nudging him back in the direction of the single girls.

In the end, the party was a huge success, and Maggie's strategic maneuvers for matchmaking worked wonderfully! Just not for Chad. But Joe, the single Titan player, and Cathy, one of Maggie's Kappa Delta sisters, sure were happy Maggie had introduced them. Things were looking really optimistic for them and that meant with Cathy taken out of the mix, there was one less single girl that Maggie knew, that would be great for Chad. She could tell some of the girls had liked him, but because he kept running off, they thought he wasn't interested in them and moved on. *That's okay*, Maggie thought with a sigh, not ready to give up. After all, Plan A *had* worked. Sort of. It just hadn't worked on the right person. So, it was on to Plan B as soon as football season ended.

∾⌘⌘⌘∾

The Titans went on to win the AFC Central title, their first title as "the Titans," with a 13-3 season again. Unfortunately they lost the home divisional playoff game to the Baltimore Ravens, who went on to win the Super Bowl. Winning the prestigious Super Bowl and the right to lay claim to the highly sought after Super Bowl ring is every professional football players goal, and Cole was no exception. Making it to the Super Bowl his first year and losing, and then coming so close his second year and losing again hadn't seemed to effect him at all, except to possibly make him even more determined.

∾⌘⌘⌘∾

Christmas that year was little Chad's first, and everything was pretty much centered around him. He was still too young to open his presents, but like most babies seemed more impressed with all the boxes and wrapping paper rather than the gifts, of which there were many! Maggie could see she was going to have her hands full trying to keep everyone from spoiling him. She just wasn't sure who was going to keep an eye on her, as little Chad wasn't the only one in jeopardy of getting spoiled, because Cole had quite the Christmas too. Though in fairness, Cole's gift was as much for her as it was for him. She'd surprised him by having part of their huge garage converted into a gym so he could work out at home, instead of having to be at the stadium gym so much. *And* Chad could join him there as well, thereby making himself more available for "Plan B". It was a win/win.

Chad's Journal
July 4, 2001

I know what she's up to.

CHAPTER 20

For months Maggie made the most of "Plan B", by 'accidentally on purpose' inviting single friends over for various reasons, when she knew the guys would be there working out, giving Chad a plethora of single girls to catch his interest. Just when she was about ready to give up, he casually questioned her about Shirley, one of the girls Maggie had met at church. Without missing a beat, Maggie invited Chad to church with them that Sunday, and he accepted.

Encouraged that he was finally showing an interest in someone, and in light of his short attention span, she was anxious for him to see how amazingly talented Shirley was. She phoned the Pastor of the church, and after getting the go ahead from him, she called Shirley and asked her what she thought of the idea she had.

Shirley was all for it, provided Maggie participated, completely unaware of Maggie's ulterior motive. So, that Sunday, before the sermon, Shirley sang *Mansion Over The Hilltop*, with Maggie playing the piano and harmonizing with her. It was a truly breathtaking rendition, and touched the heart of every member of the congregation. However, no one appreciated it more than Chad. It just so happened that it was his favorite gospel song. The very first time he'd heard *Mansion Over the Hilltop* was at his Granny Hazel's funeral, played because it had been her favorite hymn. It had been *his* favorite from that moment on. *Imagine that!* he thought.

Leave it to Maggie to have gone to the trouble to find out that little tidbit of information. So, in lieu of a job well done, not only with the performance but also her investigative abilities, to appease her and hopefully catch a break from her matchmaking, after the service he asked Shirley out for coffee. After all, Maggie knew him well enough to have chosen well for him, he'd probably enjoy it. As it turned out, he did.

Shirley was sweet and very personable, and they got along great. Without giving it *too* much thought, he asked her to dinner later in the week, and to a movie a little over a week after that. Then he surprised Maggie and all the family members, by bringing Shirley to little Chad's first birthday party a week later.

The whole gang attended the milestone birthday party. Little Chad, who was beginning to walk now and getting a few words out here and there, was taking advantage of his audience, showing off all he had learned. At the moment he was sitting in his high chair, having just blown out his candle on his own personal little cake. Everyone applauded and took pictures of him grinning and clapping over his accomplishment. Maggie removed the candle and with some encouragement from his family, he proceeded to grab two fists full of his cake and take his first bite, getting most of it everywhere but his mouth. After a few bites, she handed him a sippy cup of milk and he took it, spreading the icing from his hands to the cup, and took a sip. Then he held the cup back out to Maggie and said, "Car want joose," as plain as day. There was a moment of stunned silence. In part because it was the closest thing to a sentence he'd ever said, and partly because he'd called himself Car. There was only one person who called him Car, and all heads turned to him.

Chad was looking intently at the ceiling like he'd just noticed it was there.

When it became obvious they were expecting him to say something, he was the picture of innocence when he looked back at them with a sideways grin and said, "What?" That got a laugh out of everyone, but he wasn't sure what else to say. He'd been calling him little Car since day one. Who would have thought with everyone else calling him Chad, he would have even noticed being called Car from time to time. He was so darned proud to have little Chad named after him, but he just couldn't trust himself that the first time he tried to say it out loud he wouldn't get choked up. Now that it had become an issue though, he knew the time had come, because he needed to try to rectify the situation. Maggie had just gotten a clean sippy cup with juice in it. Chad took it from her and sat it on the tray of the highchair beside the cake. "Here you go, little Chad. Some juice," he said, glancing around at everyone, like, "There, I said it. Problem solved".

"*Car's* juice." Little Chad corrected.

Several more attempts elicited the same response from little Chad. So on his first birthday, he became known to all who loved him as "Car".

∾⌘⌘⌘∾

Chad continued to see Shirley about once a week. He told himself it was just so he and Cole could work out in peace, but as time went on, he had to admit it was because he genuinely enjoyed her company.

∾⌘⌘⌘∾

The Titan's first game of the season was on Sunday, September 9th , against the Miami Dolphins, which they lost 31-23. Not a good start. Then on Tuesday morning, September 11th, tragedy struck in the form of terrorist attacks. Thousands of lives were lost in the attacks on the Twin Towers, The Pentagon, and Flight 93. There is no way of knowing how much worse it would have been, if not for the selfless acts of the innocent souls on Flight 93 bravely trying to overtake the terrorists that had hijacked the flight, thereby causing the plane to be detoured from its intended target, saving countless others. The world watched in horror as the death toll mounted, and waited in fear of more attacks.

Out of respect for those who lost their lives that fateful day, the National Football League postponed games, resuming scheduled play on the 23rd of September, hoping to bring some semblance of normalcy back to American lives, though in reality, America would never be the same.

Cole and Chad wanted to go to New York and volunteer wherever they could help, but were respectfully convinced they would better serve America by fulfilling their obligations to the team, and getting *their* lives back on track by example. So, they tried, but the Titans struggled through the difficult season, ending up with a 7-9 record, leaving Cole and Chad wondering if their instincts to go to New York would have been time better spent.

Chad's Journal

August 6, 2001

I couldn't be prouder if Car were my own son.

Chad's Journal

September 11, 2001

I am sickened by today's tragic events,
and heartbroken for the families of
those who lost their lives.
Thank you God,
that my family
and loved ones are safe,
please embrace those who were not as fortunate.

CHAPTER 21

In early February, Shirley broke the news to Maggie over lunch, that she was going to be leaving in March to be a missionary in Peru.

Jolted by Shirley's unexpected announcement, Maggie's usual poise and tact was momentarily forgotten when she burst out, "What about Chad?!"

"What about him?" Shirley asked confused, wondering what Chad had to do with Peru.

"Well I...I thought you two were, were...I thought things were working out! That you two were an item!" Maggie stammered.

"Oh!... no, I mean, he's a friend, and we'll stay in touch, for sure, but...,"she hesitated, surprised by Maggie's reaction. "He's *known*..." she started to try to explain and looked at Maggie apologetically. "I'm sorry, I thought you knew too. He's known from the beginning of my desire to do this. I told him up front that I didn't want any kind of serious relationship, and he was okay with that. In *fact,"* she added, remembering, "he said *he* didn't want one either, because he had a lot on his plate, too."

With the picture becoming clearer, Maggie slowly nodded her head, putting the pieces together. "Huh," she said to herself. He was on to her. She chuckled. So, *that's* how he wanted play. It looked like it was time for 'Plan B, Part Two'.

Regaining her composure, she apologized to Shirley for her reaction and inquisition, then congratulated her on the new and exciting journey she was about to embark on. The two of them spent the remainder of their lunch discussing Shirley's exciting plans and expectations, and promising to see each other as much as possible before her departure.

∾ℋℋℋ∾

Chad truly was busy at school. He was preparing to graduate in August, and he would have his Doctorate degree. It seemed like it took forever, but was actually only about a year more than a Masters. And then there was his job with the team that occupied a large part of his time. Neither of these, however, took up so much of his time that it prevented him from pursuing a serious relationship.

∾⌘⌘⌘∾

As a going away gift for Shirley and a birthday present for Maggie, Chad bought four tickets to the Grand Ole Opry. Brad Paisley was going to be performing, and he knew both Maggie and Shirley loved his new song, *I'm Gonna Miss Her.* He liked it too, and besides, both girls had been wanting to go to the Opry, so it was an easy choice of gifts. It turned out to be a fantastic show and he and Cole enjoyed it as much as the girls did. Well, *almost* as much. He and Cole didn't think Brad was *quite* as cute as the girls did.

∾⌘⌘⌘∾

They said goodbye to Shirley in May, but heard from her regularly, mostly through email, as phone service was pretty unreliable where she was. She really enjoyed the missionary life. She said it was very rewarding, and one of the best decisions she'd ever made, though she did miss everyone. She made no mention of coming home any time soon.

∾⌘⌘⌘∾

Before the guys knew it, training camp rolled around again. That kept Cole busy because he was determined to pull the team together and not have a repeat of last season, and Chad was in the home stretch at school. Maggie had her hands full as well. Car was walking, and it was a full time job just keeping up with him. She had her students that were such a joy to her, and she was planning a surprise graduation party for Chad, under the ruse of a party for Car's second birthday.

Once she had confirmations all the family members could attend the party, she got on the phone to make reservations for some extra rooms, in order to accommodate everyone.

Chad was expecting the guests for Car's birthday party on the weekend, but had told everyone that he understood it would be difficult for them to make his graduation during the week. So he had no idea that the whole gang was coming two days earlier to witness *his* big day, and he was genuinely astounded at the commencement, when he heard all the cheers coming from the audience as his name was announced. After the ceremony, he was nearly moved to tears when everyone gathered around to commend him and be one of the first to call him "Doctor". When he found out all that Maggie had done to orchestrate the whole thing, he felt truly blessed.

∾⌘⌘⌘∾

Chad arrived at the party to find that the surprise extended to there as well. There were graduation gifts, balloons, and cake, along with resounding congratulations. He was very happy that he and Car got to celebrate their special days together. It would be quite the memory. It also gave Maggie the perfect opportunity to introduce him to several more of her friends, who just *happened* to be single, but after all she had done to make his graduation so special, he had to let her have her fun.

One of the girls he was already somewhat familiar with because he'd seen her on T.V. Her name was Bobbye and she had auditioned for a new reality show, in huge part, due to Maggie's urging. So Maggie made sure they watched every episode and it fast became her new favorite show. Chad thought Bobbye was not only very attractive, but really talented as well. The show was *American Idol* where singers competed before a panel of judges. After a series of try outs, the judges making eliminations each time, the contestants got whittled down each week until only ten remained. At that point, the judging was done solely by America phoning in votes for their favorite contestant. Every contestant strove to at least make the top ten, where they were assured a spot on a tour after the finale, no matter how much farther in the competition they made it. The contestants with the lowest number of votes were eliminated each week until only the winner remained. Out of thousands of contestants, Bobbye made it to the top twenty-four before being voted off by the judges. Everyone they knew who had been watching the show, felt like the judges made a huge mistake because she was better than a few who had made the top ten. But since she hadn't made the top ten she could try again the following year, if the show was successful enough to have a second season. At this point, it seemed like all of America was watching and voting for their favorites, so she'd probably get the chance. Chad was pleased to meet her in person.

∾⌘⌘⌘∾

The Edwards/Rivers gang had long since considered each other family, and the Thompsons had fit in from day one, all meshing together, sharing a common bond. The Birthday/Graduation party had gone off without a hitch and they all enjoyed the rest of their weekend together, making the most of it. They hated to see their last day with each other come to a close. Reluctantly, everyone bid their farewells, and promised to get together again soon.

∾⌘⌘⌘∾

With their friends and relatives all back home safely, Maggie, Cole, and Chad's daily routines resumed.

On Sunday, September 8th , the Titans played their first game at home, against the Philadelphia Eagles and won 27 to 24. Off to a good start, Cole's optimism was put to the test, when they lost the next three games in a row. He was so wrapped up in working to turn things around, he wouldn't let up, even to celebrate his birthday. Then, three days after his birthday, they lost the next game to the Washington Redskins, 31 to 14. During their bye week, he was relentless, watching play tapes and pushing the team during practice. This time it paid off. Out of the next ten games, they only lost one, to the Ravens in December. Then they won the divisional playoff against the Steelers, but lost the conference championship game to Oakland, ending their chance for the Super Bowl once again.

Chad's Journal
August 8, 2002

I can't believe all Maggie did to make my
graduation so special.
There's no lust in my heart, Lord
only love, for the love I cannot have.

CHAPTER 22

To celebrate Cole's skipped birthday—and his perseverance and dedication to the Titans—Maggie took him to Four Corners Marina on Percy Priest Lake, and presented him with his present. A 24 foot cabin cruiser he had been looking at for some time. He hadn't had a clue and was so ecstatic, Maggie was glad she had put her reservations aside and gone ahead with it. She'd gotten a really good deal on the boat, because the dealer was making room to bring in the new models, *and* he really liked Cole and the Titans. She'd also gotten a special deal at the marina. By paying for twelve months slip rental, she got a month free. The money she saved not only paid for the safety course, but all the essentials to stock the boat. Cole was impressed with her determination to be so savvy with money in spite of the money he made. She just flat out refused to be a spendthrift and he vowed to make sure she was with him whenever he made any major purchases in the future.

After smothering her with kisses and telling her how much he adored her, he called Chad right away to tell him the news. He also wanted to see if he would like to take the boating safety course with him. He had promised Maggie that if they did purchase a boat, before taking it out, for everyone's safety, especially Car, he would take the boating course the Coast Guard Auxiliary offered.

Chad agreed to take the course too. He'd finally earned some free time because, before the season had ended, he passed his exam to become a Certified Athletic Trainer. He was now a bona fide employee on the medical staff for the Titans. So what was a little more school? It sounded like it would be fun. After hanging up, he left to go to the marina right away so Cole could show off his new present. When Chad saw it, he had to admit it was a beauty, and Cole was like a little kid with a new toy.

The boat had a cabin with a bathroom—one of Maggie's requirements—so Car wouldn't suffer any setbacks with his potty training, and he could nap if needed. Maggie outfitted the boat with life jackets, making sure Car had several, and even though they didn't take the boat out, she let him try one on and had a hard time convincing him to take it off when they were leaving.

Now that Cole had his boat, he was anxious to find out how soon he and Chad could take the course and get it out on the water. Maggie knew he would be and was one step ahead, informing him that the classes started Tuesday, and were already paid for, with their spots reserved. All they had to do was sign up on Monday. She had purposely timed giving him the gift by the boating course schedule, not wanting him to have to wait too long to get to enjoy his present. It was a good thing too, because it turned out that Car wanted to "make the boat go" as bad as Cole.

She didn't consider herself a Nervous Nellie, but she'd always had a bit of a fear of senseless tragedy after a boy she had a bit of a crush on in grade school dove into a lake and broke his neck. It had affected her deeply, and since then she preferred to err on the side of caution so that, hopefully, she never had to wish "if only" again. If only he had checked the depth of the water first. If only he'd checked to make sure there wasn't something under the water he didn't see. With that in mind, she also made arrangements for Car to have swimming lessons while the guys were completing the boating course, trying to cover all the bases for everyone's safety.

After spending most of the day at the marina, they went back home to grill some burgers and watch two movies Maggie rented. Cole started to complain when he found out the movies were *Shallow Hal* and *My Big Fat Greek Wedding* but he shut up pretty quickly when Chad gave him a warning glance and mouthed the word 'boat' to him. Cole got the message and went on to mumble something about how long he'd been wanting to see those movies. Maggie smiled smugly to herself, having witnessed the silent exchange, and proceeded to start the first movie. The name of it was *Shallow Hal* and it was about a guy who was so shallow minded, that even though he was somewhat overweight himself, he was only interested in beautiful slender women. Then he gets hypnotized by Tony Robbins to see "inner beauty", and he meets a very pretty girl who looks like the slender, svelte girl of his dreams. In reality the girl weighs about 300 pounds, but he can only "see" her inner beauty. At the end of the movie he is able to see what she really looks like, and he realizes that he has fallen in love with the beautiful person she really is. It was very humbling.

The second movie they watched, *My Big Fat Greek Wedding,* was about a mousy young Greek woman who undergoes a self makeover, then catches the eye of a handsome "non" Greek guy, and when they fall in love she has to get her family to accept him. Both movies had hilarious scenes, but were still extremely heartwarming. Maggie loved both of them and much to the guys surprise, they really enjoyed them too, and promised they wouldn't complain the next time Maggie picked out movies.

∾⌘⌘⌘∾

After the guys completed their course, and Car had his swimming lessons, they spent every moment they could exploring the 42 miles of Percy Priest Lake. Maggie invited friends along from time to time, and Chad always seemed to enjoy himself, but didn't show any particular interest in any of the girls afterward. Maggie didn't give up.

∾⌘⌘⌘∾

Before long, it was training camp time again. The season was just around the corner. The Titans first game was at home against the Oakland Raiders, and they won, 25 to 20. They went on to finish the season with a 12-4 record, and made the playoffs, winning their wildcard game over the Ravens, 20 to 17, but then lost the AFC Divisional, to the New England Patriots, 17 to 14. The Patriots went on to win the Super Bowl. Cole won the MVP Award that season, and it took some of the sting out of coming so close to the Super Bowl again and not making it, but he was as determined as ever to make it the next season.

Chad's Journal

June 19, 2003

What does she see when she's looking at me?
Am I able to hide, or does it show,
this love she can't know,
the one I keep buried inside.

CHAPTER 23

Chad wasn't surprised when Maggie 'suddenly discovered' that she loved to workout, *or* that she didn't like to work out alone. Nor did it surprise him with her inability to remember when he and Cole were supposed to be working out, and scheduling a work out with one of her 'single' friends at the same time. After about the fifth or sixth accidental overlap in scheduling, he decided that he had better pick one of the girls and ask her out before Maggie started to look like Arnold Schwarzenegger.

A few days later, he casually asked her about Bobbye—the girl who had tried out for *American Idol—k*nowing that the very next time Maggie knew he was coming over, Bobbye would just *happen* to be visiting. Bobbye was pretty and seemed very nice, but his main reason for choosing her was that he knew she had priorities, so to speak—with her ambitiously working on her singing career—so it seemed safe to ask her out. As he expected, her life was very full at the moment as a singer/songwriter trying to get her foot in the door of the music industry. And as he had hoped, she didn't have a lot of time for a serious relationship, she told Chad over coffee, but wouldn't be opposed to seeing him occasionally as a friend. He decided she was perfect.

∾⌘⌘⌘∾

Cole couldn't wait to get the boat back out on the lake, so they made it happen on the first day it was going to be warm enough. Chad invited Bobbye along, which mollified 'Maggie the Matchmaker'. They got the boat launched with absolutely no issues, in spite of it having been stored over the winter months. Once they were out on the water, Car finally got to steer the boat. He had so much fun, he didn't want to stop until he was utterly worn out and had to go lay down for a nap. It was an exhilarating start to welcoming the springtime, and it was Bobbye's first opportunity to see the breathtaking mountain scenery from the vantage point of a boat. She was given the complete tour, and it was as if they were all seeing it for the first time again, through her eyes. It made them appreciate it all the more.

They went out in the boat as often as they could that summer, taking full advantage of their free time. Sometimes, during the week when Maggie had lessons with her students, Cole and Chad would take the boat out and do some fishing. They threw back whatever they caught, just fishing for the sport of it. Neither one of them were big on cleaning and gutting fish, and Maggie was thankful for that.

∾⌘⌘⌘∾

On the way home from the marina one day when the four of them had gone, Maggie was sitting in the back seat with Car. They were stopped at a traffic light, when she noticed a woman crossing the road in front of the line of cars they were in. She looked just like Charlize Theron, except she was heavy set. Surprised at the likeness, Maggie pointed her out to the guys who quickly looked where she indicated, peering anxiously to get a look at the woman who looked like Charlize Theron.

When Cole spotted her, he almost choked. "Yeah, if you're 'Shallow Hal'!" he burst out, laughing after he said it.

Chad knew he shouldn't, but try as he might, he couldn't keep from laughing at Cole's remark. Maggie slapped Cole's shoulder. "That was cold! I *meant* that she looked like Charlize Theron *in the face*, you goof," she said, admonishing him. But then she found herself giggling too. Apparently it was contagious. Then feeling guilty, she said a silent prayer that God understood they were laughing at Cole's warped sense of humor, and not at the unsuspecting woman.

∾⌘⌘⌘∾

Chad and Bobbye went out from time to time throughout the summer, and he found that he really liked her. *If*, and that was a big *if*, he ever decided to try his hand at love again, she could possibly be the one to make it happen. She was getting ready to go to Cincinnati, Ohio, to try out for *American Idol* again in August, but by that time, Chad would be busy with the team, so the timing was good.

∾⌘⌘⌘∾

Maggie and Cole discussed putting Car in Pre-K, for a few hours a day, so he could adapt to being around other kids his age, before he actually started Kindergarten. He was already pretty advanced with his counting and reciting the alphabet, because Maggie had been devoted to teaching it to him by making it a playful game. So playful in fact, he had learned them without even realizing he was being taught. After talking it over, they came to the conclusion it would be good for Car all around. It would also enable Maggie to dedicate some quality time to her students, so they decided to go ahead with it. It was what she wanted, but now that the decision was made, she was conflicted. She would miss having him with her every day—even though he would only be gone for a few hours—but at the same time she was really excited for him to go and meet some playmates. In her heart she knew they made the right decision.

∾⌘⌘⌘∾

The Titans season began on a Saturday that year, against Miami, at Miami. The Titans won, 17-7. Back at home, the next game was against the Colts, which started a three game losing streak. On a Monday night game against the Packers at Green Bay, they pulled out a win, beating them, 48-27. But the Titan's had several key players injured, and saw only three wins out of the next eleven games, ending the season with a 5-11 record. For the first time in his professional career, Cole's confidence seemed to be slipping.

Chad's Journal
July 12, 2004

Do I dare try to love another?

CHAPTER 24

Chad was coming as close as he ever had, to opening his heart to love again. It just sort of happened without him realizing it. He certainly hadn't made a conscious decision to let it happen. Bobbye was different from Maggie in several ways, the first and foremost being that she wasn't married to his best friend. Beyond that, she was about four inches taller than Maggie, almost the same height as himself. Bobbye had short dark hair, in contrast to Maggie's long blonde hair. Bobbye had brown eyes, Maggie's were blue. Bobbye's voice was strong and kind of gravelly, like Pat Benetar—in fact, she kind of resembled Pat Benetar—where Maggie's voice was soft and smooth, more like Sarah McLaughlin or Alison Krauss. The one thing they did have in common was that they were both extremely beautiful women. In completely different ways.

Bobbye auditioned for *American Idol* again in August in Cincinnati, Ohio, and was asked to go Hollywood, where the contestants competed again, and were either asked to stay for further rounds of elimination, or sent home. She made it again, to the top 36. Chad and Maggie watched and cheered her on, when the first show aired on January 19th. Cole spent the evening watching play tapes in one of the guest rooms, desperate to get his team back on track this season.

Bobbye kept in touch with them over the next weeks, calling after making it through each elimination, and asking for feedback concerning her performances. By March, she made the top ten, meaning that no matter how far she made it now, she would be going on the *Idol* tour. It was really exciting watching and voting for her, and they pulled all of their family and friends together to support her too.

During this time, Car was doing great in Pre-K. Everyone at the center adored him, and Maggie received nothing but good reports about him. That is, after the initial incident with the staff calling him

Chad, and him insisting that they call him Car. Once that was cleared up, everyone was happy, and Car was progressing effortlessly. He got along with the other kids like a champ, and was showing signs of following in his mother's footsteps with her love for teaching, by helping other kids along who were just beginning to learn the alphabet or to count.

Though Cole spent a great deal of time with his playbook and game tapes, he still made time for his family. Taking the boat out whenever their schedules allowed was still one of their favorite activities. That summer he got Car a little football that fit his small hands pretty good and began tossing it to him. Even though Car was only four and a half years old, you could tell he'd definitely inherited his dad's arm. He could pretty much throw the ball exactly where he wanted it to go. He just couldn't throw it very *far* yet. He'd apparently inherited his father's love for the sport too, because as soon as Cole got home every day, Car would grab the ball and say, "Wet's frow ball, Daddy." Cole loved it. It didn't *completely* take his mind off the Titans last season, but it came close.

Cole had another memory of that summer near and dear to his heart. He and Car were playing hide and seek in the back yard, and Cole had hidden in a big box a piece of gym equipment had come in. When Car got near, Cole burst out of the box, and yelled, "Boo!" Car jumped and squealed. "Whoa! Daddy! I fought you was a gowilalala!"he said, nearly breathless. Then he kept asking Cole to do it over and over and each time collapsed in a fit of giggles.

One night a few weeks after that, Car put up a fuss about going to bed, but Maggie finally got him tucked in and went out to watch some T.V. with Cole. Apparently, at some point in time, Car had come to the conclusion that if he couldn't see you, then you couldn't see him. The next thing they knew, this little figure draped in a blanket came slowly into the room, making its way silently across the floor in front of them. They watched, trying not to laugh out loud, to see what Car was going to do. He bumped into the coffee table, and without making a sound, turned in another direction, and continued on around the room. Each time he bumped into something he would change course and head in another direction. Finally Maggie had to stop him just before he walked into a wall. They couldn't stop laughing long enough to even dream of reprimanding him. When they got him back to bed this time, he went to sleep almost instantly, his little adventure having tired him out.

During those few months, Bobbye made it to the top six on *American Ido*l, before being eliminated, leaving a girl named Carrie Underwood to go on to win the title a few weeks later. On July 12th, she began the tour and would be on the road, well into September. Chad and Bobbye kept in touch mostly through email, and she would call when she had a break in her rehearsals. He was surprised to find that he missed her, and hoped she would be home soon.

CHAPTER 25

In the off season—because the Titans were well over their salary cap—several key players were cut or traded. With these players replaced by rookies, the 2005 Titans were the youngest team in the NFL. They lost their first game on the road to the Steelers, but they won their home opener game against the Ravens. Cole was working hard with this new team to mold them, to lead them, to take them to the Super Bowl, but they lost the next game on the road to the Rams, 31-27.

Today they were playing their divisional rival, the team Cole's hero, Johnny Unitas, had led. The illustrious team that, in his youth, he had dreamed of playing for. The Indianapolis Colts.

By the end of the first quarter, the Colts scored a touchdown, and the Titans had to settle for a thirty-four yard field goal. The second quarter started with the Colts scoring a field goal, making the score, 10-3.

Maggie and Car, Cole's parents, and Cheyenne were cheering Cole on from the stands. They knew how important it was to him to come through with a win. This game, against this team, particularly.

The Titans called for a fair catch on the punt, getting the ball on their twenty-eight yard line. Cole ran back on the field, with Car yelling from the stands, "Frow the ball, Daddy!"

After two downs, the Titans gained only six yards from a very stingy Colt defense. Cole was determined to make this a scoring drive, hoping to tie the score before half time. Two rushing plays later, Cole lines his team up. Coming up to the center, he doesn't like the way the defense is lined up. He gives an audible, drops back into a shot gun formation, and sets up to pass, but everyone is covered, and his only option is to run. After a five yard gain, making the first down, Cole is sandwiched between two Colt defenders. The impact knocked Cole's helmet off.

A flag was thrown, presumably for unnecessary roughness, but upon review of the play, it was determined that the second tackler, #86, Darren Archer, was in forward motion, and unable to stop. During the review, slowly getting back to his feet, Cole motioned Chad and other medical staff back when they started onto the field, and then waved to the fans, indicating that he was okay.

Maggie, holding her breath, breathed a sigh of relief when he waved. Car didn't understand what had happened, so she picked him up and cupping him in her right arm, pointed Cole out to him. "See? Daddy's okay! Wave to Daddy. Do you see him?" she asked. He grinned, nodding when he spotted Cole, and clapped his little hands together. After Car was satisfied, Maggie turned to Cheyenne on her left and hugged her, then, weak in the knees, had to sit down. With Car on her lap, she reached over to Cole's mom on her right and squeezed her hand, then reaching past her, did the same with his dad, the worried looks on their faces giving way to thankful smiles.

No penalty was issued and play resumed, with Cole handing the ball off for another gain of three yards. In the next play, Cole drops back and sets up to pass, when #86 breaks through the defenders and heads straight toward Cole for the sack. Cole scrambled and pulled the ball back to make the pass, but instead of completing the pass, he just stood there, his receiver wide open. Seconds before #86 sacked Cole, he noticed the dazed look on Cole's face, and stopped short, holding other players back from making contact with Cole, his gut telling him something wasn't right. #86 motioned to the sidelines for help, and as Cole began to go down, he grabbed him and laid him gently on the field.

A whistle marked the end of play, and medical personnel rushed onto the field, with Chad leading the way. Cole's dad asked, "What happened? What did I miss?"

Maggie said, "You didn't miss anything, but something's definitely wrong."

They waited anxiously for a few minutes, but Cole didn't get up. When they saw the ambulance driving out onto the field, Maggie grabbed Car, and followed by Cole's family, ran from the stadium, rushing desperately to get to her car and cell phone.

The fans were silent as Cole was being placed on a stretcher. Many had witnessed players being carted off the field to the locker room in golf carts before, but never had they seen an ambulance come right to the injured player. The silence was deafening.

When they got to the Tahoe, Cheyenne took Car while Maggie pushed the remote to unlock the doors, then frantically opened the rear door to get her cell phone and purse she had hidden in the back. Cole's dad took her keys and started up the vehicle, while Cheyenne got Car strapped in his seat, then she and her mother got in on each side of him. Maggie got in the front passenger side and buckled up while listening to a message from Chad, letting her know that Cole was being taken to Vanderbilt Medical Center. She relayed the information to her in-laws. Mr. Rivers backed the SUV out and headed to the hospital, while Maggie tried to get back through to Chad. It went straight to his voicemail. She disconnected and as soon as she did, her phone beeped indicating she had a new message. She hastily entered her code to hear it. It was from her parents who had been watching the game on T.V., wanting her to call them right away. She tried Chad again but when she was still unable to get through, she called her parents back and told them she didn't know anything more than they did, except that he was on his way to Vanderbilt Hospital. Her father assured her that her mother was already packing them a bag and they would be leaving right away. Maggie thanked him, but said she was almost to the hospital and asked them to please wait at home with the landline where she could be sure to reach them, and she would call them back just as soon as she found out anything. He promised that they would.

Mr. Rivers drove straight to the emergency room and was relieved to find a parking spot right beside the entrance. Inside, they were sent up to the tenth floor, to the Trauma and Surgical Critical Care Unit. Maggie rushed to the nurses' station. While inquiring about Cole, Chad emerged through a set of double doors, marked personnel only. Maggie rushed to him. "Chad, where's Cole? What happened? Is he okay?" she asked, desperation in her voice.

Chad, clearly upset, raked his hand through his hair, and looked from Maggie to Cole's parents. Cheyenne stayed back with Car, keeping him occupied, so he wouldn't see how distressed his mother, Chad, and grandparents were.

"He's in surgery. He lost consciousness on the way here, Maggie." He took her hands in his. "They're doing everything they can. All we can do is wait," he said, feeling helpless.

"But what happened?! He was fine! He waved saying he was fine. What happened?" she asked, on the verge of hysteria, her voice rising with fear. Cole's parents stepped closer to Maggie, putting their arms around her, trying to comfort her, their eye's pleading with Chad to give them some sort of answer.

"All I can tell you right now, is that he must have suffered some sort of head trauma during the tackle when he lost his helmet. It's possible that he didn't realize it and thought he was okay," he offered in explanation to Cole waving off medical help.

A nurse from behind the counter approached them. "If you'll follow me, I'll take you to the waiting room. You'll be more comfortable there and have some privacy while you're waiting for an update. I promise, I'll let you know the minute we hear anything," she assured them.

As they made their way down the hall, everything was a blur to Maggie. In the waiting room, she remembered she needed to call her parents. When she told them what was happening and that she still didn't really know anything about his condition, they said it didn't matter, they were walking out the door as soon as they hung up the phone. She thanked them and asked them to drive safely. She was grateful for their support, but hoped they would be making the trip unnecessarily.

She glanced at Cole's parents who were lost in thought, concern etched on their faces, and then to Chad who tried to smile at her in reassurance, but she could see the same worry reflecting in his eyes.

A chill settled over her and she shivered as she looked across the room at Cheyenne, who was keeping Car busy in a corner with a coloring book, bravely holding her fear in check for his sake.

CHAPTER 26

After they had time to compose themselves somewhat and try to get a grasp on what was going on, they began trying to convince each other everything was going to be okay. In spite of their best efforts, the uncertainty and fear in the room was tangible. Car was getting tired of coloring, so Cheyenne decided to take him down to the cafeteria to get a snack and something to drink, but it was more to occupy him until they knew what was going on.

"That's a good idea," Chad said, standing to make eye contact with her so that he could silently ask if she was ok. He mouthed the words, and she nodded and smiled, but it was weak and unconvincing. Not wanting to press the issue and test her resolve for being strong for Car, he just gave her a quick hug. Then he knelt down to Car. "Come here and give Uncle Chad a hug," he said, realizing Car was doing as much for Cheyenne as she was for him. Car hopped up and gave Chad a big squeeze. "Wow! That was a good one! Ok, you go with Aunt Cheyenne, and check out the cafeteria, alright buddy?" Car nodded, eager to explore, and Chad added, "We'll be right here. Give Mommy some of that love you gave me before you go."

Car went to Maggie, and she leaned forward to pull him close and he wrapped his little arms around her neck. It was all Maggie could do to keep from breaking down. "I love you, honey," she said, her voice shaky.

"I love you too, Mommy," he said, letting go and going over to take Cheyenne's hand.

On their way out, Chad said, "I'll walk them to the elevator, and check at the nurse's station for any word."

"Thank you," Maggie said gratefully, and Mr. & Mrs. Rivers nodded their heads appreciatively.

Out in the hall, Car was hanging onto Cheyenne's hand so Chad grabbed her free hand and escorted them down the corridor. At the junction they turned to the left, where four elevators, two on each side, were located. He pushed the call button and while they waited in silence, Cheyenne fidgeted nervously, brushing through Car's hair with her fingertips. When an elevator arrived, Cheyenne pushed her nerves aside and in a cheery voice that belied the worry in her eyes, said, "Okay Car! Here we go!" Stepping inside, she showed Car which button to push to take them down to the cafeteria. As the doors slid closed, Chad looked from Car—who was smiling proudly for getting to push the button—to Cheyenne. For the briefest moment they each tried to give the other their most confident smile of encouragement, until the doors met, bringing their act to a close.

Chad's smile vanished and he stood staring at his reflection in the doors, but it wasn't his reflection he was seeing. It was an instant replay of Cole getting tackled. Suddenly the elevator beside him opened, jarring him out of his trance. He quickly turned on his heel and headed to the nurses' station to check and see if there was any word on Cole yet. The nurse—whose name tag identified her only as Janice R.N.—informed him they hadn't heard from the doctor, but would let him know the minute they did. Reluctant to face Maggie with no news, Chad slowly made his way back to the waiting room to find her wringing her hands, pale from worry. She looked up hopefully when he walked in.

He shook his head. "Nothing yet," he said apologetically, looking first at her, then to Cole's parents. He sat down beside her, taking one of her hands in his. He looked around the room and wondered how many people had sat here, helpless, waiting for news about their loved ones. The room was decorated in warm colors with picturesque photos on the walls, in an attempt, he imagined, to soothe the spirits and occupy the minds of family members as they waited, but as he looked around the room, he realized it was a futile effort. It did nothing to soothe his spirit, and Maggie and Cole's parents' minds were miles away. Minutes passed. He tried to focus on the medical facts he was familiar with that could pertain to Cole's injury. If he hit his head when he lost his helmet, there could be bleeding, causing intracranial swelling. But they had gotten to the hospital quickly, and if that was the problem, they should be able to correct that with surgery. His train of thought was interrupted when Maggie pulled her hand free, to get her cell phone out of her purse.

She called down to Cheyenne to see if Car was okay. She'd known he was fine, they had been gone less than twenty minutes, but she just had to do something. The waiting and wondering was driving her crazy. After hanging up with Cheyenne, and having promised to call as soon as they knew anything, Maggie stood, and began to pace around the room. After a few minutes, she looked at Chad, unable to wait idly anymore. "I can't take it, I've got to go find out *something,*" she said with desperation.

"I'll come with you," Chad offered, looking at Cole's parents, silently questioning if they wanted to come as well.

"We'll wait here," Mr. Rivers said.

Just as they stepped into the hallway, a doctor dressed in surgical scrubs rounded the corner from where the nurse's station was located and beyond that, the surgery area.

"Mrs. Rivers?" he asked Maggie, coming to a stop in front of her.

"Yes," she replied quietly, afraid now.

"I'm Doctor Anderson," he stepped closer, placing his hand on Maggie's elbow, in an attempt to lead her back to the waiting room. "Why don't we go in and have a seat?" He gestured toward the doorway.

Maggie didn't move. "Please. Just tell me if he's okay," she begged.

When Mr. and Mrs. Rivers heard them speaking, they quickly stepped out into the hallway. The doctor acknowledged them with a nod, before turning his attention back to Maggie. His face, unreadable just moments before, now looked, at once, both uncomfortable and extremely sympathetic.

With a sigh, he said, "In addition to the trauma to his head, your husband suffered a cerebral aneurysm before he got here." He paused. "I'm sorry, we did everything we could."

When Cole's mother heard the doctor say that he was sorry, her knees buckled. Mr. Rivers wrapped his arms around her tightly to hold her up as they sobbed in each other's arms.

Chad felt as if all the air around him suddenly dissipated, leaving him fighting to take a breath. With his lungs screaming, he looked at Maggie, but her expression hadn't changed. She looked as if the doctor hadn't said anything yet.

"He's going to be alright isn't he?" she asked, looking confused now.

Recognizing signs of shock, Dr. Anderson added gently, "I'm sorry, Mrs. Rivers, he didn't make it."

Maggie slowly took a step back, then another, backing into the wall, shaking her head. "No," she said, as if there was some mistake. "No!" she said emphatically, refusing to accept it. She looked at Chad, her eyes glassy. "No!" she said again, shaking her head frantically. "Noooooo!" she screamed in anguish. Her legs refused to hold her and she slid down the wall to the floor, crying uncontrollably.

Chad and Doctor Anderson knelt beside her, and when a nurse came to see if she could be of assistance, Doctor Anderson asked her to bring Maggie a mild sedative to help calm her. He looked at Chad for approval to medicate her, as he was ordering it.

Chad nodded, then gathered Maggie in his arms trying to console her. In shock himself, he couldn't stop the tears from streaming unchecked down his face. He held Maggie until the nurse returned, then he and the doctor carefully helped Maggie to her feet and into the waiting room.

Through her sobs, she was begging, *pleading*, for them to tell her it wasn't true. After getting her settled into a chair, Doctor Anderson was able to convince her to take the offered sedative, promising it would help to calm her, holding a cup of water to her mouth to help her get it down.

After several minutes—with the medication beginning to take effect—Maggie was still crying, but quietly now, and barely able to keep her eyes open. Chad pulled two of the chairs that had no arms together, and helped her lie down on her side, her knees drawn up in a fetal position. He waited until she drifted off, then turned to Cole's parents, and the three embraced and wept in each other's arms. As soon as he could pull himself together, Chad quietly asked Mr. Rivers if he would look after Maggie for a moment, while he went to find Cheyenne.

When he entered the cafeteria, he spotted Car and Cheyenne seated beside each other in a booth against a wall of glass, overlooking a parking lot. Cheyenne had her right arm draped across the bench behind Car, who was closest to the window. Leaning toward him, their heads close together, she was pointing something out to him in the parking lot beyond. She smiled at something he said, then straightened up and looked around and saw Chad making his way over to them. Her smile faded when she saw his red swollen eyes. The question on her face hung in the space between them. An almost imperceptible shake of his head confirmed her worst fears. She tried to hide behind her hands when her face contorted with pain, so that Car wouldn't see. Chad slid in the booth beside her, and took her in his arms, her sobs muffled in his shoulder. Car turned around then, surprised to see Chad there now.

"Hey, Uncle Chad!" Car said.

"Hey there, Car." Chad replied, his voice breaking, while he shielded Cheyenne from Car's inquisitive eyes.

"Is Daddy okay now?"

CHAPTER 27

Chad had prayed for God to give him the strength to do what needed to be done, and say what needed to be said. He thanked God now, for helping him through the past couple of days, as he sat at his dining room table reflecting on them. His parents left to go back home that morning, and he realized it was the first time he'd been alone since...well, since before the game on Sunday. He looked around at his home, but it was as if there was a veil over his eyes because all he could see was images from the past few days. The image of Cole going down on the field, twice, hearing Car ask if his Daddy was all right, and every agonizing second in between. Damn it! There was just no indication that Cole had been injured, no sign! He should have made Cole get checked when he lost his helmet in that tackle. That's what he was there for, what he'd gone to school all those years for, and when Cole had needed him most, he'd let him down!

He remembered the look on Cheyenne's face when she saw him coming to get her and Car from the cafeteria. It tore his heart out. He'd planned to tell her privately, but his face betrayed him. He thought about when he took them back up to the waiting room and Cheyenne ran to her grief stricken parents. He was holding Car and Maggie was sitting up, eerily quiet, her hands limp in her lap, staring down at the floor, her mind someplace far away. When she looked up at Chad, then to Car, a single tear escaped and ran down her cheek. He could see the pain he was feeling magnified in her eyes.

Car didn't understand what was wrong, but picking up on everyone else's emotions, he laid his head on Chad's shoulder, unusually timid, unsure what to do, never having seen adults cry before. When Maggie saw this, she took a deep breath and, for her son's sake, found an inner strength she hadn't known she possessed. With effort, she stood and carefully took Car from Chad and told him she loved him, hugging him to her tightly. Then she sat him in one of the chairs, and knelt in front of him, holding his little hands in hers.

"Honey," she began, then stopped, swallowed, and took a deep breath. "Honey, Daddy had an accident at the game and bumped his head, and the doctors...they tried to fix Daddy, but they couldn't—"

Car interrupted, "Uncle Chad can fix Daddy! Uncle Chad's a doctor. Uncle Chad can fix anything," he said, matter of fact.

He remembered Car looking up at him expectantly, and the look of apology on Maggie's face, and knew as long as he lived, he would never forget the agony he felt at that moment.

"Honey," Maggie cupped Car's face in her hands to bring his attention back to her. "Uncle Chad didn't get to try to fix Daddy, because he doesn't work here, but the doctor's who *do* work here tried very hard, and they..." her voice broke, "they couldn't fix Daddy."

Car looked confused. "But Uncle—"

"No," Maggie shook her head, stopping him before he said it again. She inhaled deeply, exhaled and tried again. Thinking of a way that might help Car understand, she asked, "Do you remember Jesus in Heaven? That you learned about in church?" Car nodded his head. "Well, Daddy went to go live with Jesus in Heaven—"

"No!" Car cried, "I want Daddy to live with me!"

"I know, baby," she pulled Car close, rocking him. "I do too," she leaned back to look in Car's eyes, "but Daddy *had* to go live with Jesus, because Jesus was the *only* one who could fix Daddy," she pleaded, hoping he would understand.

Car's bottom lip began trembling and his eyes filled with tears as he asked, "Can we go live with Jesus, too?"

Maggie glanced up at Chad, searching desperately for words. In an effort to try to help, he sat down in the chair beside Car and put his hand on his tiny back, but he was lost as to what to say to this precious little boy. The action, however, gave Maggie a moment to think of something to say.

"Well, one day," she began, "when we get older, and we've been good, then we'll get to go live with Daddy and Jesus." She forced a smile for Car, hopeful that he would accept that explanation.

Car started to smile, but then suddenly looked apprehensive. "But what if I forget to be good?" he asked, worried.

"Oh, honey," Maggie pulled him into her arms. "You won't forget. You're a good boy, and Daddy loves you, and he'll be watching us from Heaven until we can go and live with him and Jesus."

Car thought about that for a second, then, finally satisfied, said, "Can Uncle Chad come too?"

Maggie kissed Car on the forehead and pulled Chad into a group hug. "Yes, Uncle Chad can come too," she said, too exhausted at this point to do anything but agree.

Thinking back, Chad didn't know how Maggie managed to get through that without breaking down, but he was so incredibly proud of her. How hard must it be to tell your child their other parent is gone? And *never* coming back? His mind drifted back to that day again.

After Maggie had her talk with Car, she asked her mother and father-in-law and Cheyenne if they wanted to go in to say goodbye to Cole. They returned, solemn and spent, but offered to take Car on home for a nap while she and Chad said their goodbyes. She graciously accepted.

Chad remembered thinking how amazed he was at how calm Maggie seemed to be when they were on their way to see Cole. But after they went in and actually saw his lifeless body in that cold sterile room, it proved to be her undoing. Her controlled façade shattered. She ran to Cole and tried to embrace him, laying her head on his chest, weeping, as reality forced itself upon her.

Chad had been so focused on seeing to everyone else's needs he hadn't allowed himself to digest the reality of what he was about to see either. Maggie seemed to fade from the room as the intensity of seeing Cole crashed over him and he sank to his knees, his grief pouring out uncontrollably. Images of their lives over the years ran through his mind like a kaleidoscope. Everything that meant anything to him involved Cole. He couldn't be dead. It had to be some sort of sick joke! He was too young to die! There were still so many things they planned to do! He couldn't imagine his life without Cole in it. Cole had so much to live for! He had a son to raise! Why was this happening? How could they be expected to just go on? But they had no choice, other than to do just that. When his emotions subsided to the point he felt like his legs would support him, he stood, and immediately felt guilty for letting his heartache overcome him when Maggie needed him so badly.

She'd asked him to come with her to say goodbye to Cole for emotional support, and he was glad she did. But now that he had tampered his own emotions enough to actually lend that support, he felt as if he was intruding, like he shouldn't be witnessing this heart wrenching scene. The feeling was only momentary, as the sound of Maggie's sobs erased any thoughts of guilt or intrusion. She was obviously in so much pain. He went to her side and placed his hand on her shoulder, in an effort to console her, and when she felt it, she raised her head and turned into his arms, weak with sorrow. Rather than offer solace, his gesture seemed to intensify her misery and she began to cry even harder, his embrace the only thing preventing her from collapsing on the floor. He felt every ounce of her torment and tears threatened to consume him again, so he concentrated on holding Maggie up. As he did, another wave of guilt washed over him, simply because Cole would never again be able to hold Maggie in his arms like he was doing now.

He wasn't sure how long they stood there, but they were both totally drained when they were finally able to bring themselves to leave. It was sheer torture for him to leave Cole there, alone. He could only imagine how hard it was for Maggie.

On the way out she stopped abruptly and looking at Chad in anguish, broke down in tears again. He thought at first it was because it was so hard to leave, but she managed to tell him with each gasp for breath, that the next day would have been Cole's twenty-eighth birthday.

∾⌘⌘⌘∾

When Maggie's parents arrived at the hospital they saw several news media vans and personnel awaiting news on Cole's condition. Anxious to get that information themselves, they hurried past them and went to the information desk, where they were directed to the tenth floor waiting area. In line for the next available elevator, they were surprised to see Cheyenne, Car and Mr. and Mrs. Rivers when the doors opened on the first one to arrive. One look told the Thompsons the news wasn't good, but nothing had prepared them to hear what Car said when he saw them.

"Papaw! Mamaw! Did you know that my daddy went to live with Jesus in Heaven?"

The smiles on their faces faded as the shock took hold, and they looked to Coles parents for reassurance that Car was mistaken, but were met with pure devastation looking back at them.

Cheyenne quickly diverted Car's attention to a nearby gift shop, giving her parents the opportunity to bring Maggie's parents up to date.

The four of them stepped around the corner to a vacant waiting room, away from the busy common area so that they could discuss Cole in private. It was a tormented conversation that, less than six hours earlier, none of them had ever dreamed they would be having. The Rivers' relayed, as best they could, what had transpired, and they consoled each other until they had a chance to recover somewhat. The Thompsons expressed their sincerest condolences, and realizing that the Rivers' had to be exhausted, wanted to let them be on their way. They alerted them to the media waiting outside, and exchanged heartfelt embraces, promising to help in any way they could.

Heavyhearted, the Thompsons were anxious to find their daughter. They could only imagine the inconsolable grief she must be experiencing and they were extremely concerned about her. They hurried to the nurses' station on the tenth floor, where Janice told them Maggie and Chad were in still in with Cole, and showed them to the waiting room. While waiting, they discussed what they could do to be of help. Mr. Thompson kept a look out for Maggie while Mrs. Thompson searched for a phone book. Locating one, she called a nearby restaurant willing to accept payment by credit card over the phone, and arranged for an assortment of food to be delivered to Maggie's home. It seemed trivial in the scheme of things, but despite being depleted emotionally and physically, everyone would still need to eat something. It was the last thing that the Rivers, Maggie, or even the Edwards' needed to be concerned with. Chad's parents were extremely close to Cole and his family, and must have felt as if they had lost a son as well. As Stella disconnected from the restaurant, she remembered that the last time they were all together they'd had such a marvelous time they looked forward to doing it again soon. It never occurred to anyone it would be under such tragic circumstances.

With broken hearts, the families clung to each other through the difficult days ahead.

Minus one.

∾⌘⌘⌘∾

Chad's thoughts briefly drifted to Cole's service, but it was still too painful for him to process. It had been standing room only. Every member of the Titan's had been in attendance, from the team itself, to the office staff, down to the water boys. Fans lined the street in a show of support, but respectfully kept their distance. Cole had touched the lives of so many, and would be greatly missed. Chad knew that he, personally, would never be the same.

Chad's Journal
October 5, 2005

Cole, I didn't write these words
but I feel them screaming out from my heart.

Was my time spent wisely?
It's hard for me to say,
But for now, I count each minute,
Since my best friend passed away.

Each memory I've recounted,
As I bow my head to pray,
For the strength to stand alone now,
Since my best friend passed away.
"W.C. (Bean) Benjamen"

Cole, you were the best friend a
best friend could ask for.
I feel terribly alone and lost.

CHAPTER 28

Coach Fisher graciously gave Chad a week off, and told him he could take more time if he needed it. He was thankful, because it was going to take every bit of courage he could muster to go back out on that field. He needed time to adjust, to come to grips with the fact that his best friend was gone. He needed some time alone.

Cole and Maggie had not discussed his wishes for his final resting place, so she accepted his parent's offer to lay him to rest in their family plot in Powell. She made arrangements for him to be transported there, and everyone would be leaving in the morning for the service there this weekend.

There had also been talk of Maggie and Car moving back home to be close to family for help and support, since there was really no reason for them to be in Nashville now. It came as another shocking blow to Chad when the possibility was brought to his attention. He had been so distraught over losing Cole that he hadn't even considered they may be leaving too. In fact, he hadn't given the future much thought at all, other than knowing he had to do whatever he could for Maggie and Car. But now that he was forced to contemplate what came next, he realized it was almost as if he had just assumed he would step in and...no, he hadn't even considered that...had he?...at least not consciously...but in wanting them to stay in Nashville...and because of the way he'd felt about Maggie all these years...did that mean that...no...that somewhere deep inside him he'd somehow wished Cole's death? So that he could step in and take his place?

The realization of that possibility was shattering. Shaken, he tried to tell himself he was being ridiculous and struggled to push it out of his mind but...could he really deny it? He wondered about the fact he'd not been interested in dating anyone, not wanted to get involved in a serious relationship. Then he tried to justify to himself that it was because of school, because he didn't have time. But was that the *real* reason? Or was it because no one measured up to Maggie? That subconsciously, on some level deep inside, he was *waiting* for her? The questions, and confusion, and guilt mounted in him until another thought occurred to him and he found himself gripped by panic. What did Cole think? *Did my best friend know how I felt about his wife?* He tried to think back over the past several years, all the time they'd spent together, all the outings and events. Car's birth. No. Cole *couldn't* have known, he realized. He and Cole had been too close. Cole would have razzed him if he'd suspected anything. And he certainly wouldn't have named his son after him. No. He shook his head. Cole couldn't have had any idea.

Finally, convinced of that much, Chad felt a momentary sense of relief, but it was short lived as the doubt in himself came rushing back to the forefront, effectively clouding any clarity he thought he'd found. Trying again to reason with the ugly accusations he hurled at himself, his mind drifted back to Maggie and Cole's wedding. He'd truly been *happy* for Cole and Maggie...hadn't he? Wasn't he glad Cole found the perfect woman? Yes! he answered to himself defiantly. Yes, he was! He exhaled, realizing he'd been holding his breath. It was a small breakthrough, but it felt monumental! Until "perfect for who?" began reverberating in his head.

Disgusted with himself, he got up from the table, and went to the fridge. He grabbed a bottle of beer, then glanced at the clock. Eleven a.m.. Too early for a beer. He started to put it back, hesitated for a moment, then opened the bottle and took a long pull. Forcing back his thoughts, searching for a diversion, he went over to his desk, sat down and logged into his email. He hadn't checked it since last Saturday, and was amazed to see he had over a hundred new messages. Opening a few—all condolences from friends of his and Cole's—his turmoil came flooding back. He scrolled down and saw Bobbye's address. He hadn't even thought about Bobbye the past few days. Did she even *know* about Cole? He felt bad all over again. He should have made sure she knew. Should have had the courtesy to get in touch with her, for Maggie's sake if nothing else.

Bobbye was in New York, and had been since the final show in the Idol tour had ended there. She had auditioned for, and gotten a role in a Broadway musical. He wished she was here now. He'd actually missed her before his world had been turned upside down. Latching onto this revelation, he sat a little straighter and grasped for straws. He *had* been a little disappointed when he'd found out that she wasn't coming back right away...There! That was it! Proof he wasn't waiting for Maggie! Subconsciously or otherwise, he thought, perking up some more. He felt the beginnings of a smile and then..."That's the best you can come up with? That's pretty lame, buddy", echoed the voice inside his head. Deflated, he slumped back down in his chair.

A few minutes later, determined to occupy himself to distraction again, he turned his attention back to the emails, answering Bobbye's first and apologizing for not getting in touch with her earlier. She answered right away. It turned out she had heard about Cole. She said she had been absolutely shocked and was extremely saddened by the news, but she told him not to worry, she'd already talked to Maggie and sent flowers too. She told him she had also been concerned about him, since he hadn't called or answered any of her emails. He apologized to her again, and this time made sure to let her know he missed her. Afterwards he refused to analyze whether he sincerely missed her or was just trying to *convince* himself that he did. Or maybe he was simply attempting to assuage some of the guilt he felt concerning his feelings for Maggie, but to keep from thinking about it, he proceeded to answer every other email he had gotten the past few days. He started with all the *female* friends first, throwing in a few from his contact list who hadn't emailed, including Shirley in Peru, who he was pretty sure probably *hadn't* heard about Cole. Hours later when he was done and feeling a little better, he automatically picked up the phone to call and check on Maggie. Halfway through dialing the number he caught himself and hesitated. *And* Car, he justified to himself. I'm calling to check on Car too.

∽ℋℋℋ∽

On Friday morning, Cole's parents started home. Maggie, Car, and her parents headed out shortly thereafter, being followed by Chad and Cheyenne. Cole was to be buried in Bells Campground Cemetery in Powell. His grandparents and other family members had been buried there before him, including some distant relatives who fought in the Civil War, with a few dating even earlier than that.

Maggie seemed to be holding up fairly well when Car was present, though more often than not, her eyes were swimming with tears she was fighting to hold back.

Chad noticed that Cheyenne was about the same, trying hard to put on a brave face and keep her tears in check. He knew exactly how much effort it was taking. He felt on the verge of losing it himself every second, but was trying to hold it together for everyone else's sake.

Normally the trip to Knoxville seemed like a short ride, but there was nothing normal about this trip and this time it seemed interminably long. He and Cheyenne made small talk for a while, trying to dance around their grief, fears, and questions, but it was somehow harder to keep up the façade between just the two of them, and safe from Maggie and Car witnessing it, Cheyenne eventually broke down, unable to hold back any longer.

"What are we going to do without Cole, Chad?' she cried out unexpectedly and began sobbing. "What's *Maggie* going to do? What about little Car? Sure, he's doing okay *now*, because he doesn't really understand, but what about later? How's it going to be for him, growing up without a father?" she choked out between sobs, not expecting or giving Chad time to answer, desperately voicing all the questions running through her head.

Chad wished he could pull over, but was afraid if he did they would lose Maggie and her family up ahead and cause them to be alarmed, so he kept driving. "I don't know, Cheyenne, I'm sorry. I am *so* sorry," he said despairingly.

Taken aback by the intense remorse in his voice, she noticed the tears streaming down his face. Seeing him this distraught, she chastised herself for being so wrapped up in her own misery that she had been completely inconsiderate of how he was feeling. She reached over and gently touched his shoulder.

"Chad? What in the world are *you* sorry for?" she asked softly. He didn't answer right away and she could see his lips trembling as he blinked away the tears but he kept his eyes on the road. "Chad?" she coaxed again and waited. When he finally answered she jumped, taken aback at the intensity of his response.

"I didn't do anything!" he cried out in frustration. "I didn't save him! All those years of school to become a doctor, and for what? I didn't save Cole. I didn't help him when it mattered!"

"Don't you dare blame yourself!" she berated him, shocked that he felt somehow responsible. "What happened wasn't your fault! It wasn't anyone's fault! No one knew Cole was hurt. *He* didn't even know!"

"I should have made him come out of the game when he was tackled!"

"Chad, he'd been tackled before and always been okay. You had no way of knowing this time was any different than any time before!"

"He'd never lost his helmet before! I should have insisted he got checked out!"Chad argued.

"Look," she tried to calm her voice, "the doctor said it was the aneurysm that killed Cole. Even if you *had* insisted and he had been checked on the field, you wouldn't have been able to detect the aneurysm. There was nothing you could have done to stop that," she said, imploring him to realize the truth.

Chad glanced over at Cheyenne, then looked back to the road. "I should have tried," he said with finality.

Cheyenne could tell when he looked at her that she wasn't getting through to him. Obscurely studying his profile, she could tell he was angry. *Really* angry. She wondered if he was angry with himself, or with Cole for dying. Contemplating that, she shifted around in her seat and stared out her window. The vibrant autumn leaves of the trees lining the highway becoming a blur of orange, red, and yellow as they passed by. Maybe he just needed some time, she thought, deciding to back off and let him calm down.

"I love you," she reminded him after a while.

"I love you, too," he said dead pan, not taking his eyes off the road.

They drove several more miles in silence, Cheyenne willing him to loosen his white knuckled grip on the steering wheel, and Chad kicking himself for going off on her.

The tension in his grip gradually abated and in a sincere but unnecessary attempt to get back into Cheyenne's good graces, he meekly asked her about school, and from then on they continued the drive in pleasant—and neutral—conversation. Seemingly back to normal. But now that she was aware of his feelings, she promised herself she would keep a close eye on him.

When they got to Knoxville, they exited the highway, and pulled into a gas station. Maggie and Car were going on to her parents' home in Parrottsville, and would come back to Powell for the service in the morning. As they said their goodbyes, Maggie thought Chad seemed a little distant with her, but when he took extra long saying goodbye to Car she figured she must have been mistaken.

CHAPTER 29

Saturday morning dawned cool but sunny, as the families gathered at Mr. and Mrs. Rivers' home before proceeding to the cemetery for the 11:00 a.m. graveside service. They began to see cars parked alongside the street when they turned onto the road to the cemetery, but it wasn't until they approached the entrance that they saw hundreds of people, some wearing Cole's old UT jersey, waiting to pay their last respects. Maggie was so touched to see all these people who loved Cole gathered together, that her resolve to be strong for Car crumbled and the tears she had been fighting to swallow back all morning broke free.

Even though it was a game day for UT, she saw the head coach and several other members of the coaching staff, as well as some teachers and professors they'd had at school. She knew Cole had been popular, but she was only now becoming aware of the extent of just how much he meant to so many people.

As they parked and made their way to the graveside, Maggie, holding Car's hand, saw many more familiar faces, and countless others unfamiliar. They all wore the same sorrowful expression, some discreetly wiping tears away, others sobbing openly. Words weren't necessary to convey the pain they felt too, and despite their varying degrees of loss and remorse, Maggie felt a comforting sense of unity, a oneness in their share of love for Cole.

The service began and Reverend Hill gave what was to have been a brief eulogy, having already had the service in Nashville, but a grade school friend of Coles asked to speak, and shared some stories about Cole in his younger days, then another person came forward, and before they knew it, over an hour had passed. The families were all seated comfortably and didn't mind. In fact it was very heartwarming. They were amazed at the tenaciousness and perseverance of the hundreds of people in attendance standing there the whole time just to listen to stories about Cole or waiting to share their own.

Over the course of another hour they learned of several more of Coles antics, many of which they had never heard before, some including Chad, that he had forgotten all about. Then a guy named Joe ratted Cole out, not only for skipping school with him one day, but also for taking a mud box that belonged to Joe's father and crossing the river in it. Everyone who knew what a mud box was listened in shocked disbelief, especially Mrs. Rivers, and for those who weren't familiar, Joe went on to enlighten them. "A mud box, or mortar box," he told them, "was used to mix mortar, made of metal, about three feet wide by six feet long, and one foot deep with curved ends." That information in itself was unsettling, but when the Clinch River was added to the equation—and pretty much everyone there knew the Clinch River—they knew exactly how dangerous it would have been crossing it in a mortar box, and how fortunate the boys had been to have made it across.

While Joe was talking, Chad was wondering how it was possible he hadn't been aware of this tale about his best friend, and especially how Cole managed to skip school without him knowing it. Then it occurred to him that it must have happened sometime during the week he'd been home sick with the chicken pox, and Cole hadn't been allowed to have any contact with him. That made sense, because by the time he had recovered and was allowed outside again, this adventure would have been old news to Cole.

Joe was almost through with his story, then he dropped the bombshell: neither he nor Cole knew how to swim at the time. Stunned amazement rippled from person to person.

Except Chad. He'd known Cole was fearless. For him the last statement merely confirmed when this adventure must have happened, because he and Cole learned to swim the summer after his chicken pox! It made him feel better knowing he hadn't been left out on purpose, and he realized then that Joe was finished talking. It was also when he realized that Cole's family, along with most everyone else there, were staring at him with raised brows as if questioning whether he knew anything about this escapade. He shook his head, emphatically proclaiming his innocence.

Just when they thought they had heard it all, another friend from high school began to tell a story that he said Cole had told him years ago, about falling into Bull Run Creek way back when he was in grade school. As soon as those words were out, Chad's chin immediately dropped to his chest. He was reeling with the knowledge that someone else knew about that! His chin stayed glued to his chest as the guy explained that, according to Cole, he'd slipped while trying to cross over to the other side of the creek, on a tree that had fallen and spanned the water after some really bad storms, and that he would have drowned for sure, if Chad hadn't saved his life by pulling him to safety.

Chad didn't have to look. He felt it, as everyone literally turned in unison to gape at him open mouthed. Unable to profess his innocence this time, he just sat there—feeling twelve years old again—with his eyes locked on a little pebble laying between his feet, essentially confirming to everyone the story was indeed true. He knew he was definitely going to have to answer for this one later on, but right now his mind was wrapped around the fact that Cole had told someone what happened at Bull Run Creek! And he was really confused. He'd always thought Cole had been completely embarrassed about that day, particularly the part about him saving his life. That's why he thought they had an unspoken agreement not to talk about it again. To anyone. Ever. But it was obvious now that Cole had told at least *one* other person.

Had Chad looked up sooner, he might have seen the knowing smile on Maggie's face, as she remembered when Cole told her about Chad saving his life. It was the night of their first date when she cooked dinner and they had gone for a long walk afterward. She recalled that, at first, Cole had been uncomfortable talking about the events of that day, but she soon realized his discomfort came from the shame and remorse he felt knowing his carelessness put his best friend in danger by having to come to his rescue. By the time he got to the part about Chad saving his life, he spoke with such fierce admiration and gratitude toward Chad, Maggie had begun to glimpse the depth of the bond that existed between the two of them. She and Cole never spoke of that day again and she had often wondered if she was the only one he had ever told about it, but now she knew that he'd obviously told at least *one* other person.

She sighed. She had been dreading this day, but all of these people coming together and sharing their memories lifted her spirits. It was plain to see Cole would live on in so many people's hearts.

For a few seconds it seemed as if no one else was going to come forward to speak, and just when the pastor rose from his seat to bring the service to an end, a woman emerged from somewhere in the crowd and made her way up front.

Chad was still looking at the ground trying to come up with a way to get out of having to answer all the questions he was going to have to answer after the service, and didn't see who had come to speak next, until she spoke.

"Hi. My name is Karen, and I knew Cole from The Old College Inn where I work."

Chad looked up then, surprised not only that Karen was there, but that she came up to speak. She looked exactly like she did the last time he saw her, which had been several years now. He wondered what she could have to say, not realizing she'd known Cole that well.

"Cole came in one Sunday night. It was close to closing time and there was hardly anyone there. He sat down and ordered a coke, and he seemed pretty upset. I went to get his soda, and when I came back, I could tell he had a lot on his mind, so I asked him if he wanted to talk. He nodded that he did, so I took a seat. I was wondering where Chad was, because I'd never seen one of them in there without the other. Then Cole told me that he'd just had words with Chad."

All heads turned to Chad again. *Good grief! There's definitely going to be an inquisition now!* he thought, wishing he could just disappear.

"But part of the reason he was so upset was because of the way he had stormed out, leaving Chad at the restaurant they were at."

Chad remembered that night. It was the Chinese night that he had tried to talk to Cole about his career and classes and Cole had gotten upset and left. Chad recalled looking for Cole on the way home, but not finding him. Now he finally knew where Cole had gone.

"I'd almost forgotten the promise I made to him that night because I never thought I would have to fulfill it, but when I heard about Cole's passing, it came rushing back." She turned her attention directly to Chad. "Chad, I wasn't sure if I should talk to you in private or tell you like this, but after hearing the others speak, I decided that I think he would want everyone to know what you did."

Once again, everyone turned to look at Chad. He didn't notice. It was as though everyone else had disappeared and this was a dream. Or a nightmare. He felt numb, like he couldn't move if he tried.

"He told me the story we just heard about you saving his life at Bull Run Creek when ya'll were in grade school. He said you saved him not only then, but also the time in high school when he'd almost gotten kicked off the football team because of his grades? I think he called it his "near death experience"?..." That elicited a few chuckles. "...and how you tutored him and helped him bring his grades back up just in time for report cards. He said that you guys never discussed it, but that you used to go to his teachers to find out what tests or assignments he'd missed or failed, and help him do the makeup work, so that he never got close to being put in that position again."

There were murmurs amongst the people, with some turning to smile at Chad, a few nearby, patted him on his shoulders. He felt strange. This was so surreal. He'd figured Cole had to have known to some extent that he didn't just magically know what assignments he'd needed help with, but they'd never talked about it. He'd known Cole was thankful for what he did without him actually having to *say* it. He wondered how much Cole really knew.

"He told me it didn't end in high school either. That, after you started college, you continued doing this by somehow convincing the teaching staff at UT to let you help him there too. But that wasn't the only thing you did. He said that whenever he had a bad breakup with a fed up girlfriend, that you almost always went to them to make sure they were okay and told them that it wasn't their fault, and tried to convince them that he wasn't a bad guy. I'm telling you all of this Chad, because he felt really bad for blowing up on you that night. He knew all you were trying to do was look out for him once again, but he panicked when he realized that you might graduate without him. He said he couldn't answer your questions about his classes because he just didn't know what else he could ever do outside of football." She sighed. "I don't know," she said, looking over at Cole's casket, "in hindsight, maybe somehow he just had a feeling it would never be an issue." She paused for a moment to wipe her eyes, and compose herself. "He said that every time he wanted to try to thank you for everything that you did for him, for whatever reason, he just couldn't get the words out. He asked me to promise that if anything ever happened to him…" her voice broke as she started to sob. "…and I never thought it would…" her breath hitched, and she apologized for breaking down. "I'm sorry. Please forgive me." she took a deep breath and said, "He asked me to promise to tell you if anything ever happened to him that he knew, Chad. He knew."

Chad couldn't breathe. He couldn't move. He couldn't do anything. He had no idea what transpired next, nor did he know that tears were streaming down his face.

In closing, the President of the bank where Cole had his first account as a boy, made an announcement that because so many people had come forward wanting to help in any way, the bank had set up a fund, and to date, several thousand dollars had been donated and was there for Cars care and education, in honor of Cole.

Maggie was comforted in that Cole's service today had turned into more of a celebration of his life than a funeral, and had it not been for that, she didn't think she would have felt so compelled to speak herself, but after the outpouring of love and support from all the people gathered there, she just had to thank them all for their generosity. While the grief of her loss was not diminished, their unselfish acts of kindness certainly made the day more bearable. and for that she needed to convey her sincere appreciation. So as the bank president finished his announcement, much to everyone's surprise Maggie signaled she would like to say something. She stood and passed Car, who had been sitting on her lap, to Cole's mother seated beside her and made her way to the podium, pausing at Cole's casket to place her hand on the top as if gathering strength to proceed. When she was ready, she stepped behind the podium and scanned the crowd, swallowing hard behind a trembling smile of gratitude. Her eyes swam with tears but, determined, she fought them back until she was able to speak.

"First of all, I want to thank Chad for being such a wonderful friend to Cole. I'm sure he wouldn't have been the person that he was without you. He loved you very much..." her voice cracked and she stopped, swallowing several times. She took a deep breath and cleared her throat. "And I want to thank each and every one of you for taking the time to come here today. Thank you to those of you who shared your stories and memories of Cole. But most of all, thank you so much for the show of love and support..." the tears that had pooled in her eyes overflowed and were pouring down her cheeks freely now. "As most of you are aware, football was Cole's first love..." she wiped the tears away with a tissue, "but what you may not know is that he was an amazing husband and father too." She choked back a sob and hesitated. "I don't know what we are going to do without him, but it would have meant the world to him, and it means the world to me, that he will live on in so many peoples' hearts. Thank you so much for that!"she said sincerely, scanning the crowd with a teary but grateful expression. As she began to walk away from the podium there was a spattering of applause from random people, as though they were unsure that clapping was politically correct at a funeral, but when Maggie managed an appreciative smile in response, everyone reacted by joining in, and for the second time that day she was taken aback by the love emanating from Cole's fans.

Car had been a trooper through the biggest part of the service, but not understanding—much to Maggie's relief—and therefore not caring that all the talking was actually stories being shared about his daddy's wild escapades, he was beginning to get hungry and fidgety. The sudden burst of applause captured his attention though and any discomfort he was experiencing was quickly forgotten and his irritability was cast aside as he enthusiastically joined everyone in the applause, clapping his little hands together with gusto. It was so cute that it really didn't matter just what, exactly, he was clapping for!

Chad searched the crowd for Karen. He needed to talk to her, to find out precisely *what* Cole *did* know, but she was nowhere to found.

The crowd began to disperse but because so many people still wanted to say a few words to Maggie and the family before they left, Cheyenne borrowed Chad's Jeep and took Car on back to the house to get him fed and put down for a nap. Maggie didn't mind the delay. It gave her the opportunity to meet a lot of other friends and acquaintances from Cole's childhood that hadn't spoken during the service and it kept her mind occupied, even though she knew she would never be able to remember all the names and faces. It was almost three o'clock before they made it back to the Rivers' home, and by then she was completely drained.

CHAPTER 30

Friends and neighbors brought all kinds of covered dishes, casseroles, cakes, cold cuts, just about every type of food you could think of, so Maggie had a little nibble of something—that her exhausted brain refused to even identify—then slipped off to wash her face and lay down for a few minutes.

By this time Car had already woken from his nap, refreshed and ready to entertain, but everyone assured Maggie he would be looked after. It was unusual for him to have an audience of this size, so he was making the most of it. There were a few other children there, including Gaby, Maggie's niece, now almost twelve years old, who still acted like a little mother to Car. She took him and the other kids out in the back yard to play catch, while several adults watched from their seats on the back porch.

Chad was one of the onlookers from the deck, but he was quiet, contemplative, as he watched the kids, not taking part in any of the conversations going on around him, which at the moment, all centered on Maggie and Car's well being, and what they were going to do now. Abruptly, he stood and went to play ball with the kids.

As tired as Maggie was, she just couldn't seem to unwind and relax long enough to let sleep take her away, and give her mind and body a rest she so desperately longed for. She tossed and turned, the same question that had been the main topic of conversation with most everyone in the house, running rampant through her mind. What was she going to do? She finally gave up chasing elusive sleep, and began to sort through her thoughts and feelings, to try to come to some sort of decision. Her parents, and a few others, had voiced their desire for her to move back home, so they would be able to help her and Car adjust. Her mother also offered to go back to Nashville with her for a while, if that was what she decided to do. She weighed her options. Move back home? Home. Where, exactly, *was* that? Most of her life,

Parrottsville was home. But now home felt like Nashville. She admitted it did sound good to be near her parents, and her brother's family, to have the comfort of their support. On the other hand, she would still have their support in Nashville, and they wouldn't be that far away. The house in Nashville was paid for. Thankfully, Cole had seen to that early on. She had enough money in the bank to live on quite comfortably for some time, and Car would be going to first grade next year, so she could always start teaching. That had been her plan all along anyway, since God had blessed them with Car. Then there was Chad. She felt she and Cole were responsible for him being in Nashville. Could she just move off and leave him there alone? She felt like she would be abandoning him, when she was sure he was hurting as much as she was. She closed her eyes and prayed for God's guidance, to help her make the right decision, not only for her, but for Car. Minutes later she opened her eyes and looked around the room. The room where Cole had spent his childhood, redecorated, now a guest room, but still adorned with mementos from his high school and college football days. A picture of her and Cole on their wedding day stood on the dresser, the two of them smiling, eager to begin their future together. Maggie wished she could go back to that day, when she'd held the innocent belief that they would raise a family and grow old together. She looked at their faces in the picture again, and wondered if she would have done anything differently if she had somehow known she was only going to have these few years with Cole. If she could have seen herself today, alone, after putting him the ground.

And then, with sudden clarity, she knew that she wouldn't have done *anything* differently. She wouldn't have traded her time with him, not one second, and she certainly wouldn't have given up the chance to have Car, even knowing she would eventually be a single parent. She knew what she had to do! With her mind made up now, she felt as if a huge weight had been lifted, and refreshed—even though she hadn't slept a wink—she changed into jeans and a sweater and went out to join the others.

Suddenly famished, she headed toward the dining room. On the way she overheard bits and pieces of conversations from concerned friends and family members.

"She doesn't know yet, what she's going to do..."

"I'm so worried about her..."

"Is she going to stay here?"

When she rounded the corner entering the room, the conversation changed to, "How are you doing, Maggie?" and "Are you okay?" and "Did you get any rest?" and "Can I get you anything?"

Maggie appreciated everyone's thoughtfulness, and a few days ago, or more accurately, up until a few minutes ago, she would have probably burst into tears not knowing the answers to those questions herself, but now she surprised everyone with a smile that was reflected in her eyes, as she told them she was fine. And starving. Several people scrambled to get her something to eat, her insistence she could get it herself falling on deaf ears. A plate of food appeared, almost instantaneously, while Maggie inquired as to Car's whereabouts. Directed to the backyard, Maggie graciously accepted the plate of food and stepped out on the porch in time to overhear her brother, Vic, talking to his wife, Ann.

"She'll probably take a while to decide what she's going to do."

"I've decided."

Startled, they both looked over their shoulders at Maggie, standing behind them holding her plate. She smiled at them briefly, before taking a bite of lasagna. Then she closed her eyes and let out a contented sigh, as she chewed.

She had everyone's attention now, and by the time her brother pulled her up a chair, word had spread inside, bringing everyone outside to hear her decision. Chad glanced up from playing with the kids, relieved to see Maggie was eating something, and he wondered why everyone had come outside.

Maggie swallowed her bite of food, set her plate in her lap and wiped her mouth with a napkin. Her mom handed her a glass of iced tea, and she took a sip of it. "Thanks, Mom," she said, setting her glass down on the porch. Clearing her throat, she looked around, meeting everyone's anxious eyes.

"I've decided I'm, *we're,* going back to Nashville." She glanced out at Chad in the yard. Her mom and dad exchanged worried looks. "I'm going to ask Chad if we can ride back with him tomorrow."

"Maggie, honey," Cole's mom began tentatively. "Are you sure that's what you want to do? There's no hurry for you to make a decision. We'd love for you to stay here with us, with all your family I mean."

"I know, and it means a lot to me, it really does," her eyes conveyed her sincerity, "but our home is in Nashville, and I think the best thing I can do right now, is not to disrupt Car's life anymore. To get him back home and back to school, back to a routine he's familiar with. That's the only home he's ever known, and where his memories of his father are. I can't take that from him," she paused a moment to let that register, then continued before anyone said anything. "We won't be that far away, and we'll come back here for Thanksgiving and Christmas. Besides, Chad will be there, so we won't be there alone, and we couldn't very well just move off and leave him could we?"Not expecting an answer, she added, "I've got my students and other commitments, and next year I can start teaching elementary school. It was what I'd planned to do anyway when Car started first grade. We'll be fine," she stated emphatically, hoping to convince everyone. "We're okay financially, and if things don't work out, we can always move back later on." She picked up her plate, "We'll be fine," she reiterated, then took a bite, signaling the end of her pronouncement.

Her mom went over and sat beside her, "Honey, I'll go back with you and stay for a little while, until you get back on your feet," she offered again.

"Mom, I thought about it, but Daddy needs you here, and I'd just be worried about him the whole time." Holding her plate with one hand, she reached over, and took her mother's hand. "Everything will be okay, Mom. I promise I will call you if I need you for anything, but I'd feel better knowing you're here taking care of Daddy."

"Well, he does need looking after, doesn't he?" she agreed, chuckling softly.

"It'll be our secret," she kissed her mom's cheek. "I love you."

"I love you too. You promise you'll call?" she asked, keeping eye contact until Maggie answered.

"I promise."

Persuaded, her mom said, "Well for heavens' sake, honey, eat your food before it gets cold!"

"Thanks, Mom," she said, picking up her fork.

Just as she finished eating, the kids came running up on the porch, hungry, so everyone that had been out there with her, followed them inside to help them get something to eat, as Chad lumbered up on the deck. He looked tuckered out, Maggie thought, and once again she got the impression he seemed to be acting a little distant when it appeared as if he were going to follow everyone else in. Shaking off the feeling, she called out to him. She swore he seemed to hesitate a split second, essentially confirming her suspicion that maybe he didn't want to be around her. But when she didn't say anything more, he began walking toward her. He was looking everywhere but at her.

"Can I talk to you for a second?" she asked as he approached, confused by his aloofness.

"Sure," he sat down in the chair next to her.

She turned to look at him, but he was still looking out over the yard, down toward the creek.

"Hey," she touched his arm. "Are you okay?"

"Yeah! Yeah," he said quickly, like *why wouldn't I be fine?* "Are *you* okay?" he asked. He sounded as if he really needed to know that she was ok. He finally looked at her, waiting for her to answer. The concern in his eyes made her feel like she was losing it.

She nodded. "I'll be fine. I wanted to ask if you would mind if Car and I rode home with you tomorrow?"

He sat forward, giving her all of his attention now. "You're going back?"

She nodded again.

To stay?" he asked, reluctant to hear the answer, but desperately needing to know.

She answered by filling him in on the conversation he'd missed while playing with the kids. Summing it up, she asked again, "So, can we ride back with you?"

"Of course you can," he said, with a sigh of relief.

Chad's Journal
October 8, 2005

Cole, this is my journal. You know, the one that suddenly
disappeared shortly after we met Maggie?
After we met her, I couldn't take the chance
you might sneak a look. It's the only time I ever came close to
deceiving you, blood brother.
It's mainly a record of the internal battles I've fought and either
won or controlled. Things that would have hurt you and Maggie.
I loved you both too much to let that happen.
But now you know it all, and I am at your mercy.
Cole, please send me a sign, tell me what you want me to do.
I am so confused, angry, hurt, lost, afraid, and consumed with
guilt. I've always loved you, brother, please help me.

CHAPTER 31

The trip back to Nashville took longer than expected. Had Maggie known she was going to make the decision to go back, she would have brought their luggage with them and stayed overnight with Cole's parents. As it was, she'd have to go back to her parents, meaning Chad would have to drive there to pick them up Sunday morning, adding about 100 miles to his drive, there and back. Maggie tried to talk him into letting someone bring them back the next day, but he insisted that it wasn't a problem. That, coupled with a cold front moving in and causing some pretty bad storms, made driving on the highway slow going.

Saying goodbye to everyone had been particularly hard this time, partly because since Cole's unexpected death, Maggie had learned that you just never know what each day would bring to turn your life upside down, and partly because she knew everyone had been hoping she and Car would be staying—and weren't convinced yet—that she had made the right decision.

It had been a long hard week, and between the dreary weather and the droning hum from the tires on the pavement, in spite of their best efforts, Maggie and Car had been lulled to sleep.

Chad glanced over at Maggie sleeping peacefully, and over his shoulder at Car, then looked quickly back to the wet road. He eased up on the accelerator, taking extra precautions with his precious cargo in the heavy rain. His emotions were in turmoil right now. He felt it was his duty to Cole, to take care of Maggie and Car, yet at the same time he felt an overwhelming sense of guilt. If he were to see Cole, right now, today, would he be able to look him in the eyes and convince him that somewhere deep down, he hadn't wished to be in this exact spot? Him at the wheel, with Maggie and Car sleeping soundly on their trip home, like a family? He wasn't sure he could. But he *was* sure if he could somehow take away Maggie and Car's pain, if he could put that sparkle back in Maggie's eyes by trading places with Cole, he would do it in a heartbeat. Keeping his eyes on the road, the battle ensued inside him until Maggie finally stirred.

"Chad, I'm so sorry. I didn't mean to fall asleep. Where are we? How long have I been out?" she asked, looking back to check on Car, still sound asleep.

"We're about twenty-five miles out, and it was good to see you getting some rest." He looked over at her and smiled.

"Well the least I could have done was keep you company."

"No, it's fine. I would have been making the trip alone anyway if you hadn't decided to come back."

"I had to come back. This is our home, at least for now," she replied, as if it had been an easy decision.

"Well, for what it's worth, I'm glad."

She smiled. "Thanks. Me too."

The sound of their voices roused Car.

"Are we there yet?" rang out from the backseat, causing Chad and Maggie to look at each other and laugh.

"Almost, buddy," Chad answered. "Are you hungry?"

"I'm firsty."

"Well, let's stop and get you something to drink then, little man."

"Chad, you don't have to do that. We're not that far from home," Maggie protested, not wanting to be too much of an inconvenience.

"There's no way I'm taking you guys home without making sure you've eaten first."

"I'm hungry," came from the back seat.

"Okay. You guys win," Maggie relented, thinking what a good friend Chad was.

"I have to go potty," Car added, prompting Chad to take the next exit. Seeing a Red Lobster just down the road, Chad called back to Car, "Is Red Lobster okay?" knowing that he loved shrimp.

"Yeah!" Car shouted, excited.

Chad looked at Maggie apologetically, realizing too late he should have asked her first.

She just smiled and said, "That's fine," reaching down to pick up her purse, while he found a parking space.

Chad took Car straight to the men's room, and Maggie put their name in for a table. By the time they returned, a table was ready and they were led back by the hostess.

Car climbed in the booth and Maggie started to slide in beside him when Car said, "I want Uncle Chad to sit next to me!"

"Oh, sorry." Maggie said nonplussed, trading places with Chad, used to playing second fiddle to Chad when Car had a choice.

"How's that?" she asked, after they made the switch.

"Good," Car confirmed, as the waitress walked up.

"Hi! My names Lucy, I'll be your server tonight. Hey there," she said, flirting with Car. "What's your name, handsome?"

"Well, my real names Chad, like his," he said, hitching his thumb toward Chad, "but you can call me Car."

"Car?" she looked at Maggie then Chad, confused, thinking she'd misunderstood him.

Maggie explained, "It's his nickname. C-A-R are his initials."

"Ohhh, okay," she said, understanding now.

"Well, what can I get for you, Car?"

"Shrimp!" Car exclaimed.

"Shrimp it is. With fries?"

"Yes please." Car said, very polite.

"Okay, and for you, Dad?" she asked Chad.

Caught by surprise, Chad looked at Maggie like a deer caught in the headlights.

"He's not Dad," Car said, correcting her. "My Daddy went to live with Jesus in Heaven the other day. Didn't he Mommy?"

With a stricken look on her face, Lucy's hand flew to her mouth, "Oh my gosh! I am so sorry. I just thought...I mean..." she stuttered, shaking her head, "I'm so sorry." She was looking back and forth between Chad and Maggie, her eyes pleading for forgiveness, sincerely mortified.

"It's okay," Maggie told her, feeling bad for her. "You had no way of knowing, and you certainly meant no harm. Really, it's okay."

Not convinced, Lucy said, "I'm sorry, I'll be right back," and she rushed off.

Maggie watched her hurry away, then looked at Chad, who looked about as uncomfortable and apologetic as the waitress. Car's face clearly conveyed that he didn't understand what all the drama was about.

"Is she getting my shrimp?" he asked, hopeful.

Unsure whether to laugh or cry, Maggie couldn't help giggling at Car's innocence, and she relaxed some when she saw Chad trying to suppress a smile too.

A minute later Lucy returned, eyes red from crying, followed by a gentleman who introduced himself.

"Hi folks, my name is Hugh. I'm the manager. Lucy explained to me her misunderstanding. She's truly sorry, and—"

"Really, it's not a problem—" Maggie started.

"Well, we would like to extend our condolences. We're very sorry for your loss, and I would just like to tell you your meal tonight is on us."

"You don't—" Maggie began, but this time Chad interrupted.

"That's not necessary. Everything is fine, it was an honest mistake. It could have happened to anyone."

"Well, it would mean a lot to Lucy and myself, if you would allow us to do this for you. In fact, I insist."

Chad looked at Maggie to see what she thought.

"Can I have some shrimp?" Car asked earnestly when the lapse in conversation gave him an opening, causing everyone to laugh, brightening the moment.

"That's fine." Maggie said, giving in. "Not necessary, but fine. Thank you."

∾ℋℋℋ∾

The rest of the meal was uneventful. Car finally got his shrimp, and Lucy, the waitress, appeased by their accepting the restaurant's hospitality, proved to be very good at her job. Chad left her a large tip hidden beneath his plate so that hopefully it wouldn't be discovered until after their departure, then retrieving the umbrella from under the table, they made their way through the heavy down pour to the dry warmth of the Wrangler. Once everyone was buckled in, they drove the last few miles of the journey home.

When they arrived at Maggie's, there was so much mail, the carrier had to put it in a box on the front porch, because the mail box was full. She realized she had forgotten to have the mail held. It was a good thing they had only been gone for two mail delivery days and came home when they did.

Chad helped her carry the mail in, then had her wait inside, refusing her offers to help, and with the umbrella in one hand, made two trips to get their luggage. Once everything was in, she asked if he would like to stay for a while, but after making her promise they had everything they needed, he headed home.

While Car was getting his bath, she phoned her students to let them know they could resume their lessons the next day. She needed to stay as busy as she possibly could for a while, to keep her mind occupied, otherwise she would be a wreck. Once that was taken care of, she let Car watch a few minutes of T.V. while she unpacked, then got him tucked in for the night. When he said his prayers, he asked Jesus to say "hello" to his Daddy for him, causing Maggie's heart to constrict with sadness.

Finishing his prayers, he said "Amen," opened his eyes and asked Maggie, "Do you think Jesus will remember to tell him, Mommy?"

Choking back tears, her voice threatening to break, she answered, "I know he will, honey." She swallowed past the lump in her throat and leaned over to kiss his forehead. "I love you." She lovingly ran her hand across his forehead, brushing the hair off his precious face. "Goodnight," she whispered.

"Goodnight," he replied sleepily, his eyes already drifting shut.

On her way out she turned out his light, and leaving his door open, she went downstairs, took one look at all the mail, decided it could wait until morning, went back upstairs, took a shower, then climbed into bed and cried herself to sleep.

Waking early after a dreamless night, Maggie got Car off to Kindergarten, then returned home to tackle the mound of mail. Sorting through it, she began separating a few bills from the junk mail, noting that the majority of it appeared to be condolence cards, when a letter from her Uncle Charles caught her eye. He was her father's brother who had moved to Florida when his ailing health made it difficult for him to withstand the cold Tennessee winters on his own anymore. She sat the letter aside, grabbed a cup of coffee, and returned to the table to read it. She'd not spoken to him in a few weeks, and as she unfolded the letter, the shakiness of his handwriting reminded her with a painful stab of his age and deteriorating health. The letter began:

"My Dear Sweet Maggie,

I heard about yer loss, and I hurt for you Mag, but the ache in my heart is nothin compared to the ache in yers. You've been cast into a battle which only you can fight. If it be man or beast, I would throw every ounce of my being to the front of the line for yer protection, and all the people who love you would do the same. But I can't take yer hurt away. Only time will tend to that. Nothin said, nothin done makes it any easier fer you. I would like to share somethin with you though, and I'll try to put it to you as it was put to me.

Maggie, when you and Cole fell in love and got married, your love was like the start of a patchwork quilt. Your love and your quilt grew and grew and you wrapped yerselves in it, and it made you feel safe and warm. But sometimes in life Mag, yer quilt gets stripped away and you get cast into a place as cold and dark as any coal mine you could imagine. So you suffer the hurt that no one can ease. But in a short time you will realize that you ain't alone. If you look you will find yer little one wrapped in yer quilt that was there all along, making him feel safe and warm. If you look a little closer you will see the big tattered whole in that quilt that needs mending, and it's those two things that will give you the strength to carry on. Honey, once the veil of your grief lifts some, you will see too, that we are all here to help you mend and add to yer quilt.

Wish I was there with you. I love you.

Yers and always,

Uncle Charles"

Maggie had a hard time reading the last of the letter, the tears blurring her vision. She got up to get a tissue, and read the letter again, noticing with a smile, the endearing way he spelled his words exactly the way he spoke them. He was such a good sweet man, and she vowed she would go to see him, and take Car, so he could get to know this wonderful man who was so dear to her.

She called her mom and dad to tell them about the letter, and to let them know she was okay, then she called her Uncle Charles. He told her he was "fantastic, but gittin' better," something he'd said for as far back as she could remember. They talked for a while, and Maggie ended the conversation with a promise to go see him soon. Then she tackled the rest of the mail.

CHAPTER 32

The next couple of weeks took some adjusting for Maggie and Car. The weekdays were the easiest, not being much different than before Cole passed away. The nights and weekends, when it was just the two of them for dinner or when she went to bed by herself, were when his absence was a glaring reminder. She couldn't stand to hear a football game on the television, but they were slowly settling into a new routine, and Car seemed to be doing okay, sending messages to his Daddy via Jesus during his prayers each night. In his little head, Cole was just living somewhere else, and Maggie supposed it was better that way for now. It was easier for him, until he was older and understood what it meant to 'go to heaven'.

She spoke to Chad several times, and while he made a few of the calls to check on them, most of the time their talking was the result of her calling him. She knew he was having difficulty at work—being at the stadium and around the team with Cole not being there—but she couldn't shake the feeling that something else was going on. He didn't seem to be himself, and she'd never seen him so distant. She'd invited him over for dinner a few times, and each time he'd begged off, saying he had other commitments, and though she was beginning to think it was just excuses, she didn't put him on the spot by asking what those commitments were.

The cards and letters were still coming in, though thankfully they were beginning to taper off. It was kind of everyone, and she knew they meant well, but there had been *so* many and it was a constant reminder of what she'd lost. A letter she received today had been particularly hard, but the pain it evoked in her had been more for the sender, than herself. It was from Darren Archer, the defensive end for the Indianapolis Colts that originally tackled Cole, then protected him from *being* tackled when he saw that Cole was having problems. Evidently he had been having a hard time with Cole's death, of feeling responsible because of his aggressiveness and being unable to stop from plowing into Cole, to the point that he had not been able to play since that day. In the letter, he asked for Maggie's forgiveness, more than once, and wanted to know if there was anything he could do for her or Car. He also enclosed a check for ten thousand dollars, and begged her to please accept it, and put it toward Car's college fund. He went on to say he had something for Maggie, and asked if she would contact him, so he could make arrangements to get it to her.

After finishing his letter she was anxious to call him. She couldn't imagine what he could possibly have for her, and she also appreciated his concern for Car—though she felt that his check was way too much for her to accept—but her desire to call him had nothing to do with either of those matters. She wanted to explain to him what happened wasn't his fault, that no one could have known. Cole could have been sleeping peacefully in bed, instead of on the field, and it wouldn't have changed anything, and hopefully that information would help him with his struggle of feeling responsible. What she *didn't* want, was for him to think she called because he had something for her, or to be put in the position of having to refuse it, especially if it was money.

What she really needed was to ask Chad's opinion on how he thought she should handle it, but she hadn't spoken to Chad in two days, and hadn't seen him since he brought her and Car home two weeks ago. Her suspicions that something was wrong were getting stronger. They'd never gone two weeks without seeing each other.

She knew he was having a really hard time with Cole's death, and in some aspects, it was probably *harder* for him because of his and Cole's lifelong friendship, and then there was his job and the daily reminder of Cole's absence on top of everything else. So was seeing her and Car without Cole just too much for him to handle? She thought about how he'd been the last time she'd seen him, how concerned he'd been, making sure that they had dinner and everything they needed, and she remembered thinking what a good friend he was. Maybe she was being paranoid, and he was only grieving in his own way. Maybe he really *was* busy with work. She knew from Cole's schedule—that was still hanging on the fridge—Chad would be in Arizona this weekend, so rather than wait, she decided to call and ask him to dinner that night, to discuss the letter from Darren and what she should do. Before she could change her mind, she called and got his voice mail.

"Chad? It's Maggie. I know you're busy, but I got a disturbing letter today, and I was wondering if you could come over for dinner tonight so we could talk it over, and maybe you could help me decide what I should do? Call me back please. Thanks. Bye." She laid down her phone, and picked up the letter again. She began to re-read the first few lines, and her phone rang.

"Hello?"

"Maggie, its Chad, are you okay?" She could hear the concern in his voice, and felt bad for thinking he'd been avoiding them. She briefly explained who the letter was from, and asked him if he could come for dinner. He told her he could come by after work on his way home, but couldn't stay for dinner. She hesitated. There was that feeling again. He'd never refused dinner before, when Cole was there. But she accepted his offer, and hung up thinking, "*What's going on with him*?"

CHAPTER 33

True to his word, Chad came over after work, and true to his word, he didn't stay for dinner. When he arrived, he seemed sincerely glad to see her and Car, and hugged them both warmly. He played with Car for a while, and then Maggie let Car watch T.V., while she read the letter to Chad. She shared her concerns for the guilt that Darren was carrying—and her desire to convince him that it wasn't his fault—along with being worried about what Darren had for her. And that she didn't want to offend him about the check he had sent, but felt it was really too much. After they talked it over, Chad offered to stay while she tried to call Darren, if she wanted him to. She glanced at the clock and it occurred to her that she might be calling him during his dinner, but Chad told her that he thought it would be a welcome interruption for Darren, even if she was. She thought about it for a second and then agreed with Chad and went ahead and placed the call. After telling the woman that answered who she was, Darren came on the line quickly. Maggie thanked him for his letter, and told him that his gift was way too much for her to accept, but after hearing how much it meant to him, she graciously agreed to keep it for Car. Then she explained to him about Cole's aneurysm and tried to assure him that it wasn't his fault, putting Chad on the line to confirm, medically, everything she had told him. When she got back on the phone, Darren mentioned he had something for her. She insisted that his check was too much already. He assured her that it wasn't anything monetary, and asked if he could make arrangements to get it to her.

Reluctantly, she said that he could, and for the first time during their phone conversation, she could tell that this seemed to genuinely lift his spirits. Before they hung up, he told her that he would call her back to let her know when to expect the delivery.

Now here she was, Monday afternoon, five days later, waiting for Chad to get there before the package, which was due to arrive around 5 o'clock. Darren still hadn't told her what it was, but it obviously meant a lot to him and having no idea what to expect, she had to admit she was a little nervous.

She talked to Chad twice over the weekend, and everything had been fine, he'd seemed like his normal self, except—the doorbell rang, and Car came running.

"Uncle Chad! Uncle Chad!" he shouted, on his way to the door.

"Wait," Maggie warned, wanting to make sure it was, indeed, Chad, before Car opened the door. "We have to make sure who it is first."

"It's Uncle Chad!" Car exclaimed.

She looked through the peep hole. "Yes, it is," she confirmed, opening the door, "but we always need to check first, okay?"

"Okay," Car answered, jumping into Chad's arms, who'd heard how excited Car was to see him and had a big smile on his face.

He stepped in and hugged Maggie, still holding Car, "Did it get here yet?" he asked.

"Not yet." She glanced at the clock. "Should be anytime now."

"Wanna see what I did in school today?" Car asked Chad.

"I sure do," he said, sitting Car down. Car grabbed his hand and began leading him back toward the family room.

Maggie followed behind. "Can I get you something to drink, Chad?"

"No. No, I'm fine, thanks."

Chad sat on the sofa and Car began showing him an assortment of paintings he'd done in school. Listening to Chad's praise you would have thought that Car had painted the *Mona Lisa,* Maggie thought, amused.

At the sound of the door bell again, Chad looked up and caught Maggie's nervous expression before she turned to go answer the door.

Chad interrupted Car, "Come on, Buddy, let's go help Mommy with her package."

"Okay," Car agreed, setting his paintings aside.

Maggie hesitantly opened the door—without looking first to see who it was—to find Darren Archer himself, standing there holding a box. He was dressed in a suit and tie, and a beautiful young woman was with him, holding a little boys hand who looked to be about Car's age, and was the spitting image of Darren. Seeing the little boy, Maggie suddenly understood part of why it meant so much to Darren for her to accept his check for Car.

"Oh my gosh!" Maggie said, shocked. "I was expecting FedEx or something. Please, come in!" she said, opening the door wider, and stepping back for them to enter. Chad and Car were standing in the foyer.

"This is Chad, who you spoke to on the phone," she said motioning to Chad, "and this is my son, Car," she said, moving to stand behind him, putting her hands on his shoulders.

"Hi," Darren said to Chad, reaching out to shake his hand. "Hi there, Car."

A pained look flashed across his face when he addressed Car, but he quickly masked it with a smile.

"Hi," Car replied, raising his right hand briefly, before placing both hands behind his back, all of a sudden bashful.

Darren's smile spread to his eyes in response to Car's shyness, and he turned to introduce his family. "This is my wife Jamie, and my son, Darrell."

Introductions made, Maggie invited them to have a seat, escorting them into the formal living room. As they were taking their seats, the boys were eyeing each other warily. Jamie complimented Maggie on the beautiful furnishings in the room, and turning her attention to the baby grand piano, asked Maggie if she played.

Maggie explained that the piano had been a gift from Cole, and that she gave music lessons during the week. Again Maggie saw the pain flicker across Darren's face at the mention of Cole's name, and her heart went out to him. By this time, Car evidently came to the conclusion that Darrell measured up to a potential playmate.

"You wanna play?" he asked tentatively, and Darrell shyly nodded his head.

Maggie figured the Archers' would be more comfortable where they could keep an eye on Darrell, so she asked if they cared to move to the family room, where the boys could play. On the way back, she offered refreshments, which everyone thanked her for, but declined.

Entering the family room, the boys made a bee-line to the toys on the right side of the room, fast friends already. On the left side of the room, there was a sofa and loveseat forming an "L" around a coffee table, and an end table with a lamp on it, nestled in the corner nook created between the two sofas. Maggie indicated with a wave of her hand for Darren and Jamie to have a seat wherever they liked, and Darren took a seat on the far end of the sofa near the table with the lamp, placing the box he was carrying on the coffee table in front of him. Jamie followed and sat to his right. Maggie walked around the coffee table and sat on the loveseat, adjacent from Darren, and Chad sat to her left.

In an effort not to worry about the box Darren had placed on the coffee table, Maggie took note of the boys playing quietly on the other side of the room and remarked, "It's amazing, isn't it? How they make friends so easily?"

"It is," Jamie and Darren nodded in agreement, smiling as they looked over at them.

They all watched the boys for a moment, then Darren cleared his throat, leaned forward and slid the box down to the end of the table in front of Maggie. Her breath hitched and she cast a nervous glance to her left at Chad, but her uneasiness about the package was momentarily forgotten when she noticed that Chad was so scrunched up against his end of the loveseat that it looked as though he was trying to extend the length of it, in—what seemed like to her—an obvious attempt to keep as much space between himself and her as possible. For a second she felt like a leper and it hurt, but the sound of Darren's voice brought her attention back to the him and the box in front of her.

He was saying, "I brought this to you, because I think, in time, it will mean a lot to you and Car."

Maggie was completely perplexed, but now, self conscious as well, with what was going on with Chad. She forced herself to push that aside and give Darren her full attention. With shaking hands she gently pulled the top off of the plain white box, to reveal a football encased in Plexi-glass. All of the worry and anticipation that had mounted in the days since her initial phone conversation with Darren regarding the contents of this box, turned into confusion, and not understanding the balls significance, she looked up at Darren in question and was surprised to see his eyes swimming with unshed tears.

"It's the ball..." he stopped, staring at the ball, his lips pursed, struggling not to break down. He cleared his throat, and started again. "It's the ball from the game. The ball Cole had in his hands before he went down," he blinked several times, fighting back the tears that threatened to spill over.

Enlightened, Maggie looked back down at the ball in silence. A gamut of emotions began running through her at once. A vision of Cole holding the football before he went down formed in her mind, and for a moment she was overwhelmingly repulsed with the knowledge that this was it, this was the same ball he'd held, the symbol of the game that had taken him from her. But almost immediately she remembered how much Cole had loved the game, and the countless conversations she'd had with Chad and Darren trying to convince them that it was the aneurysm, not football, that had caused his death. Suddenly the ball before her took on a whole new meaning, and she realized then, how incredibly thoughtful it was for Darren, not only to have gotten the ball in the first place, but to have brought it to her and Car personally.

"I don't know what to say," she finally managed. "I can't thank you enough," and she leaned over and wrapped her arms around him. She held the embrace a beat or too longer than she normally would have, trying to convey to him she was sincerely thankful, and hoped her heartfelt gratitude would possibly assuage some of his pain. Darren returned the embrace with equal fervor and sincerity, but for him it was an attempt to express how truly sorry he was. When they finally released each other, she looked into his eyes. "This really means a lot to me," she said, placing her hand over her heart.

"I only wish I could do more," he said, with a helpless expression in his eyes.

Then a thought struck her. Lighting up, she said, "You can! You, Jamie, Darrell, and Chad," she cast a glance at Chad without making eye contact when she included him, "can all stay and have dinner with Car and myself!"

"Oh, we don't want to im—"

"Please? We'd love to have your company, and I promise I'll put you to work!" she said, with laughter in her voice.

Darren smiled, unable to resist such an earnest invitation, and looked at Jamie, who nodded.

"It would be an honor," he answered.

Maggie turned to Chad. She refused to let herself think about his apparent newfound loveseat extending capabilities *or* Leprosy. Instead, she boldly met his gaze, and with a slight raise of her chin—that she hoped on the outside looked like she almost dared him to say no—asked, "Would you help Darren fire up the grill?", while on the inside she was fully expecting another excuse for him not to stay.

"Absolutely," he said, standing.

Taken aback momentarily, a second passed while Maggie thought, "*Huh. I can't believe that worked!*" but she quickly gathered herself and stood up too. "Steaks, baked potatoes, and salad okay with everyone?" she asked, to a chorus of yes's.

Darren took off his jacket and tie and laid them on the arm of the sofa, then followed Chad out onto the deck, while Jamie offered to help Maggie in the kitchen. On the way, Maggie correctly guessed—based on Car's eating habits—that Darrell would prefer a burger to a steak as well, which Jamie verified, so they added a couple of burgers to the steaks on the platter for Chad and Darren to grill. While Jamie was cutting up lettuce for the salad, Maggie ran the platter of meat out to the guys, checking on the boys on the way. They were still playing peacefully together, oblivious to anything going on around them. It did her heart good to know they had befriended each other so easily. Car was going to need the distraction of his friends in the coming days, she thought, though she knew a whole bevy of friends could never take the place of his father. Vowing to do everything in her power to see to it that Car suffered as little as possible for not having his father in his life, she stepped out on the deck. As she did, she overheard Chad explaining Cole's aneurysm to Darren again, so mouthing a silent prayer that Chad would get through to him, she quickly slipped the steaks to them and hurried back inside without breaking stride, and, she hoped, without interrupting their conversation.

When the food was ready, they had an enjoyable dinner and spent the rest of the evening getting to know each other better, and parted knowing they would be lifelong friends. Chad seemed to be himself all evening, and Maggie went to bed—for the first time in the weeks since Cole's death—without crying herself to sleep.

CHAPTER 34

They had more than their share of ups and down during the next few months. Thanksgiving and Christmas were difficult. For Thanksgiving, Maggie and Car rode with Chad to Maggie's parent's home, where all three families shared the holiday together. At Christmas, Chad had to be in Miami on Saturday for a game, so Maggie and Car made the trip alone, spending Christmas Eve and Christmas Day with her family, and spending Christmas night with Cole's family, seeing Chad when he flew back from Miami that evening.

One day in between Thanksgiving and Christmas, Maggie called Chad in tears. She'd gone out shopping for gifts, and after arriving home, wrapped Car's presents and went to the guest room closet to hide them, only to find the presents she'd bought for Cole for his birthday. She had forgotten all about them, not having had any reason to go into the closet since his death. It completely overwhelmed her at the time. Chad had rushed over and took the gifts away, donating them to a charity at Maggie's request.

In January, Maggie's mother, Cole's mother, and Cheyenne came to stay with Maggie for a weekend, to help her clean out Cole's closet and dressers. Sorting through his things had been really hard—harder than they imagined—but they got through it together, putting some of his personal items away for Car to have some time in the future, and packing other things to donate. Afterwards Maggie was absolutely sure she could never have done it without their help.

∾⌘⌘⌘∾

Maggie hadn't made a decision about what to do with the boat. She knew Car really loved it, but she also knew it being only Car and herself, she wouldn't dream of taking it out. Just the thought of the two of them going out and getting stranded or something, made her shudder. So she put it on the back burner, to wait and see if maybe Chad would be interested in doing something with it.

No one had used the gym equipment in the garage either since Cole's passing, but again, she couldn't or *wouldn't* make a decision about it, wanting to see how Chad felt about it too, yet not wanting to ask him about it. She remembered how hard it had been going through Cole's things and she didn't want to subject Chad to that. It just wasn't that important, and would still be there when the time was right to address it.

One thing she *had* made a decision on was Cole's Camaro. She was going to keep it for Car. It was already a classic, and it was something she could maintain easily enough. It would *really* be a collectable by the time Car was old enough to appreciate it, she mused.

Maggie often reflected on Chad's behavior of late. At times, like with Cole's birthday present's, he went above and beyond, and was just as sweet as he could be. Other times, he seemed very distant, and days would go by without her hearing from him. She was concerned, but wasn't sure she wanted to say anything to him about it. Maybe it was just part of his grieving process.

One evening she called to check on Bobbye, who was still performing on Broadway. During their conversation she found out that Bobbye was keeping in close contact with Chad, so she asked for *her* opinion on how Chad seemed to be holding up. She said, other than missing Cole, he seemed fine. She hadn't noticed anything unusual.

Not convinced, Maggie called Cheyenne. After voicing her concerns about the way he'd been acting, Cheyenne shared with her the discussion she and Chad had about his not being able to save Cole, and how guilty he felt. Maggie was stunned to hear this! He had been so instrumental in helping Darren realize *no one* was to blame for what happened! Cheyenne responded by saying that she *thought* Chad had gotten better about feeling somehow responsible. Maggie hoped that was true. But if it was, there was something else going on.

A few days later, Maggie ran into a mutual friend of hers and Chad's at the grocery store. After exchanging pleasantries, the friend casually mentioned she'd heard Chad was dating a lot. This was news to Maggie! Riddled with curiosity, Maggie asked her if she knew who Chad was dating.

"Oh, no one in particular. Playing the field I guess you could say!"

Perplexed, Maggie murmured, "That doesn't sound like Chad."

Their friend agreed, but added she had heard it from several people, including some of the girls he had taken out.

This new information raised more questions about his behavior than it answered. Maggie was glad to hear he was going out, goodness knows she'd tried enough over the years to get him to go out once in a while. But now, dating with such wild abandon? It was totally unlike him. She didn't know what to think. She could only hope that maybe time would tell.

CHAPTER 35

February came with several pleasant surprises for Maggie. Everyone was so thoughtful, going out of their way to see that she didn't spend her 30th—and first birthday without Cole—alone. But there was one surprise in particular that would always stand out in Maggie's memory.

To take her mind off Valentine's Day, Stephanie and Maresa, Maggie's close friends and sorority sisters, got together and made arrangements to travel to Nashville and spend Saturday, Sunday, Monday, Tuesday (Valentine's Day), and Wednesday with Maggie. Afraid to drop in unannounced and take a chance on Maggie having commitments, Maresa called and asked if she could come to visit. Maggie was elated and said other than a few hours on Monday, Tuesday, and Wednesday with her students, she had no plans. She offered to pick her up at the airport, but Maresa insisted on taking a cab. She couldn't explain to Maggie she needed time for Stephanie's flight to arrive so they could surprise her together. Maggie couldn't have been happier when she saw the two of them on her doorstep.

It was just like old times! They enjoyed catching up with each other, watching what most guys would call 'chick flicks', and just hanging out. They celebrated Maggie's birthday early, making a big deal of it being her 30th. Car loved the added attention of two beautiful women, winning their hearts immediately, and Chad had even come over for dinner one evening! It was fantastic, and Maggie wouldn't have traded a second of it for anything.

The following weekend, Maggie's brother Vic, his wife Ann, and Gabrielle, drove over on Saturday to take Maggie to dinner for her birthday. They stayed overnight with her and Car, and went home on Sunday. It meant a lot to Maggie to see them, too. They had a great time together, and she would never forget it. But still, the best was yet to come.

On Monday, Chad called her and asked if she would keep the coming Saturday night open, so he could do something for her birthday. Pleasantly surprised, she promised him she would, but then shortly after that, Cheyenne called to ask if she could come for the weekend. Maggie smiled to herself. It felt good to have so many wonderful people in her life that cared for her, but she was disappointed she couldn't somehow spend the weekend with both Cheyenne *and* Chad. Regretfully she told Cheyenne she would have loved for her to come, but she'd just promised Chad she would keep Saturday evening open for him.

"Then it will be perfect!" Cheyenne exclaimed, "Because I'll be there to watch Car!" She was careful not to let it slip she had just gotten off the phone with Chad and knew Maggie would be needing a sitter. After working out the details they hung up, with Cheyenne promising to drive over on Friday evening after school.

When Maggie spoke to Chad during the week, he confirmed they would definitely be going "out", and she should get "dressed up". So on Saturday, Cheyenne, Maggie, and Car spent the day shopping. Maggie was going to treat herself to a new outfit, having not been shopping for herself in over six months. She still didn't have any idea where Chad was taking her, but when Cheyenne kept pushing her from sensible pantsuits to elegant cocktail dresses, she had a feeling that Cheyenne knew, and surmised he was probably taking her to a really fancy restaurant.

Finally, after some serious persuasion from Cheyenne, she decided on a beautiful ankle length strapless satin and silk chiffon dress. The dress was two layers, with the bottom layer being a form fitting straight sheath of brilliant white satin, covered with a layer of sheer silk chiffon. The bodice was white on white to a strip of glittering rhinestones around the empire waist. From there the sheer chiffon began the slow transformation from white to a deep midnight blue. In contrast to the straight skirt of the satin layer underneath, the chiffon skirt widened as the color deepened, into a flowing float away hem, with the white satin beneath showing through. It had a little midnight blue, sheer, chiffon shrug to top it off. It looked stunning on Maggie, and she had to admit she loved it, but was afraid it was *too* dressy. Cheyenne insisted it was perfect.

After they returned home, Maggie flip flopped over her decision to buy the dress and voiced her concerns that it was much too elegant to wear to a restaurant, but each time Cheyenne assured her it would be fine. Until that evening, minutes before Chad was due to arrive, when Cheyenne was overcome by a sense of panic. Maggie was dressed and sitting at the vanity. Cheyenne was standing behind her, pinning the last bit of her upswept hair in place, when Maggie made a last second decision to change out of the dress.

Frantic she was going to have to reveal Chad's surprise in order to keep Maggie from changing, Cheyenne blurted "No! I won't allow it!"

Maggie stilled, startled by the sudden outburst, and stared past her own bewildered reflection in the mirror to Cheyenne's. Car looked up from the trucks he was lining up on the carpet behind them, but when all was quiet, decided there was no cause for alarm, and went back to the more important task at hand.

Cheyenne, seeing Maggie's dumbstruck expression, realized not only had she maybe overreacted a tiny bit, but that she'd just *ordered* Maggie not to change. Sheepishly, she chuckled a what-I-*really*-meant-to-say kind of chuckle and said, "What I *really* meant to say was, whaaat? No! You can't change now! Chad is going to be here any second!"

There was a hesitation—with the two of them gazing at each other in the mirror—but eventually Maggie said, "Well, *okay* then," like *she'd* finally convinced *Cheyenne* the dress was perfect!

Pure relief washed over Cheyenne's face and she began to giggle under her breath. Slowly it evolved into a heartier laugh, and before long she was laughing uncontrollably. Maggie watched warily in the mirror as tears began to run down Cheyenne's cheeks from laughing so hard. Having a contagious effect, *she* felt giggles begin to bubble up inside and erupt. Their peals of laughter mingled and echoed throughout the room, the tension from the unexpected outburst a moment before, dissolving in an instant.

This time Car was unfazed by their antics, intent on getting his trucks lined up and parked just right.

With perfect timing, the doorbell rang—proving Cheyenne's point—which was made abundantly clear by the expression on her face, bringing with it a new bout of nervous giggles. Quickly recovering, Maggie hastily checked her makeup, and turned to Cheyenne for her approving once-over. With a thumbs up signal, Cheyenne hurried down the steps, taking them two at a time, so she could open the door in time for Chad to see Maggie descending the stairs. Car was right behind Cheyenne, anxious to see his Uncle Chad, as usual.

Any nagging doubts Maggie had about her dress were silenced when Cheyenne swept open the front door dramatically, to reveal Chad, as handsome as ever in a black tuxedo, with a sleek, shiny, black limousine waiting at the curb over his shoulder.

"Wow," Maggie and Chad said simultaneously, both clearly delightfully surprised by the others appearance.

Cheyenne was grinning broadly, looking back and forth at the two of them.

"Wanna play catch, Uncle Chad?" Car asked excitedly.

Chad tore his appreciative gaze from Maggie and knelt down on one knee, eye level to Car, giving him his full attention. "Buddy, I can't tonight because I'm taking mommy out for her birthday," he apologized.

Trying to avert any problems or heaven forbid tears on this special night, Cheyenne jumped in to volunteer playing catch in Chad's place. "*I'll* play catch with you, Car!" she suggested with a 'it'll be fun' look on her face, hoping to convince him she could be as fun as Chad.

Car looked doubtful, but when Chad promised to come back and play ball the next day if Cheyenne could take his place "just this once", he relented. "Okay", he said with a sigh. "But she frows like a girl," he added as an afterthought, and looked at Cheyenne with a twinkle in his eye.

"Why you little tease! I'll show you a thing or two!" she said, rushing over to grab and tickle him. He doubled over in a fit of giggles trying to wrestle himself away from her.

Maggie made her way down the rest of the stairs, and now with Car's blessing, they said their goodbye's and started out the door.

With their modest upbringings, neither Maggie nor Chad had ever had the occasion to warrant a limousine before, so it was a new adventure for both of them. The chauffeur held open the door and they climbed in. Chad had taken the time on the ride over to Maggie's, to familiarize himself with all the perks, and Maggie now took everything in. There was champagne nestled in a silver ice bucket, and Chad uncorked the bottle, pouring them each a glass. Accepting the sparkling liquid, Maggie tried to get him to tell her where they were going, but he refused to reveal their destination, so they sipped the Champagne and brought each other up to date on how they were doing, any family news, and of course talked about Car.

Before long the limo slowed to a stop, and the chauffeur got out and opened the door for Maggie and Chad to exit. Once out of the car, Maggie looked around and thought Chad was playing some sort of prank on her. The building in front of them looked decrepit and abandoned—although she saw cars parked nearby—and as she was taking it all in, the door opened, and an elderly gentleman in a suit emerged from the building to escort them inside. Intrigued, Maggie accepted Chad's offered arm by wrapping hers around his securely, as she allowed him to lead her through the open door. When her eyes adjusted to the dimly lit interior, it proved to be as antiquated as the outside looked, but instead of looking neglected, it was brimming with an air of old world elegance. She was immediately drawn to a marvelous huge sideboard occupying one of the walls in the reception area, crafted from rich dark mahogany and graced with a scattering of fine antiques. Tearing her eyes from it, she took in the comfortable looking ornately carved benches, with thick cushions covered in burgundy linen, that lined the other walls. She could easily envision them and several more like them, housed in some glorious old cathedral hundreds of years ago. The walls were adorned with beautiful oil paintings of breathtaking landscapes, in glittering gilded frames. She barely had time to scan the room, before being ushered directly into the dining room where she noticed, appreciatively, how the windows, draped with floral chintz curtains and the candlelit tables covered with hunter green linen, gave the room a warm and elegant ambiance. She thought it was simply charming, and quite a surprise, considering her first impression with the exterior. Despite this—and the fact Chad was in a tuxedo—Maggie felt the stirrings of her earlier concerns of being over dressed. She glanced around at the other patrons, and while everyone appeared to be well dressed, they were all *casually* attired, not black tie. Perplexed by Cheyenne's insistence on her gown and Chad wearing a tux, she considered the possibility that maybe he had expected the restaurant to be more upscale, but he appeared to be perfectly at ease and comfortable in his tuxedo, so she decided just to go with it and enjoy the evening.

Led to a cozy corner table, they took their seats and were given a wine list, which Chad perused briefly and took the liberty of ordering from without having to consult Maggie, already familiar with her preferences, selecting her favorite. A moment later a waiter appeared with a platter of freshly baked bread, and while he uncorked the bottle and served their wine, they sampled the bread and found it to be heavenly. Placing their orders, Maggie chose the petite filet mignon with a baked potato, and Chad ordered the same, only opting for a larger cut of filet. After ordering, they nibbled on the bread and sipped their wine, and when he complimented her again on how beautiful she looked, she made a mental note to thank Cheyenne for flipping out earlier, and not letting her change.

While they were waiting, they were each given a complimentary serving of one of the restaurants specialties, a savory French onion soup. They agreed it was the best they'd ever had, and by the time their meals arrived Maggie had completely forgotten her initial misgivings in regards to the cosmetically challenged exterior of the restaurant. She was pleasantly surprised to realize how much she was looking forward to the rest of her meal, as the waiter placed it in front of her. After commenting on how good everything looked, she sliced easily into her filet mignon and took a bite. She wasn't disappointed. It was delectable. The texture was perfect and the flavor was incomparable. Astounded, she looked at Chad, who had been quietly watching for her appraisal.

"This is delicious!" she said, in disbelief.

Pleased, Chad said, "I'm glad you like it," with a sincere smile on his face.

Maggie went on to try the light, fluffy baked potato, and perfectly sautéed green beans, savoring every bite. She had no idea how Chad knew about this place, but it was definitely the best kept secret in Nashville, and *okay*, she admitted, looks *could* be deceiving. It was one of the best meals she had ever had, over dressed or not.

After dinner, as they enjoyed the last of the wine, she thanked him for the exquisite dinner and the exciting limousine ride, telling him it had been a wonderful birthday present.

From seemingly out of nowhere, he produced an elegantly wrapped package and placed it in front of her. "This was just dinner. *Here's* your present."

"This wasn't "just dinner", it was divine!" she exclaimed, before turning her attention to her gift.

The package was so beautifully wrapped she almost hated to open it, but her love of surprises won out and she picked it up, gently untied the ribbon, and lifted the top. Nestled in delicate tissue paper, she found the most exquisite pair of antique opera glasses that took her breath away.

"Chad, they're amazing," she said in awe, carefully picking them up. "Thank you so much!" she breathed. She took her time admiring them, thanking him over and over again, before reluctantly starting to place them back in the tissue paper.

"That's not all," he said. "There's more, under the tissue."

She eased the paper up to uncover what appeared to be two tickets. Holding them up to read them, her eyes lit up as she slowly read out loud, her voice rising in excitement with each word, "Phantom of the Opera. Saturday, February 25, 8:00 P.M.! Chad! Are you kidding me? Oh my gosh! Phantom of the Opera? Do you have any idea how much I've wanted to see this? Thank you!" she gushed, then looked around to make sure she hadn't made a spectacle of herself. All of a sudden she realized their attire made perfect sense! Cheyenne *had* known!

Chad hadn't seen her smile like this in too long, and it was the best thanks he could have asked for. "You're welcome," he said, truly thrilled to see her so happy. He glanced at his watch. "Your chariot awaits," he said gallantly.

She couldn't contain her excitement on the limo ride to the theater, and was positively beaming. It warmed Chad's heart to see her so happy. After they arrived and were making their way to their seats, Maggie couldn't help admiring all the beautiful gowns the other women were wearing and felt a brief twinge of remorse for all the grief she had given Cheyenne. She would make it up to her, she promised herself before getting caught up in the moment again.

When the performance began, Maggie was spellbound and Chad positioned himself in his seat where he could also observe her, without her noticing and making her uncomfortable. Sitting this way, he was able to see her facial expressions, watch her looking through the opera glasses, witness her emotions and reactions to the actors and the music, ranging from elation, to laughter, to the tears she softly brushed away. He was reminded of a time, once before, when he had done this very thing. It was at the fireworks on the fourth of July, shortly after they had met. He hadn't been able to take his eyes off her then either. Maggie raised the opera glasses he'd gotten her to her face, pulling him out of his reverie, and in that instant it became clear to him that no matter how hard he tried, he would never stop loving her.

∾⌘⌘⌘∾

On the limo ride home after the show, she couldn't stop talking about the performance, the costumes, the actors, the whole production. And the dinner! She would never forget this night, she told him, and he believed her.

CHAPTER 36

Chad walked Maggie to her door, where she hugged him warmly and thanked him again for the wonderful night. The house was dark except for the porch light and he waited for her to unlock the door and go inside. After watching him ride away in the limo, she shut and locked the door quietly, careful not to wake Cheyenne and Car. Her mind was replaying the night's events as she turned to make her way upstairs. She about jumped out of her skin when she saw Cheyenne standing at the foot of the steps.

"Oh my gosh, Cheyenne! You scared the daylights out of me!" she cried out.

Giggling, Cheyenne shushed her and said, "You'll wake Car! You didn't think I could go to sleep did you? Come and tell me all about it!"

Maggie spent the next few hours describing every glorious detail of the dinner and the opera, to which Cheyenne happily confessed she *had* known about and was glad to have been a part of it. Maggie thanked her and apologized for not completely taking her word that the dress was perfect. They finally had to force themselves to go to bed and get some sleep.

When they got up Sunday morning, Maggie didn't need any coaxing to resume talking about her night out, especially since she now had Car to tell all about it. Car was about as interested in the opera as he was clothes shopping with them the day before, until Cheyenne whispered in his ear reminding him that his Uncle Chad was coming over soon to go to church with them and to play ball afterward. That perked him up enough to listen happily. When Chad arrived, *Phantom of the Opera* was still the topic of discussion. During breakfast and on the drive to church…the opera *remained* the topic of discussion.

They got to church a little early, giving them time to mingle with their fellow parishioners before the service began, and after the initial pleasantries were exchanged, Cheyenne overheard Maggie start talking about...the opera. She bumped shoulders with Chad when Maggie wasn't looking and said, "You did good!" Chad smiled happily in response.

When they began making their way to find a seat, several people commented to each other how pleased they were to see Maggie and Car had Cole's closest friend to look after them. They knew the family well enough to know Car was very fond of Chad, and they all thought it was good for Car to have Chad's male influence in his life.

After church, Chad came home with Car to play ball as promised, but something changed in his demeanor during the service. He'd been completely wonderful the night before, and appeared to have still been his old self that morning, but Cheyenne and Maggie both noticed a marked difference since returning home from church. Maggie mentioned it while they sat out on the deck watching the boys play ball, and Cheyenne admitted she had seen it too. But now that he was alone with Car, he seemed to be okay again. Maggie's parents arrived while they were discussing the bizarre change in Chad's behavior, so they put their conversation on hold for the moment, and went to welcome Clarence and Stella. On the way back out to the deck, Maggie stopped in the kitchen to fix everyone iced tea, then joined them.

Her dad was saying how amazed he was at Car's ability to throw the ball so well at his age. They all agreed he *was* extremely good.

"He's going to take after his Dad, that's for sure," Clarence commented.

"I'm not sure I want him to," Maggie said quietly, her thoughts taking her back to the day she watched Cole collapse on the field. She didn't realize she'd spoken out loud, until she heard her father.

"Why, honey?" her father asked.

She looked up to find them all staring at her with concerned expressions on their faces, waiting for her to answer.

Forcing the image out of her mind, she said, "I don't know. I mean, I appreciate that he's like his father, I'm just not sure I want him to play ball, you know? It scares me."

"Maggie, you may not be able to stop him," Clarence said gently.

"I know, and if that's what he really wants to do, I'll support him. I just may not be happy about it," she said with a sigh. Getting a grip on her emotions, she pulled herself together. "Look, I know that "football"," she made quotation marks with her fingers, "didn't kill Cole, but I just can't help wonder if he hadn't been tackled…" her voice trailed off, as she remembered how many times she'd assured Darren that his tackling Cole had not been a factor. "Well, time will tell. If that's what he wants to do, then I know we'll all be there for him." Standing, she asked "Now, who's hungry?" essentially ending the conversation.

She went inside, followed by Cheyenne and her mom. Her dad went out with Car and Chad, to toss the ball with them a bit, while the girls fixed sandwiches for everyone. A few minutes later, Chad came in.

"Hey, Mrs. Thompson," he said, kissing her on the cheek.

She pulled back with a frown. "I've told you to call me Stella," she admonished him.

"Sorry," he said, wincing. "How are you, Stella?"

"That's better. I'm fine" she answered, her frown turning into a smile. "How are you?"

"Good," he replied, turning to call out to Cheyenne and Maggie, "but don't make anything for me. I've got to run."

Maggie and Cheyenne exchanged glances.

"Why?" Cheyenne asked boldly, tired of the cat and mouse game, unconcerned at this point, about putting him on the spot.

Her question evidently threw him for a second. "I…I've got things to take care of," he said, recovering quickly. He hugged and kissed Stella on the cheek again, and before Maggie and Cheyenne could react, standing at the counter with their hands full, he gave them both glancing kisses on their cheeks. "I've already told Car and Mr. …uh…I mean Clarence, goodbye," he said, backing out of the kitchen. Then he was gone.

Stella watched the strained exchange, and when Chad left, she asked, "Did I miss something here?"

"Nothing to worry about, Mom," Maggie said, brushing it off, not wanting to go into it again. "Chad's just been busy a lot lately, that's all. Now," she said cheerfully, gathering up the sandwiches, "let me tell you about last night!"

∾⌘⌘⌘∾

They had just finished lunch and started clearing the dishes, when a questioning look from Clarence reminded Stella she had a surprise for Maggie.

"Oh! I almost forgot! We have a surprise for you out on the car!" she said, rushing out to get it. She came back in with an apple stack cake Aunt Sylvia had sent with them for Maggie's birthday and set it on the table. "No way your daddy was going to let me forget that!" she said chuckling, and he licked his lips as he waited for a piece.

"Well I ain't no dummy!" he replied, and they all laughed.

"Aww... that was so sweet of her!" Maggie said. "I'll call and thank her as soon as we're done. I know these aren't easy to make!"

"Mm, mmm! Glad I didn't miss this!" Cheyenne said, getting clean saucers and forks, and a knife to cut the cake. She grabbed a few candles she found in the drawer, left from Cars birthday, and stuck them on the cake for Maggie. They lit them and sang the birthday song and Car helped her blow out the candles. When they were done, Cheyenne helped clean up and then had to get on the road to Knoxville, having classes in the morning. After saying good bye to everyone, Maggie walked her out to her car.

"I see what you mean about Chad now," she told Maggie. "I'll be having a little talk with him, you can bet on that," she said, matter of fact.

"Well, go easy on him. I'm just worried about him."

"All right. I'll let you know if I get anywhere."

"Okay." They embraced. "Be careful driving home."

"I will. Now you go celebrate your birthday with your parents, and stop worrying about Chad," she ordered.

"Yes ma'am." Maggie saluted, laughing. "Love you!"

"Love you, too," Cheyenne said, waving as she drove off.

Chad's Journal

February 26, 2006

I saw the looks and whispers in church, this morning. Seeing Maggie so happy last night, made me drop my guard.
It can't happen again.

CHAPTER 37

Maggie had a great time visiting with her parents. They went out to an early dinner and to see a movie. Her parents stayed the night and planned to go home on Monday, Maggie's birthday, but seeing she had no plans other than her students after school, they decided to stay over one more night so she wouldn't spend the evening of her birthday alone.

The phone started ringing early that morning and continued off and on throughout the day with birthday greetings and well wishes from friends and family, including one from Chad, who called around noon. He wished her a happy birthday and asked if they needed anything. She told him they were okay, and thanked him again for her wonderful present. He told her she was welcome and he wished her a happy birthday again, then abruptly said he had to go. She'd hung up feeling a little bit hurt, and a lot frustrated. She couldn't wait for Cheyenne to get out of her classes to find out if she had talked to Chad or not. She finally got the call she had been waiting on around six o'clock that night.

"Happy Birthday!" Cheyenne sang out when Maggie answered.

"Thank you!" Maggie said, but without missing a beat she asked, "Did you talk to Chad, yet?"

"Yeah, I talked to him last night, but by the time I got hold of him, it was so late I was afraid to call you."

"Well, what happened? What did he say?"

"I don't know Maggie. I couldn't get anything out of him," Cheyenne said, sounding exasperated. "I told him how you and I both noticed how one minute he seemed to be fine, like Saturday night, and Sunday morning, then the next minute he was treating you like a leper on Sunday afternoon, when he just cut and ran, wanting to get away as quick as he could."

"Okay, and what did he say?"

"That he was sorry if he gave you the impression you were a leper, and he was just busy with work and stuff."

"Just busy with work and stuff, huh?" Maggie repeated.

"Yeah, that's what *I* said." Maggie heard her sigh in frustration. "I told him he needed to be a little more considerate of your feelings."

"And?" Maggie prompted.

"He said, "What, she didn't like *Phantom of the Opera*?"

"Well, he kind of had you there," Maggie admitted.

"Yeah, what could I say to that?"

"Well, thanks for trying, anyway."

"No problem. I'm just sorry I didn't get anywhere with him."

"That's okay. We'll have to wait and see, that's all."

"Did you have a nice birthday today?"

"Yes I did. It's been very nice, all things considered," Maggie said, trying to be positive.

"What do you mean "all things considered"? Chad?"

Maggie told her about Chad's brief birthday call, and they hung up promising to let each other know if either one of them were able to find out why he was acting so strange.

Maggie's parents went home Tuesday morning, and she and Car got back to their routine. She started checking into nearby elementary schools where she could apply to serve her internship. She was hoping to start teaching the next school year, when Car started the first grade.

That Saturday, she and Car had plans to help the Kappa Delta Sorority put on a Children's Art Show Benefit, for the prevention of child abuse. Car had been looking forward to it all week. It turned out to be a lot of fun, was a huge success, and Car the best time. He didn't really understand the nature of the cause, just that it was to help kids, and he was really motivated. He even offered to take some of his toys to give to the kids. Since it meant so much to him, Maggie decided to plan an outing to the children's ward at the Cancer Center, for Car to visit the kids and take them some gifts. She was very proud of him and his compassion for others.

Sunday, after they got home from church, Chad called to see how they were and asked if they needed anything. Maggie felt like telling him she needed him to tell her, or *somebody*, what was going on with him, but instead, she just said they were okay. She was curious to see how the conversation would go, not expecting that to *be* the extent of the conversation. There was no small talk, no comments about the weather, nothing. She hung up as confused as ever.

That was four weeks ago, and since then she'd only had three other phone calls, all almost identical to that one. It was almost as if he was just doing what he felt—or thought others would consider—to be his duty to Cole. To check in on them. No more, no less.

Chad's Journal
March 31, 2006

Tomorrow's April Fool's Day,
and I am the biggest fool of all.
She doesn't need me.
She hasn't even called me.

CHAPTER 38

Car was beginning to ask questions about Chad and why he hadn't been to see him. He'd also been asking if they could go out in the boat soon. Maggie hadn't told him, but she had no intention of taking the boat out by themselves, and though she was concerned about the fact it hadn't been started in months, the only alternative was to ask Chad to take them out, and the way he'd been acting, that simply wasn't an option. She had considered asking him if he would care to take it out with her and Car, to celebrate his birthday coming up in a couple of weeks, but decided against it. She didn't want to know how many more excuses he could come up with.

She felt bad she hadn't called to see how *he* was lately, but his aloofness was getting really painful. She considered him her closest friend, besides Cheyenne, someone she could really depend on, but she was afraid *he* had decided he didn't want to be *her* friend, and she didn't think she could handle it if that was the case.

But was it fair to just wait on him to call her? Friendship worked both ways, she decided, picking up the phone to call him. It rang several times, and just when she thought she was going to get his voice mail, he picked up.

"Hey, Maggie," he answered.

Startled, she said, "Oh! Caller I.D. huh?"

"Yeah. Is something wrong? Is Car okay?" he asked. He sounded concerned, Maggie thought. That was a good sign.

"Everything's fine. I was just calling to see how you were."

"I'm good."

Silence.

Okay. So much for filling her in on the current events of his life or anything. Maggie thought if she could reach through the telephone line, she would strangle him with it. Deciding he couldn't possibly upset her any more than she was now, she decided to go ahead and take a chance. She took a deep breath.

"Car and I were wondering if you'd made plans for your birthday yet?" she asked quickly, before she chickened out. She exhaled slowly. It had been so long since she'd asked him for anything, surely he'd come up with a new and improved excuse to tell her no.

"Well, Chris and Savannah are planning to come spend the weekend."

"Oh. Okay," she said disheartened. She had to give him credit though. That *was* a new reason. Here we go again, she was thinking, but realized that them coming was perfect. "Well, that would actually be good, if you're game."

There was a hesitation. "Game for what?"

"Um, well, Car has been wanting to see you, and he's been driving me crazy about taking the boat out. We could take Chris and Savannah out on the lake for your birthday, if you haven't made other plans with them," she asked, and waited, prepared for the real rejection this time.

"Yeah, we could do that," he finally said.

"Really?" she asked, caught completely off guard.

"Sure, sounds like fun. I've been wondering about how to entertain them while they're here."

Was this the *old* Chad she was talking to? "Okay, great! Are you sure you don't want to check with them first?" she winced and kicked herself for giving him an out after he'd already agreed.

"No, they'll love it. Besides, we can't let Car down, can we?"

This *was* the old Chad! Elated, she almost asked him over for dinner, but stopped herself, afraid to push her luck. "Car will be one happy little guy when he hears this!" she said instead. "So, Saturday after next?"she confirmed.

"Sounds like a plan," he said, sounding completely normal, maybe even a little excited.

She couldn't believe her ears. "I'll pack a picnic lunch, and stock the cooler. Is there anything in particular that they don't like?"

"No, Chris will eat anything, and Savannah's easy to please."

"All right then. Will you come by here, so we can follow you guys out?" she asked, still feeling a bit like she was walking on eggshells.

"I'll do better than that. We'll come pick you up."

"You don't have to do that! Besides we won't all be able to fit in the Jeep."

"We don't have to. I just bought an Expedition. We can break it in. There's plenty of room for all of us."

"Really? That's great Chad! I'm so happy for you! But what about Bessie?" she asked, referring to his Jeep. "Did you trade her in?"

"No. I couldn't do that. But she's got a lot of wear and tear on her. I decided to give her a rest and a little T.L.C."

"Oh, good." Maggie said, relieved. "I would hate to see you get rid of her."

"Yeah, I couldn't do that. Too many good memories."

"More than I know, I'm sure," she laughed, teasing him.

"We won't go there," he answered, laughing too.

It was so nice talking to him, she hated to hang up. "Well, I'm sure you're busy—" she started saying, before Chad cut her off.

"Actually, would you and Car be up for going out for ice cream later?" he asked.

Now Maggie hesitated, but not because she didn't know what to say. She was just so surprised she couldn't get the words out of her mouth right away. "Car would love that, Chad. *I* would love that."

"Is six o'clock okay?"

"Perfect. We'll see you then." She hung up in utter shock. She called Cheyenne right away and told her all about the conversation.

"Well, well," Cheyenne mused. "Maybe our boy's coming around."

"From your mouth, to God's ears," Maggie replied, hopeful.

CHAPTER 39

Maggie could hardly believe how sweet Chad had been in the weeks since that Sunday. Car had been tickled to see him, and even happier that he took them out for ice cream. They'd played a quick game of miniature golf before Car had to get home for bedtime, since he had school the next morning. It was like old times.

They were in touch almost every day since. Chad even took them to get submarine sandwiches the next Saturday and they picnicked at a park where Car could play on the jungle gym. Maggie wanted to invite him to church with them the next morning, but was still too afraid to 'rock the boat', no pun intended. Whatever had happened before, that caused him to avoid them for so long, had happened at, or shortly after, they'd been to church together. She didn't know. Everything had been going well lately. So well, in fact, she thought that possibly he *had* just been busy with work and stuff, and not avoiding them at all. She decided not to risk it yet.

Car woke up early the following Saturday morning, so excited that they were finally going boating, he eagerly agreed to go to the farmer's market to get some fresh fruit for their outing. Normally shopping for fruits and vegetables didn't rank real high on his favorite things to do list. Maggie was glad to have found such a good selection of fruit this early in the season. She'd gotten strawberries, grapes, cantaloupe, watermelon, pineapple, kiwis and some bright yellow bananas. She was cutting it all up now, remembering, with a smile, a trick her mother had taught her about tossing the bananas in lemon juice to keep them from turning turn dark and unappealing.

She'd cooked a small turkey breast the night before, purposely so that she could refrigerate it overnight. There was just something about leftover turkey sandwiches, one of the many things she loved about Thanksgiving. She already had it sliced and ready to go, opting to make the sandwiches on the boat when it was time to eat, rather than taking premade sandwiches that would be soggy by then.

She packed the food in a cooler, then checked to make sure she had plates, cups, napkins, utensils, and anything else they may need. It had been so long since she'd been on the boat, she couldn't remember what she already had there, or if any of it was even still usable. Satisfied she had everything, she put the finishing touches on Chad's chocolate birthday cake—with lots of chocolate icing—his favorite. It would be too early to have the cake before they left, since they were supposed to pick them up at 10:00, so she got individual containers out and ready, and after he blew out his candles, she would cut everyone a piece to have after lunch.

She checked on Car in the den watching cartoons, then, even though she doubted the water would be warm enough for a swim, she went to put her swimsuit on under her shirt and shorts, just in case. Dressed, she got towels, sun block, a change of clothes for Car, and grabbing Chad's gift, she started downstairs with everything.

She was really pleased with Chad's birthday present and, though it paled in comparison to *Phantom of the Opera,* she hoped he would like it too. Car picked out a really cool captain's hat with her help, and she was secretly hoping Chad would take the hint and want to take the boat out more often with them now. Just as she reached the bottom step, the doorbell rang. She sat everything down and opened the door with a smile.

"Happy Birthday!" she said, hugging Chad enthusiastically.

"Thanks," he grinned, hugging her back.

Was it her imagination, or did he hug her back just a little longer than usual? When he let go, she hugged Chris and Savannah, standing behind him.

"It's so good to see you two!" she said, "Come on in! Chad has to blow out the candles on his cake before we can go."

Before they got in the door, Car came racing out. "Uncle Chad!" he said, jumping into Chad's arms. "Happy Birfday! Can we go to the boat, now?" he asked, in the same breath.

"Uncle Chad has to get his present first, and blow out the candles on his birthday cake," Maggie reminded him.

"Oh yeah! Wait till you see what we got you!" Car exclaimed, anxious now to give Chad his present.

Before Maggie could usher everyone in and get the door shut, Car grabbed the package, handing it to Chad. "Open it, open it!" he urged.

They all stepped inside and Maggie closed the door. Chad looked up at her and with her nod, he hastily tore the paper off and opened the box. "Well, what do you know!" he said with a big grin, as he pulled the hat out and put it on his head. "I've always wanted one of these! It fits perfect!" he said, a big grin spreading across his face.

"Now you can drive the boat!" Car informed him, as if he couldn't *without* the hat. "Can we go now?" he asked again, patience eluding him.

Everybody laughed. "*Candles*," Maggie sang out, reminding Car. She led them to the dining room, and lit the candles. Chad promptly leaned over to blow them out.

"WAIT!" Car cried out, startling everyone. "You have to make a wish!"

Once everyone's hearts started beating again, Chad closed his eyes for a moment to make his wish, then blew all the candles out.

"Yay!" Car cheered. "That was close," he added, with a relieved chuckle. "Now can we go?" Everyone laughed again. Cars brows furrowed as he wondered, *What do they think is so doggone funny?*

"Let me just slice us all some cake to take with us. The coolers are over there, if you guys want to get them loaded," she told Chad and Chris, pointing to the ice chests. While they did that, she filled the waiting containers with cake, and they were on their way.

At the marina they easily transferred everything to the boat, and Car didn't waste any time getting his life vest on and secured. Finally, it was time to see if the boat was going to start. There was a collective silence and lots of crossed fingers. Chad turned the key. It cranked right up, eliciting applause and cheers. Chad carefully maneuvered around the marina to get gassed up and they were on the lake in short order.

The weather was beautiful. The sun danced on the glassy surface of the water, causing it to appear deceptively warm. In reality it was still way too cold for them to go swimming without freezing. It wasn't a big disappointment. They were having such a great time scouting out every inch of the lake, stopping only long enough for lunch. Maggie got glowing compliments on the food she'd prepared for them and after everyone finished their chocolate cake for dessert, they were off again.

Chad loved his hat. Maggie only saw him take it off once, just for a second, to brush his hair back with his fingers. It was long enough for her to realize he must have forgotten to put sunscreen on, noticing a distinct line across his forehead halfway between his brows and hairline. Where the cap had blocked the sun…winter white. The rest of his face was beet red. She suppressed a smile but didn't point it out, figuring he'd see it soon enough. She *did* hand him the sunscreen she'd brought though, and told him she thought maybe he should put some on. At least it wouldn't get any worse, she hoped.

Car had taken a nap after lunch, but was awake now, and had his second wind. They explored a little longer and as they were heading back to the marina, Chad slowed down to a crawl, pulled Car up onto his lap in the helm seat, put the Captains hat on him, and said, "Now *you* can drive the boat."

Maggie watched the exchange, and cringed inwardly, quickly looking around for a spare hat to give Chad before anyone noticed his forehead, when he glanced over his shoulder, flashing them a noble smile.

Chris, seated closest to Chad in the front of the boat, saw it first. "What the—"

"Chris!" Maggie interrupted. "Um, can you give me a hand with this?" she asked, putting a finger over her lips when he looked, in an attempt to keep him quiet. She wasn't sure why it meant so much to her. It wasn't that big of a deal and everyone was bound to see it sooner or later, but it just did. She didn't want Chad to be embarrassed. Things were going really well and it was his birthday celebration, and she wanted it last as long as possible. Chris started back to her and by this time Savannah was curious as to what she'd missed.

"Did you see—"he started to ask them.

"Shh! Yes! Please don't give him a hard time about it! At least not now," Maggie asked, her voice a whisper.

"See what?" Savannah asked, confused.

Chris pulled Savannah over where she could see, without Chad noticing. "Chad's face," he said in her ear. Her mouth dropped open, then she covered it with her hand, and stepped back over next to Maggie. Chris was cracking up. Maggie punched him lightly on the arm and said quietly, "Be nice! Give him a break, it's his birthday!"

Savannah took over, pulling Chris to the back of the boat where they pretended to watch the scenery until they could keep straight faces. Maggie took Chris's abandoned seat across from Chad, watching and waiting for Car to notice it and blurt something out, but fortunately the hat actually prevented him from looking above him to see Chad's face. When he was finally ready to relinquish the wheel and hat back to Chad, he was so intent on describing his exciting experience to everyone, Chad had the hat securely back in place, and Car never noticed anything amiss.

Navigating the last mile or so back to the marina, Chad backed the boat into the slip with ease and Car commended him.

"You did that just like Daddy!"

Chad grinned proudly.

No one was prepared for what Car said next.

"Will you be my *new* daddy now, till I go live with my other daddy in heaven?"

CHAPTER 40

Shaken by Cars innocent but unexpected question, Maggie hastily diverted his attention by pointing out a fish swimming in the water beside the boat. Chad stood transfixed. For a moment he gazed at the two of them with pure longing in his eyes. Then caught himself, and instantly the look turned to guilt. Maggie was so focused on saving him from being put on the spot, she didn't see it.

But Chris did. And he was overwhelmed. He'd had no idea. His little brother not only loved Car, but he was *in* love with Maggie! So many things that had never added up, suddenly did. All the years the family had wondered and worried about why Chad didn't seem to be interested in finding a girlfriend, falling in love, settling down, and starting a family. They'd all made excuses for him, saying it was because he didn't have time because of school, and then because of his job, but it hadn't really made any sense. Especially after he graduated and started working with the Titans. Personally, he couldn't figure out why Chad hadn't hooked up with one of those hot Titan cheerleaders. Not that *he* thought they were hot, he amended quickly. He was *strictly* thinking of Chad. He cast a sidelong glance at Savannah, lest she read his mind like he sometimes swore she could do. She was busy helping Maggie gather everything up and he breathed a sigh of relief.

He jumped out on the dock to help Chad tie off the boat, a telltale grin on his face, but Chad never met his eyes, pretending to be concentrating intently on what he was doing. That's okay, Chris thought, we'll talk about this later. He shook his head. He just couldn't get over it. Had his little brother been in love with Maggie all along? Wow. That would really be something. It would certainly prove to the family Chad didn't have a problem with commitment! But the important thing was that Chad was in love with her now! Maggie was awesome! They would be perfect together, and everybody knew how much Chad loved Car. He didn't know why he hadn't thought of the two of them getting together before now.

Once the boat was secured, they all pitched in carrying stuff back to the Expedition. Even Car, who was making a big show of doing his part by strenuously lugging a half empty bag of potato chips.

Chris noticed Chad was purposely preoccupied, intent on packing everything just right. He had not, as yet, met anyone's eyes, and he wondered why his little brother was so embarrassed. He decided he'd talk to him later, when they had some privacy.

The drive back to Maggie's was uneventful, and once there, they carried in the coolers, helping her unpack them and put everything away, despite her insistence she would take care of it. Before they left, Maggie wrapped up the rest of Chad's cake to send home with them.

When they were ready to go, Maggie hugged Chris and Savannah, asked them to keep in touch, and to come back soon. They promised they would, thanking her for her generous hospitality, wonderful food, and for an all around great day on the lake. Chris nonchalantly watched, curious now, as Maggie hugged Chad, kissed him on the cheek, and told him Happy Birthday again, but Chad's face gave away nothing during the embrace. He could have been hugging the mailman, Chris thought, his curiosity really piqued now.

Maggie called Car, who had gone to the den where his toys were, to come say goodbye, and he came running. Straight to Chad.

"Tell everyone goodbye, and thank you," Maggie told him.

"Goodbye, and thank you," mimicked Car. He finished hugging Chad, and turned to hug Chris and Savannah, repeating it twice more, sounding like a little mynah bird, then ran back to his toys.

On the ride back to Chad's, Chris thought he seemed kind of quiet, so to get a conversation going, he asked him where he wanted to go for his birthday dinner. Chad thought about it for a second, then asked if they felt like just having a pizza delivered and chilling out, adding that he was kind of beat. They agreed that sounded good. They were pretty tired themselves.

Chad, being a considerate host, sent Savannah and Chris to the shower first, while he ordered the pizza. After they were done, he went in to get his shower, before the food arrived. A short while later he hesitantly emerged from the bathroom with his glaring two tone forehead, to find them sitting on the couch waiting for him, looking quite amused.

"Don't say a word," Chad warned them.

"What?" they both asked innocently.

∾⌘⌘⌘∾

After dinner, they decided to watch a movie on HBO that none of them had seen, called *Second Hand Lions.* They didn't realize, until too late, that it was about a boy who didn't have a father and was spending the summer with his two uncles. It was really good, but Chris wondered what kind of an impact it had on Chad.

They made small talk for a while after the movie, then Savannah gave Chris a kiss, and said she was going to turn in.

It gave Chris the perfect opportunity to talk to Chad privately. He asked him if he wanted to have a beer with him, and when Chad agreed, he got two from the fridge, and they went out on the back porch to drink them. Taking a seat, Chris opened his beer, and took a long swallow. He glanced at Chad who was gazing out across the manicured lawn of the condominium complex and seemed a million miles away. He debated on whether or not to say anything to him while he was in this melancholy mood. Then he decided that's what big brothers were for. He quietly asked, "Have you told her yet?" He waited so long for Chad to answer he was beginning to think he hadn't heard him.

At first Chad started to play dumb, but figured it was no use. He'd never been able to hide anything from Chris. "No," he said simply.

Chris figured as much. When it became evident Chad wasn't going to say anything more, Chris went on. "When do you plan to?"

"I don't," Chad answered, emphatic, taking a swig of his beer.

Chris couldn't believe his ears. Flabbergasted, he sat forward, and said, "Are you kidding me? Why? Maggie's awesome!"

"I know," Chad answered, ignoring the first two questions.

"You guys would be perfect together," Chris went on, stating the obvious.

"I know."

"You love Car. He's *named* after you, for crying out loud."

"I know."

"And he's obviously crazy about you."

"I *know*." His voice was starting to ring with impatience.

"You won't find anyone else like Maggie," Chris warned.

"I KNOW!" Chad answered loudly, setting his beer down on the table beside his chair so hard that it foamed up and spilled over the mouth of the bottle.

He was obviously annoyed, but his cryptic answers were beginning to annoy Chris too. He knew this wasn't a winning combination and he should back off, but he just didn't understand why Chad was being so hardheaded. "Then what's the problem? Why don't you just tell her how you feel?" he asked, exasperated.

Chad finally looked at Chris. "Don't you get it?" he asked, his voice raised. "I *know* Maggie's awesome, I *know* I won't find anyone else like her, I *know* Car loves me, and I love him. I *know* he's named after me, and yes, I love Maggie! I've loved Maggie since the first time I saw her. I've loved her for the past seven years! I loved her the day she married Cole, and every day since. *That's* the problem. There wasn't a day that went by that I didn't wish I was in Cole's shoes. That *I* was the one married to Maggie, that Car was *my* son. Not one day, subconsciously or otherwise, that I didn't wish that I was in his place. *That's* the problem, Chris. Every day, one way or another, I wished him out of the picture. Well, it looks like I got my wish, doesn't it?" he stood abruptly and went inside, slamming the French door behind him.

Chris jumped up, opened the door and called out to Chad, but was met with the sound of Chad's bedroom door slamming. Shaking his head, he stepped back out on the porch, and let out a long sigh.

"Nice going, big brother," he said to himself, as he sat down and picked up his beer. "Happy damn birthday, Chad," he muttered under his breath, kicking himself, feeling like dirt.

CHAPTER 41

Chad wrestled with the demons in his head for sleep, but finally gave up the fight, pulled a t-shirt over his head and slipped on a pair of jeans. Barefoot, he quietly opened his door, and crept out into the kitchen. He rarely drank coffee, but he always kept some on hand for his company, and was craving a cup now. He thought about putting a pot on, then decided the aroma of fresh brewed coffee might rouse Chris and Savannah, and he wasn't ready to face Chris yet. Besides, it was only four a.m., he noticed, glancing at the clock. He grabbed a bottle of water from the fridge, and made his way in the dark to the porch, noticing when he stepped out, that Chris had cleaned up the evidence of his outburst. His stomach knotted up at the thought of it again. He took a seat and began to think about how he was going to apologize to Chris.

In the quiet, he could hear the sound of water, and squinting his eyes, he could make out the fountain in the small pond the condos in his section backed up to. The water glistened as it bravely escaped the confines of the pond to race toward the sky, before turning into little droplets that sparkled like diamonds in the moonlight on their way back down, disappearing into the obscurity of the darkness that engulfed them. He sat mesmerized by the calming dance of the water, and slowly felt some of the tension drain from his body. He had no idea how long he had sat there lost in thought, before he realized that dawn had released the pond from the shadows, and he could see clearly now. Both visually and emotionally. He was suddenly anxious to talk to Chris and apologize for his behavior. As if summoned by some magical force, the door opened and Chris gingerly stepped out onto the porch. Encouraged by the lack of flying objects aimed at his head, he took the seat he'd been sitting in last night.

"I'm sorry," the brothers said in unison.

Chris opened his mouth to speak again and Chad held up his hand.

"Please, just hear me out first."

Chris nodded his head in assent. Chad took a deep breath, and exhaled slowly, trying to decide where to begin. While Chris was waiting for Chad to gather his thoughts, he flashed back to the previous night, when Savannah had softly slipped out to join him on the porch, after being awakened by the slamming doors. He filled her in on everything that had transpired, beginning with Car's question at the marina, up to the moment she came out, and then he confessed to her his own guilt for not having been aware of the struggles Chad had been facing. To give her a clearer picture of his and Chad's relationship, he explained that because of their five year age difference they had gone to different schools, and had completely different sets of friends. When he was eighteen and graduating from high school, Chad was just becoming a teenager, so they had never been extremely close. He had always given Chad a hard time, because it's just what big brothers do to pesky little brothers.

And even though they were grown men now, he'd never really thought of Chad as a adult. Until last night he was still just his 'little brother'. It made him realize he had never really been there for Chad, and he expressed his desire to Savannah to change that, to be able to help Chad through this and to be there for him from now on, no matter what. And he sat here now, ready and waiting to make good on his promise. But the very first thing Chad asked of him, he was unable to do.

He was crestfallen when Chad finally broke the silence, and asked, "I need to ask you to keep last night between us."

Chris sighed. "It's too late," he admitted.

Chad started to say something and he looked upset again, so Chris hurried to explain. "Savannah heard the doors slam and she got up to see what was wrong."

"Couldn't you have made something up?" he asked, knowing the answer before the words were out of his mouth.

"No, I couldn't," Chris replied, emphatically. "We *talk* to each other, we're open and honest and don't keep things from each other. That's part of being married and having a good relationship. Honesty. That's why I think you should talk to Maggie and tell her how you feel."

"Well, first of all, Maggie and I aren't married, and we don't *have* a relationship other than being friends," Chad retorted, his voice tinged with sarcasm.

"But *that's* where it begins! With friendship!" Chris said, incredulous.

"Yeah? Well don't lay another guilt trip on me okay? I've got enough of those to deal with already."

Chris could see Chad was beginning to get worked up again. Not wanting things to end up the way they did last night, he lightened his tone. Sedately, he asked, "So what do you want me to do?"

"Just please don't say anything to anyone else about this. I need some time to—"

"Done," Chris interrupted.

Chad looked at him warily. "Yeah?" he asked dubiously, thinking that had been way too easy. He'd expected Chris to give him a hard time, like he'd always done.

Chris smiled. "Yeah" he confirmed. "But you don't have to do it alone. Things are going to change. I'm gonna be here for you. And Savannah is too. I don't care if it's two o'clock in the morning, if you need to talk, you call me."

Chad's expression went from wariness to 'who are you, and what have you done with my brother?' as he continued to stare at Chris in silence.

"I mean it," Chris added reassuringly.

Chad kept waiting for the punch line or for Chris to start cracking up, but when it didn't come, he visibly relaxed, not only convinced that Chris really did mean it, but relieved to have someone he could actually talk to now. "Thanks," he said sincerely.

"That's what big brothers are for," Chris said simply.

This was news to Chad. Until now, big brothers were for teasing you, giving you wedgies, and pulling pranks on you to the point of just making your life miserable in general. This was going to be a nice change, he thought.

Chris stood up. "Now, let's go see if Savannah's got some makeup to fix that forehead of yours," he said, going inside.

Chad sat there for a second, thinking *what happened to "things are gonna change"?* "Guess we're going to *ease* into it," he said to himself, laughing as he got up to follow Chris inside.

CHAPTER 42

Over the next five or six months, Chad *did* see a lot of change in Chris. They had grown a lot closer. Yeah, Chris still teased him every now and then, like old times, but Chad knew firsthand some things *were* hard to change. Chris was becoming more of a 'friend' like Cole had been, and less of the older brother who always just told him what to do. And Savannah was being really sweet—of course she always had been—but they were much closer now too. She would even call sometimes when Chris wasn't around just to check on him, to talk if he wanted to, or just to say a quick "hi".

At least with Chris it was a big difference than when they were kids. Chad remembered one time in particular, when he was about six or seven years old. It was right after he'd met Cole, but Cole hadn't been able to play that day, so Chad wanted to hang out with Chris and some of his buddies. After pleading with them for several minutes, they graciously decided to play hide and seek with him. He thought it was so cool. He was hanging out with the big guys! So, excited beyond words, he found a hiding spot in his dad's tool shed, where he curled up tightly in a cabinet under the table saw. Just in time too, before he'd heard Chris yell, "Ready or not, here I come!"

A few minutes passed and he thought he must have found the best hiding spot ever, because Chris hadn't even come close yet. A few more minutes passed and he'd had to wriggle and squirm around to get more comfortable, because it was really cramped in there. After a little while more, he lost track of time and dozed off. When he woke up, he could barely unfold himself to get out. He'd limped into the house, where his mom informed him that Chris and his friends left to go to the movies about thirty minutes earlier. "Right after you went out to play," she'd said. He didn't know what made him remember that after all this time, but now that he had, he decided he was going to have a little talk with Chris about it, and just maybe, get some payback.

∾⌘⌘⌘∾

One thing that *hadn't* changed, was how he felt about Maggie and Car. He called them twice a week to make sure they were okay, and even though he was trying to keep his distance, once or twice a month he did something with them, preferably *away* from their house. Things like going out to dinner, going to the park, miniature golf, to get ice cream, anything away from the house, because *it* was more like home to him than his own home, and it was way too hard to leave.

On Car's sixth birthday, Chad took him and Maggie out in the boat again. That was all Car had asked for, and even though Chad would have preferred not to, he just couldn't bring himself to let the little guy down. So they'd gone and had a really great time—like he'd known they would—which was exactly why he hadn't thought it was such a good idea.

Since then, he'd been trying to stay busy, and thought that by now, he should have learned how to master it, but it still took constant effort. He'd joined a bowling league with a couple of trainers from work, Aaron and Rafael, and surprisingly, he actually enjoyed it, but it was only one day a week. That left a lot of free time for renegade thoughts to assault his unoccupied mind.

So he made himself start going out on dates again. Not on the scale he'd done a few months before, that was just crazy. He didn't know what he'd been thinking. Actually, he realized, that was the problem. He *hadn't* been thinking. It was all in an effort to stay so busy that he didn't have time to think. He'd gone on dates, three or four times a week, but it just never felt right. There were a few second dates, but never third, because that was way too risky.

One day he'd inadvertently overheard a few girls in the break room at the stadium, discussing over their lunch, the merits to the rumors they'd heard, and the possibility of him really being gay. He hadn't stuck around to hear what their consensus was. Instead, laughing at the preposterousness of it, he'd called Chris, figuring he'd get a real kick out of it too. Chris chuckled, but admitted there was a time when the whole family had considered that possibility as well. It was a little sobering for Chad, until he realized it was a perfect out! Let everyone continue to watch and wonder, and he'd put the whole dating thing on hold for a while! He joined a gym instead, and worked out every night after work. It took a lot less effort and was way more satisfying. He could have gone back to working out in the gym at the stadium, but spending most of his time there already, he needed a change of scenery that wasn't a constant reminder of Cole. He really hoped Maggie wouldn't find out about it. He felt sure she probably wouldn't understand, since all the weights and equipment were exactly as they were when he and Cole had last used them, but he couldn't work out there for obvious reasons.

Besides, something was going on with Maggie he couldn't quite put his finger on. He knew she was staying busy too, but it was more than that. She'd been fine for a while, but lately she'd been acting kind of distant, and it had him worried. Which was strange, because distance was exactly what he'd wanted. The thought crossed his mind that maybe she'd met someone, and he, literally, got sick to his stomach. He couldn't even think about *that* possibility. He decided it had to be because the anniversary of Cole's death was coming up, and that was going to be extremely hard for both of them.

CHAPTER 43

Maggie and Car were doing pretty well. They had full schedules, between doing charity work with the sorority and their church, and Maggie had taken on extra students for the summer. She was so proud when Car began showing an interest in music. He was now officially one of her students with his own appointment on her schedule, which he thought was really neat. He was doing great too, much to her delight.

Car had become good friends with a little boy named Luke in his Kindergarten class, and twice over the summer, Luke had stayed the night with him. They'd gotten along great and had lots of fun, but so far Car hadn't expressed any desire to stay over at Luke's house. Maggie hoped it wasn't because he didn't want to leave her alone.

He still talked to his daddy every night by sending messages via Jesus in his prayers. One night after finishing his prayer, it nearly broke Maggie's heart when he looked at her with the saddest look in his big brown eyes and asked, "Mommy, why doesn't Daddy send *me* any messages?"

She got such a lump in her throat, she couldn't have answered even if she'd had the words. Her eyes were brimming with tears before she was able to come up with an answer.

"He does, honey. You just have to listen with your *heart*. You won't be able to hear it, but you'll be able to feel it," she explained, laying her hand on his little chest. "Here, in your heart."

She was relieved her answer seemed to satisfy him, instead of starting a whole new series of questions she couldn't handle. He nodded his head, seriously considering what she'd said, and turned over to go to sleep. She kissed him and told him goodnight. He was already drifting off, before she'd turned off the light.

Sleep had not come so easily though, for her that night. She laid awake in bed, worrying about Car and her ability to answer his future questions. She was really concerned about her role as a single parent, and how Car was coping without his father. How it would affect him in years to come, not to have his dad. At least he had *some* male influence with Chad, and for that she was grateful, but she couldn't impose upon, or rely too heavily on Chad, any more than she already had. He had his own life, and slowly, it seemed, she and Car were becoming less and less a part of it. She didn't understand why. When he was around, he was wonderful, but when he was away from them, it was like he turned into someone else. It was so frustrating! Sometimes she just wanted to scream at him, to shake him until only the *old* Chad remained. But then she would feel like she was being selfish, because Chad didn't owe them anything, and he certainly had the right to pick and choose who he spent his time with. For Car's sake, she would only ask of Chad what he was willing to give, even though she desperately missed the friendship they once had. All she could do was pray for God's guidance. And she prayed earnestly. Eventually she drifted off to sleep.

∾⌘⌘⌘∾

Summer drew to a close, and now they were excited to be getting ready for their first day of school. Maggie couldn't believe her good fortune for getting hired as the music teacher at Car's elementary school! It was more than she could have asked for! Not only would she still be near Car, but most importantly, it solved her dilemma about her getting him to school on time. She'd been worried about having to drop him off too early at his school, in order to commute to her job at a different school. And then, even if she figured a way around that, how was she going to be able to pick him up, when school ended for them both at the same time? Even if she was able to make arrangements for him to wait in the office, what happened if she got held up at work? Or stuck in traffic somewhere? Now, all he had to do was come directly to her class to wait until she was finished. It was the perfect solution, and they were both eager to start a new chapter in their lives.

CHAPTER 44

The anniversary of Cole's death came and went. It was hard on Maggie, but with God's help, and her family and friends, she was surrounded by loving, caring people who helped her through it. Car wasn't aware of the significance of the date, and for now, Maggie felt nothing would be served by spelling it out to him. It would just make him sad, and she wanted to spare him that if she could.

Chad called her twice on the second, and twice on the third—Cole's birthday—to check on her. She was truly touched over his concern for them. She could tell by his voice he was having a hard time too. She made a mental note to let him know the next time he called, how much his calls meant to her, but then she didn't hear from him for a week. He was evidently staying true to his modus operandi of late. His normal sweet self one day, and gone the next. No warning, no excuses, just gone. As the days passed, the frustration with his behavior morphed into concern. She had been trying to give him space, not pressure him into keeping them in his life, but she was worried, so she called him. Sorry, he'd said, he didn't mean to make her worry, he'd just been busy. Same old, same old, she hung up thinking.

∾⌘⌘⌘∾

The Thanksgiving holiday was upon them before they knew it. It had been so nice the year before, they all decided to keep it the same this year. Everyone, including Cole's and Chad's families, got together at Maggie's parents on Thanksgiving Day. All the women gathered in the kitchen to cook a feast, while the guys spent the time catching up, watching football, and getting shooed *out* of the kitchen. Even though they all missed Cole, it had been easier on everyone to be together, and they made some wonderful memories.

∾⌘⌘⌘∾

Christmas was beautiful. It snowed on Christmas Eve. That was the best present of all for Car. They spent Christmas Eve and Christmas morning at her parents, then drove to Cole's parents house to spend the rest of the day and night with them, and to see Chad and his parents.

Since Thanksgiving, there wasn't one day between then and Christmas that Chad didn't call. He'd been so attentive and sweet. On one of those momentous days, he'd left Maggie speechless when he accepted a dinner invitation at home with her and Car. It was the first time that just the three of them had dined together there. It was lovely, and Chad appeared to be his old self and to have genuinely enjoyed it. Maggie and Cheyenne had a long discussion about it at Christmas. While neither of them were able to get to the root of his bizarre behavior, both were relieved to see he was finally coming around.

Driving home after the Christmas holiday, Maggie reflected over the past month. For the first time in a long time she felt content. Things were going well for her and Car, both at home and at school. Most of all, she was happy to have her friend back, and more than a little surprised to realize how much she'd missed him. She didn't want the holiday festivities to come to an end and break the spell. A thought occurred to her then, giving her an excuse to continue to the celebration. She decided it was time to have a dinner party. And what better time than to ring in the New Year!

She called Cheyenne right away to see if she could come, hoping, as the phone rang, that she hadn't already made plans since New Year's Eve was only a week away. Cheyenne answered, confirmed she had no plans as of yet and said she thought it was a great idea! Since she was out of school for Christmas break, she decided she would come the day after next and help. It was going to be so much fun, they told each other like two giddy teenagers.

As soon as Maggie hung up with Cheyenne, she immediately called Chad, who was following behind her, having insisted on making sure they made it home safely. When Car heard, Maggie knew he would be asking if he could ride with Chad. It was the way he did it that took her by surprise. Her heart swelled as she dialed Chad's number, remembering the conversation.

"Mom," he'd said, with a serious grown up look on his six year old face.

"Would you be awfully, terribly alone if I rode with Uncle Chad?" The sincere concern in his eyes was so heartwarming, she couldn't have refused him if she'd wanted to.

"That will be fine, if Uncle Chad said you could," she answered.

"Yes!" He threw both arms up in victory, the seriousness from a moment before obliterated by the fervor of a happy little boy.

Chad answered his phone, "Hey Pretty Lady."

Maggie's stomach did a little flip flop. How long had it been since he'd called her that? Catching her breath, she said, "Hey! How's Car doing back there?"

"Zonked," Chad said.

Maggie laughed. "What a surprise!" They both knew riding in a vehicle for any length of time was like a sedative for Car. She went on, "Have you, by any chance, made plans for New Year's Eve yet?"

"No, why? Have you got something in mind?"

Even though the past month had been great, Maggie was still a little taken aback at his open ended response, but she didn't miss a beat. "As a matter of fact, I do! Cheyenne's coming over, day after tomorrow, and we're going to put together a little New Year's Eve dinner party. I was wondering if you would come."

"Sounds great! What do you need me to do?"

"Just show up," Maggie said happily.

"You got it" he replied.

"Okay, then! It's settled. See you at home?"

"See you at home."

They both hung up smiling.

∾⌘⌘⌘∾

Cheyenne showed up at Maggie's as expected and they got busy planning the dinner. But as the plans evolved, they decided to forego the quaint dinner party and have a full blown New Year's Eve party, so they could invite more people. Before they went ahead with that idea though, they both thought it would be the right thing to do by running it by Chad first so that he wouldn't be blindsided, and once they had his seal of approval, they spent the rest of the day calling everyone who was invited.

The two of them had a blast as the week progressed, shopping for food, decorations, party supplies and making preparations in general. When New Year's Eve finally arrived, they spent the better part of the day making hors d'oeuvres, and other assorted finger foods and pastries, as well as a huge pan of lasagna for the guests wanting something with a little more sustenance.

Once the food was completed and in warming dishes or being chilled, they arranged the empty platters and bowls on the tables, making sure there was room for everything. With that done, they surveyed the end result and were pleased with their efforts. The decorations were perfect, and every dish was ready and waiting to be filled before the guests arrived, with chips, dips, pretzels, and all the other goodies they'd made. They consulted their list again, to make sure nothing had been overlooked. Satisfied that every item was checked off, they had time to relax and unwind, before getting a shower and dressed for the party.

Cheyenne's boyfriend Jim, was the first to arrive, having volunteered to set up and be in charge of the music. Chad arrived shortly after. A new friend of Maggie's from school, a third grade teacher named Carolyn, and her husband Frank, arrived next, and then Car's little friend Luke, and his parents.

By nine o'clock, everyone invited was there, and the party was off to a great start. The hors d'oeuvres were a hit and dwindling rapidly, but the real star turned out to be the lasagna. Since it was a joint effort between Cheyenne and Maggie, they both shared in the accolades, but the real credit went to Maggie's mother since it was her recipe. Maggie promised to pass along everyone's compliments as well as the recipe, of which she would receive requests for, for weeks to come.

The guests were enjoying themselves, mingling and socializing. Some were even dancing in the family room, in the space the girls made earlier in the day by rearranging the furniture, in the hopes someone would want to kick their shoes off.

The boys were playing up in Car's room, and came running down every fifteen minutes to check and see if it was time for the ball to drop yet, determined to stay up and witness the event. When they missed their checkpoint at 10:30, Maggie went up to look in on them and found them both curled up on the bed, sound asleep. Knowing they would be upset if they missed it, she decided to let them nap for now and wake them up before midnight. She went back down to the party and let Luke's parents know. At eleven forty five, they woke them up and the boys scrambled downstairs in a rush, to get situated in front of the television.

Jim took a break from playing music, and the volume on the T.V. was turned up as everyone gathered around for the countdown. When it began, they joined in with Dick Clark, "Ten, nine, eight…" As the countdown continued, Maggie glanced around the room. And though she was surrounded by so many of her friends and loved ones, it didn't stop the wave of loneliness she felt wash over her. It hadn't occurred to her until that moment that everyone there were couples, ringing in the New Year together. With the exception of her and Chad.

"…three, two, one! Happy New Year!" Cheers erupted and *Auld Lang Seine* rang out, and the couples embraced, sharing the customary kiss with their significant others. Maggie started to turn away, suddenly uncomfortable watching the displays of affection, and stopped short, finding herself face to face with Chad.

Before she knew what was happening, he cupped her face with his hands and kissed her tenderly on the lips for several seconds. She opened her eyes when he pulled away, surprised to realize they had been closed. Unable to move a muscle, her surprise turned to confusion as she watched him disappear among the guests.

Someone said, “Happy New Year!” and gave her a big hug. Then she was caught up in a flurry of hugs, as one after another of her friends extended their New Year’s best wishes. Maggie reciprocated each embrace, all the while searching the room for a glimpse of Chad. When Cheyenne popped up for a hug, Maggie asked her if she had seen Chad, but she was barely able to shake her head no, before they were both swept up in someone’s else’s arms. As soon as Maggie could slip away, she went to look for him, but he wasn’t anywhere in the house. Wondering where he could be, she opened the front door and looked out at the parked cars, her eyes drawn to a glaringly empty space amid all the other vehicles. It was suddenly very clear why she couldn’t find him. He had left without a word.

Chad's Journal

January 1, 2007

Cole! I need to talk to you! Please! Talk to me Cole! Come to me in a dream,
tell me who I kissed tonight.
Was it my friend, the woman I love, or my best friend's wife?
In reality, it was all three.
Where do I go, Cole? What do I do?
You know I've tried not to love her the way that I do.
I've told myself over and over, it's not real,
it can't be, it's not right.
No matter what my mind says, my heart won't listen.
Tell me Cole, how do I trick my heart?

CHAPTER 45

Maggie was having a bad day. It started with her spilling her cup of coffee all over the papers she was grading that morning. Then she realized she had forgotten to get milk at the grocery store the night before, which wouldn't have been the end of the world, except that she had let Car talk her into a box of Cap'n Crunch cereal to have that morning. She diverted that little problem by taking him to McDonald's for breakfast, the only thing he liked better than Cap'n Crunch. After breakfast, they went to the grocery store to pick up the forgotten milk, and when they got back to the car, she discovered she'd locked her keys inside. No big deal, she thought, she'd just use her spare key she kept in her purse. Then she remembered—as she looked at the wallet in her hand—her purse was at home on the kitchen counter. She'd just grabbed the wallet and her cell phone that morning, not wanting to tote the heavy purse she carried everything but the kitchen sink in.

With a sigh, she reached into her pocket for her cell phone. Finding her pocket empty, she reluctantly looked through the car window to see her cell phone lying on the console. Groaning, she looked around, but there wasn't a pay phone anywhere in sight, so they went back in the store to ask to use their phone. She called AAA, who took all the information, put her on hold, and when they came back, told her it would be at least an hour before anyone could get to her location. Having no choice but to wait, they headed back out the car. On the way she spotted a woman who had her hands full trying to manage four little kids *and* load her groceries in her car. Maggie gave her their milk, knowing it would never last until they got the car unlocked and made it home.

She and Car went to find a bench in the shade, where they could watch for the locksmith. After an hour, the sixty degree weather was beginning to feel a little cool in the shade, so they went back out to the car to wait in the warm sun, figuring help would be arriving any minute. Forty-three long minutes later, the locksmith finally showed up, and within two minutes, Maggie had her keys in hand.

Beyond eager to get back home now—especially Car, because he was missing cartoons—they buckled up and Maggie carefully eased her way through the crowded parking lot. It seemed like they had to wait forever until, at long last, there was a break in the traffic and Maggie was able to pull out on the busy road. It wasn't until then that she remembered they still had no milk, and they'd had to turn around and go back.

What a frustrating morning, Maggie thought on the drive home. It just topped off the frustratingly similar week. Tomorrow, or more accurately, tonight at midnight, would mark the two week point since the New Year's Eve party and the mysterious kiss and subsequent disappearance of Chad, making it the last time she'd seen or talked to him. She left messages he hadn't returned, and Cheyenne, who was aware of what transpired that night, hadn't been able to get in touch with him either.

After a few days with no luck, Cheyenne didn't want to worry Mr. and Mrs. Edwards, but she was concerned enough to call Chris. He told her Chad was okay, he'd "just been busy". When Cheyenne relayed to Maggie what Chris told her, Maggie shook her head in frustration and said, "Famous last words."

Fine, she decided. If he wanted to play that game again, she'd deal with it. But it was easier said than done. She'd run out of excuses to tell Car why Uncle Chad hadn't been over, and that morning when Car kept asking her to call Uncle Chad "cause he could get the keys out", had almost been the breaking point, because that was precisely what she'd *wanted* to do. She'd resisted the urge to call him the entire time they were waiting for the locksmith, and even though she wasn't as sure as Car was that Chad could have gotten the keys out, her first instinct *had* been to call him.

So back home now, she was sitting at the dining room table sipping on a much needed cup of coffee, when Car comes in and asks her if she would call Uncle Chad to see if he would come play ball with him. Maggie calmly asked him to excuse her for a moment, set her coffee cup down very gently, walked up the stairs to her bedroom, quietly shut the door, sat on the side of her bed, covered her face with her hands, and broke down. After a moment or two, she pulled two tissues out of the box on her nightstand and blew her nose. Then she calmly picked up the phone sitting next to the box of tissues, and dialed Chad's number. It went straight to his voice mail—just as she expected—and at the tone she began to leave a message.

"Chad," she began, "I really need..." her voice broke and she choked back a sob. "I really need to talk to you. Please. Call me back," she said earnestly. She slowly placed the phone back in its cradle, and as soon as she let it go, it rang.

"Hello?" she answered, her voice husky from crying.

"Maggie! What's wrong?" Chad was asking, sounding panicked, before she finished saying hello.

Maggie's breath rushed out in a huff as she bit back a sarcastic are-you-kidding-me? retort. "What's *wrong*? WHAT'S *WRONG* CHAD?! I've been calling you for two weeks, and you haven't returned one single call. Not one! You haven't called to talk to Car, who, I might add, has been asking for you *every day!* You haven't returned Cheyenne's calls, and she had to call your family to find out if you were even *alive*, for crying out loud, and *you're* asking *me* what's *wrong*?" Her overwhelming sadness dissipated rather quickly when she first began speaking, each word raising her up to the verge of hysteria. By the time she was done venting, her state of mind had escalated into full blown disgusted anger. She was nearly shouting when she finished.

"I'm sorry," he said simply, when he had the opportunity to respond. "I've just been busy."

"Just been busy," she slowly repeated, vowing to scream if she heard that one more time. Biting her lip and nearly drawing blood, she sighed. "Okay," she started, speaking very calmly, "well, *I've* got to go now, because *I* have to figure out how to explain to a six year old boy that his Uncle Chad has *"just been too busy"* to spare him two minutes for a phone call." Her voice was starting to rise again. "And you know what Chad? I'm tired of trying to explain your disappearing acts to him. If you can't decide whether you want to be in our lives or out of them, then spare us the heartache, and just stay out!" she cried, slamming down the phone.

CHAPTER 46

Maggie's anger vanished the instant she let go of the phone. She couldn't believe what just happened and what she'd said to Chad. She sat in shock as a blanket of remorse settled over her, and the gamut of emotions she'd endured and bottled up for the past two weeks, came rushing out in a torrent of tears. She didn't know how long she sat there crying, but at the sound of the doorbell she ran to the bathroom to try to wash away the evidence of her emotional breakdown. Unable to do anything about her red, puffy eyes, she gave up and hurried to get to the door. On the way she heard Car downstairs, shout "Uncle Chad!" apparently assuming Chad had come play ball with him like he'd asked. Before she could get down the stairs to tell him otherwise, he made a mad dash across the foyer and opened the door. She stopped short, just a few steps down, when she saw that it actually *was* Chad standing in the doorway. He looked slightly disheveled and very tired. Or maybe sad. She couldn't be sure, because he was looking down at Car. She was frozen where she'd stopped, but, as if sensing her presence above him, Chad's eyes turned up to gaze directly into hers.

"Uncle Chad! Did you come to play ball with me?" Car asked, thrilled to see him.

It was killing Chad to see her face all red and splotchy from crying, knowing it was because of him. Without taking his eyes off her, he answered Car. "Yeah, I came to play ball," he said, as though it was a matter of fact, but a haunted questioning look appeared in his eyes as he waited, it seemed, for her to say otherwise. It felt like an eternity to him before she gave the slightest nod of her head, pardoning him from her recently imposed sentence of life without them, and his knees nearly buckled in relief.

Car grabbed his hand and pulled him inside, oblivious to what was going on between the two adults, but Chad's eyes stayed locked on Maggie until Car pulled him past her, on their way to the back yard.

As soon as they were out of sight, Maggie sank down to the step behind her, her legs weak and shaking, her head swimming. She had no idea what was going on, nor could she identify all of the emotions she was feeling, but most of all she couldn't believe how fast Chad had gotten there. All she knew for certain, was how glad she was that he had. She could sit there for hours trying to analyze the events of the day, of the past week, the last month, even over the last year, she realized, and still not know any more than she did now. The last time she remembered feeling like she had two feet planted firmly on the ground—and was actually in charge of her life—was the morning before Cole's final football game. But, rather than waste any more precious time worrying about it, and especially since she had feeling in her legs again, she stood up—holding on to the banister just in case—and went to see if applying some make up would help her appearance. Then she went out on the deck to watch Chad and Car play. She waved when they looked up, and her heart melted at the sight of the huge grin spread across Car's face. After a while, she decided to go inside and start dinner, having a feeling that Chad wouldn't decline her invitation. By the time they came in, she was putting dinner on the table and she sent Car to wash up.

She glanced at Chad wondering if she was going to have to ask, but when she saw him looking at the third place setting on the table, and then saw each side of his mouth curl up to form a little smile, she knew everything was going to be okay.

∾⌘⌘⌘∾

While she cleaned up the kitchen after dinner, Car regaled Chad with his entire repertoire on the piano, and judging by what she could hear, they were both enjoying it immensely. When she joined them, they had time for one game of Go Fish, before Car had to take a bath and get ready for bed.

When the game was over, Car asked Chad, "Will you wait for me to finish my bath so you can help mommy tuck me in?"

Chad looked at Maggie questioningly before answering. She nodded that it was okay. "It would be an honor, little man," he answered.

"Promise?" Car pressed, wanting a more binding answer before he would leave the room.

"I promise," Chad confirmed solemnly, a stab of regret piercing his heart for making Car feel like he couldn't trust he would still be there without that extra affirmation. The pain subsided a little though, when, reassured with that promise, Car rushed off, one very happy little camper.

They headed on up to his room behind him, and he was already brushing his teeth when they got upstairs. By the time they got to his bedroom they heard the shower running, which surprised Maggie because he normally took a bath. They had just begun to discuss how quickly Car had taken to the piano, when—after what had to be the fastest shower in history—they heard him emerge from the bathroom. Maggie was about to call out to him that he had to actually step *into* the shower for it to count, when he came into the room with his hair still wet and dripping, soaking the top of his pajamas. She was going to send him back but caught the scent of soap, and not wanting to keep Chad waiting, she decided to just make sure he took a better shower, or bath, in the morning before church. Shaking her head at his antics, she grabbed a towel and dried his hair and got him a dry pajama top to put on. When he was done, he knelt by his bed to say his prayers.

"Dear God, thank you for letting me win at Go Fish, and please tell my Daddy he doesn't have to worry, cause since I've been practicing with Uncle Chad, he's learning to throw the ball pretty good now. Oh, and me and mommy are doing just fine since we got the car keys back. Amen." Then, with a little more zeal than he usually had at bedtime, he pulled the covers back and climbed into bed, ready to be tucked in.

Maggie pretended to yawn to hide her smile at Chad's expression when Car mentioned his apparent lacking-but-improving-football-throwing-ability. She hastily bent down to kiss Car goodnight, ignoring Chad's now questioning look regarding the car keys remark. Fully aware he probably wasn't going to just let that one slip by, she told Car she loved him, and stepped back to let Chad take over.

Though he was new to this nightly ritual, he passed with flying colors. Car was content and already drifting off to sleep when they pulled his door to, leaving it ajar a few inches. As they descended the stairs Maggie was mentally preparing herself for Chad to make a hasty retreat, but hoping he would stay for a little while because they had a lot they needed to straighten out, and wondered if she should push the envelope by asking him.

When they reached the foyer, Chad took a few steps toward the door, just as Maggie feared, but then stopped abruptly and turned. "Do you have a few minutes? There's something I'd like to talk to you about," he asked.

Greatly relieved, Maggie said, "Absolutely. I need to talk to you too." They made their way to the den, both prepared now to clear the air of all the mixed signals and misunderstandings of the past few weeks. Maggie took a seat on the far end of the sofa, and Chad went to the adjacent loveseat, sitting down at the end closest to Maggie.

Chad began before Maggie had a chance to, hoping to spare her any discomfort. "I'm sorry I didn't call you or return your messages, and I know it's no excuse, but *because* of your messages, I knew you and Car were okay."

Maggie interjected, nodding her head, "Physically yes, but not emotionally, as you were witness to this afternoon, and I'm so sorry for what I said." She looked as though she were about to cry.

"Maggie, you have no reason to apologize. You were just reacting to my actions, and I promise I will never do that to you and Car again. When you hung up on me, I was scared to death I had lost the two of you forever. It made me realize nothing could stop me from wanting to be in your lives. My life wouldn't be complete without you and Car in it." He stopped there, unsure of how much he should confess.

"I'm glad, because we want you in our lives, Chad. If it hadn't been for Cheyenne these past few weeks, I don't know how I would have coped. You two are my best friends."

At Maggie's mention of the word "friend", Chad had his answer. He was thankful he hadn't revealed too much about his feelings. He went on. "Well, I'm glad Cheyenne was there for you, and if you'll give me a second chance, from now on I will be too. You have my word on that."

Maggie reached over and squeezed his hand tightly, still swallowing back tears. "Thank you," she said sincerely. "Will you forgive me for what I said before?"

"I forgave you before you hung up the phone."

She smiled. Everything in his expression conveyed he was being sincere. She wanted to ask him why he had behaved so oddly, there one minute and gone the next, but decided he was there now, for good, he'd said, and that was all that mattered.

Sensing that particular issue was cleared up, he said, "I quit the Titans."

"What?! Why?" she asked, stunned.

He shook his head. "It just wasn't the same without Cole there, and I was getting really tired of all the traveling, so I decided to open my own practice."

"Are you serious? That's fantastic! Do you have a place yet?"

It meant a lot to him that she not only approved of his decision, but was so excited for him too. "I put a deposit on a place over by Vanderbilt Hospital last week. It used to be a doctor's office, so the set up in the front is pretty good. Renovations on the back are supposed to start next week, before I have equipment delivered."

They talked for over an hour, and finally Maggie asked with a sly grin, "So, do you need a decorator?"

CHAPTER 47

Several months flew by in what seemed like a handful of days. Chad kept his promise—though he really was busy setting up his practice—and was in contact with Maggie and Car every day, either by phone, or more often than not, in person. It took eight weeks to get the clinic open, and Maggie had the best time redecorating the waiting room and offices. The placement of the equipment in the therapy room had been left to Chad, but otherwise Maggie had carte blanche, and the end result was beautiful. It was classy, warm, inviting, and above all, practical. Chad wondered if there was *anything* she couldn't do.

The clinic had only been open five weeks, but was already a huge success. In addition to his office staff, Chad had to hire two other physical therapists, in order to cover the work load. He couldn't have been happier. In spite of their busy schedules, with Maggie juggling school, her music students after school, various church and sorority charity events, and helping Chad with the clinic, they planned some sort of outing or special activity each weekend for the three of them.

They had been boating three times, and Maggie had almost laughed out loud the first time when Chad showed up with his captains hat on, and a tube of sunscreen hanging from a string around his neck. Not wanting to embarrass him by letting on she knew about the two toned forehead incident, she hadn't said anything then, or the second time, or the third, but it made her smile each time. Evidently he'd learned his lesson.

One of their weekend outings was to a rodeo. Car had been so fascinated with the bulls and riders he decided then and there that was what he wanted to do. Ride bulls. Big, bucking, irate bulls. Chad chuckled and told him that he thought it might be a good idea to learn how to ride his bike without training wheels first, figuring that would be the end of it. He thought the silence that ensued confirmed his theory, until Car said, "You know, Uncle Chad, you're right. Will you take my training wheels off?"

He was still adamant about it by the following Saturday, so Chad took them off and spent the day helping him learn to ride without them. By the end of the day when Car could ride down the sidewalk a ways, turn around and ride back without assistance, he announced he was now ready to begin his career in bull riding. In spite of his enthusiasm, he did agree, however reluctantly, to continue practicing on his bike throughout the week due to the lack of available bulls. He worked all week honing his newly acquired skills, so by the next weekend he was feeling pretty confident. But during one particular maneuver, he slowed down a bit too much attempting a turnaround and it caused him to take a little tumble. He wasn't hurt very bad, especially by bull riding industry standards, just a scrape on the palm of his hand and his knee. But that little tumble, that barely required two band-aids, brought his dreams of a bull riding career to an abrupt end.

Two or three weekends later the circus came to town. The three of them attended and Car immediately fell in love with the lions and tigers, marveling at how the ringleader could make them jump through the flaming hoops at his command. Maggie and Chad glanced at each other, suddenly apprehensive, remembering the bullet they'd dodged a few weeks earlier regarding Car and bull riding. Realizing now that may not have been the worst of it, they kept expecting throughout the act for Car to announce his next big career move, but after the fierce cats were led away and the elephants were putting on their show without any new career decisions from Car, they began to relax. By the end of all the animal acts they had completely forgotten about it and were enjoying the show as much as he was. The amazing tightrope walkers and trapeze artists concluded the show and they were inching their way to the exit, each holding on to one of Cars hands so they didn't lose him in the throng of people, when they heard a determined voice say, "I'm gonna be a tight rope walker." They looked at each other, trepidation etched on their faces, then burst out laughing.

∾⌘⌘⌘∾

Sunday mornings had long since been reserved for church Maggie's entire life, and it remained so during her marriage—as much as Cole's travel schedule would allow—but especially during the devastating aftermath of his passing. She rarely missed a Sunday, and since the morning after her and Chad's relationship had been put to question, Chad attended every service with them. The difference now, was when he saw people talking, he knew they were saying *good* things, because not only had he been welcomed warmly and accepted into their church family with open arms, but mainly because they told him as much. He was finally coming to terms with the demons that had haunted him for so many years, and it felt great.

Car's aspirations to be a tight rope walker turned out to be even shorter lived than his bull riding dreams, when, as they were leaving church the day after the circus, he was practicing his skills on an extremely treacherous curb in the parking lot, and mis-stepped, causing him to twist his ankle, lose his balance and fall down. He tore a hole in his pants and scraped his knee again, and after a brief examination by Chad, it was determined nothing was broken, but his ankle did need to be iced. He carried Car to their vehicle.

At home, after some serious deliberation and with his ice pack firmly in place, Car requested a meeting. Once he had Maggie and Chad's undivided attention, he said, "Mommy, Uncle Chad," making eye contact with each of them in turn, "I don't want to let anyone down, but I think it would be a pretty good idea, if maybe, instead of being a tight rope walker, I became a doctor like you, Uncle Chad."

Maggie looked at Chad for a split second, but decided to play along with Car before he changed his mind. "I think that would be a fine idea, Car," she said, nodding her head and looking at Chad again for confirmation, hoping that Car's quest of becoming a daredevil overnight was behind him. But instead of Chad agreeing with her like she had expected, she found him just staring at Car, beaming with pride. She realized it was what Car said about him and the 'doctor' thing. She was a bit surprised at how much the comment seemed to mean to Chad, but before she could give it any more consideration, her attention was drawn back to what Car was saying.

"See, that way would be more better, because then I can fix up the bull riders and tight rope walkers when they fall!" he was saying, in an earnest attempt to lessen the blow from his announcement. After a brief pause for that sink in, he said, "So, can I borrow your school books, Uncle Chad?"

Maggie looked at Chad again, but this time he was looking at her, grinning. He shrugged. "At least he's motivated," he said.

∾⌘⌘⌘∾

Maggie and her students had been working the entire school year toward for the music recital, scheduled on Monday, April 15th, and it was finally here. Car was going to have his first performance on stage. A solo on the piano.

A few hours before the show, Chad called Maggie and Car to wish them luck. While on the phone with Car, he started to tell him to "break a leg" but thought better of it. Instead, he said, "I wanted to wish you luck, and let you know I'll be there soon, buddy."

"Okay, thanks a lot! Hey, Uncle Chad? I think you're really going to like it," Car told him.

"I know I will! I'm looking for a forward to it. Well, you'd better go get ready. I love you, little man."

"Love you, too" Car said happily.

"Can I speak to Mommy again, real quick?" Chad asked. He could hear Car handing the phone to Maggie.

"Hey," she said, a little breathless.

"I know you're busy, but I just wanted to let you know I'll be there early."

"Okay, great! I've got a seat reserved for you on the front row," she told him.

"Good! Get back to what you were doing. I'll see you soon. I can't wait!"

"Okay, see you in a bit. Bye-bye."

"Bye," Chad said, disconnecting. He had a few things to take care of, then head to the school, but he got held up with an unexpected patient, and now it was thirty minutes before the show. As he was locking up, he glanced at his watch. "So much for getting there early," he said to himself. If he hurried he could still make it on time, at least, he thought.

Fortunately most of the rush hour traffic was over, and he couldn't believe his luck at catching every light green so far, but no sooner had that thought transpired, the light ahead turned red. "Until now," he groaned. As he began to slow down for the stop light, it turned green. "Yes!" he said, grinning. He accelerated, and looked at his watch again. I'm going to make it!

He never saw the dump truck coming from his left, that didn't stop for the light and hit him broadside in the intersection.

CHAPTER 48

It was printed in the paper that the funeral service was going to be on Thursday at 1 p.m. Maggie wanted to be sure to send flowers. The day after the accident, the wife of the man driving the dump truck, told Maggie her husband had a massive heart attack. He had just turned sixty-five years old. It was believed he had died before he'd entered the intersection. She was grieving deeply over the loss of her husband, but had come to the hospital in search of the person he'd collided with, to check on their condition, pray for them, and if possible, convey her husband's apologies, because that's what he would have wanted, she'd said.

∾⌘⌘⌘∾

At the recital the night before, when Maggie saw the still empty seat after the show had started, she'd gotten a little upset, thinking Chad was playing his old tune. Then she thought about how he had been lately, and the phone call he'd made a few hours earlier, and as the show went on she became deeply worried. Car's part came, and he'd played perfectly, but she noticed he kept searching the auditorium for Chad whenever he could. She remembered wishing desperately she'd had her cell phone with her instead of in her purse, locked in the classroom. As soon as the final curtain fell, she'd asked another teacher to keep an eye on Car for her and rushed to get her phone. For some reason, on the way, she had a flashback of rushing from the stadium to her vehicle to get her cell phone once before, in an emergency, and she vowed from then on to carry her phone in her pocket at all times.

She'd gotten two messages. One from the paramedics—who'd found her number, in case of emergency, in Chad's phone—saying he had been in an accident and was being transported to Vanderbilt

Hospital, and one from Mr. and Mrs. Edwards, who had gotten an identical call. Running back to get Car, she'd returned Chad's parents call, but they hadn't been able to get any more information regarding his condition, or reports on the severity of the accident. They'd said they were on their way, but were still about two hours out. Maggie told them she would call them back as soon as she got to the hospital. In the auditorium, she'd found her friend Carolyn, and after explaining the situation, Carolyn offered to keep Car for her, while she went to the hospital. At first Maggie declined, but then decided maybe it would be best, at least until she found out what happened and that Chad was okay. Carolyn had hurried Maggie on her way, telling her not to worry about Car, she would keep him safe and occupied until they knew more.

Without even realizing it, Maggie drove right to the sight of the accident on her way to the hospital. Stopped in the traffic, she saw the dump truck sitting in the road, but Chad's Expedition had already been towed, so she didn't connect the two. Finally getting through the detour, she rushed on to the emergency room. As she was being directed to the Tenth Floor Trauma Unit, a place she was all too familiar with, she started to get sick to her stomach, realizing it must be very bad. When the elevator door opened, she was suddenly overcome with fear. She'd had push back the rush of bad memories and force herself to step out to make her way to the nurse's station.

As she approached, one of the nurses looked up and Maggie recognized Nancy, a nurse who was there when Cole had been. Nancy was one of Cole's biggest fans, and knew who Maggie was immediately. She also noticed that Maggie was white as a sheet, and looked scared to death. She stood and hurried to meet her halfway.

"Oh, Mrs. Rivers, I'm so sorry," Nancy said, as she hugged Maggie. "This has got to be so difficult for you." She stepped back and had such a look of concern on her face that Maggie was afraid to ask.

"Is he…" her voice trailed off, unable to say the word.

"He's alive and in surgery, honey," Nancy interjected quickly, allaying Maggie's fears to the contrary.

Maggie's knee's almost buckled with relief.

"If you'll wait right here, I'll go see if I can find out anything."

Maggie could only nod her head as Nancy hurried off. She was still standing in the same spot, when Nancy returned.

"I'm afraid all I can tell you is that he's expected to be in surgery for some time. He was in pretty bad shape, honey," she relayed gently, "but he's alive!" she reminded her optimistically. "Now if you want to go to the waiting room, I'll come get you as soon as I know anything else. Are you expecting anyone to come be with you?"

Maggie remembered she needed to call Chad's parents back. "Yes," she answered, distracted. "Yes, his parents are coming from Knoxville. They should be here in just over an hour or so," she said, as they were walking to the waiting room. "Do you know what happened?" she finally thought to ask.

"I was told that he was broadsided by a dump truck," Nancy answered as gently as possible, expecting the look of horror on Maggie's face in response. "The other driver didn't make it."

"Oh my gosh," she said gravely, the realization sinking in that the detour with the dump truck must have been where the accident had happened.

They reached the door, and as Maggie turned to enter, Nancy said, "Okay, well hopefully we'll have some good news for you and his parents by the time they get here. Is there anything I can get for you, honey?"

"No, thank you." She tried to smile. "I'll be fine."

"Okay, if you change your mind, you know where to find me, and if I hear anything, I'll let you know right away," she promised as she turned to go.

Maggie went inside the waiting room to sit down and call Chad's parents, and fill them in with what little information she had. She omitted the part about the dump truck and the fatality, because she didn't want to upset them anymore than they already were, while they were on the road. They were still over an hour away, and she told them exactly where to go when they arrived. She had forgotten to ask if anyone had called Cheyenne yet, so she called her next and found out she was on her way as well.

After Maggie called her parents and then Carolyn to check on Car, she waited, trying to figure out how this could be happening. How she could be sitting here again in this very room, where she had unknowingly waited for hours to receive the most devastating news of her life, on the eve of what would have been Cole's twenty-eighth birthday.

She felt like the walls were closing in on her, and a deep sense of déjà-vu engulfed her when it suddenly struck her that tomorrow was *Chad's* birthday.

CHAPTER 49

Sometime between nine and ten o'clock that night Mr. and Mrs. Edwards arrived, but Maggie still hadn't had any word about Chad's condition other than he was still in surgery. About an hour or so after that, Cheyenne got there, and together they prayed, while waiting for any news.

Maggie had spoken to Carolyn earlier, and Carolyn offered to take Car back to his house where he would be more comfortable and she would stay the night with him there. If Maggie wasn't home by morning, she would take him on to school, and have the school call in a substitute teacher for her. Carolyn was such a blessing. Maggie knew she was fortunate to have a friend like her, and was so thankful for all her help. Car was fine with the arrangement, but worried about his Uncle Chad. Maggie had promised him she would let him know as soon as she heard anything and asked him to be brave, and to remember to say his prayers.

Around one a.m., Maggie and Cheyenne went down to the snack room to get cups of coffee for everyone, checking in at the nurse's station on the way back, before continuing their vigil in the waiting room.

Finally, at twenty after four in the morning, the doctor came to see them. They were told that Chad's injuries were so extensive that he had been in surgery for over nine hours. He looked at each person he was addressing to make sure they grasped the severity of Chad's condition, then settled on Mr. and Mrs. Edwards, before continuing.

"I have to tell you, your son's injuries are extensive and we're doing everything we can to keep him stable. We had to do a craniotomy to relieve the intracranial pressure, due to the trauma to his head..."

Mrs. Edwards' hand flew to her mouth to stifle a sob, and Mr. Edwards held her close. Maggie felt faint and nauseas when she heard him say "trauma to the head", but tried to stay focused on what he was saying.

"...which was successful, and he'll be monitored very closely to make sure there is no recurrent swelling. He is currently on a ventilator, and we had to perform a splenorrhaphy to stem the bleeding to his spleen, which also appears to have been successful. We didn't want to remove it, if at all possible, because as you may know, the spleen plays such a vital role in the immune system, and with the injuries he's sustained we want him to be able to fight off infection." He paused a moment, letting them process what he'd explained, then he took a deep breath and continued. "He has a fractured hip and pelvis, as well as several broken ribs, one of which punctured his lung. His left arm was fractured in three places, and had to be set. He was unconscious when the paramedics arrived at the scene, and did not regain consciousness during the transport here. Due to the extent of his injuries, he's being administered very strong medications to temporarily deepen his level of unconsciousness in order to control his breathing, blood pressure, and other vital functions."

Maggie and Cheyenne were both crying quietly, overwhelmed, as the doctor went on.

"He is in critical condition, but as I said, stable, and if we don't encounter any setbacks during the next twenty-four hours, we'll begin to bring him out of the drug induced coma. Until then, I'm afraid we won't be able to determine if there was any brain damage, temporary or permanent. I'm sorry, but we just have to wait and see." He looked sympathetic and very tired. He gave them a second to take everything in. "On the bright side, given everything he's been through tonight, he's doing remarkably well."

Mr. and Mrs. Edwards looked at each other, and voicing the question in her eyes, Mr. Edwards asked, "What do you think his chances are?"

"I can't answer that right now. However, we'll be able to determine more during the next twenty-four to forty-eight hours." He placed his hand on Mr. Edwards shoulder, in a gesture of support.

"Your son is in good hands here. Some of the best trauma surgeons in the country work in this trauma unit, and will do everything possible to get him through this. Unfortunately, the hard part is waiting."

"Thank you," Mr. Edwards said.

Mrs. Edwards nodded her head, "Yes, thank you."

"I'll be happy to try to answer any other questions you may have."

Unable to think clearly, they looked at each other helplessly, shaking their heads.

The doctor looked sympathetic. "I understand. You may find it helpful to write down anything that comes to mind, and I'll do my best to answer it when we talk again." He shook Mr. Edwards's hand, then turned to go.

And so they waited.

Maggie didn't know what was running through everyone else's minds but all of Chad's injuries kept echoing in her head. Cole had *one* artery rupture and he was gone now. How in the world could Chad survive all of his injuries? But she was determined to stay positive, and do whatever she could.

At seven a.m., Maggie called Car to tell him his Uncle Chad was out of surgery, but was still sleeping, and then she called the school to make sure a substitute had been arranged since Carolyn had called in for one earlier. After that, she began calling her home students before they went to school, to let them know she wouldn't be able to give them their lessons for at least a few days.

While the others were making calls of their own to fill everyone in on Chad's condition, Maggie called her mom and dad, who were making arrangements to come to Nashville, so they could stay with Car while Maggie was at the hospital.

With the phone calls made, Maggie and Cheyenne insisted that Mr. and Mrs. Edwards go down to the cafeteria to get coffee and something to eat, promising that they too, would go when the two of them returned. Reluctant, they finally agreed to go, with cell phone in hand in case there was any more news or changes with Chad.

They were barely gone twenty minutes, and came back just as Maggie's parents got there. A few minutes later, a young nurse named Makayla, came to let them know Chad was still in stable but critical condition, and one of his parents could see him for just a few minutes. Exchanging a glance, words not necessary, Chad's mother nodded in assent for Mr. Edwards to go and see their son. After the two shared a brief embrace, he let Makayla lead the way to see Chad.

When he returned, he was clearly shaken and pale. As gently as he could, he shared with them how Chad had looked, obviously trying to prepare everyone for when they got to see him, especially Mrs. Edwards, and hopefully lessen the shock when they did.

It was about this time that the wife of the man—who apparently had a heart attack resulting in the collision—had searched them out. She introduced herself as Sally Marie Raley, and conveyed her concern for Chad. She apologized for her husband's role in the accident, explaining that was what he would have wanted her to do, and that if he hadn't died in the crash, it would have broken his heart knowing someone's life hung in the balance because of him. She was so sincere and as sweet as she could be, and every one of them assured her they harbored no ill feelings toward her husband. They were genuinely sorry for *her* loss. When she asked if they would mind if she stayed to wait and pray with them, they told her she was absolutely welcome any time.

Because Chad was in critical condition, only immediate family was allowed to see him. Mrs. Edwards was given permission around one o'clock. She was anxious to go to him, but scared, and in spite of her husband's attempts to prepare her for what she would see, actually seeing all the tubes and machines connected to her sons bruised and battered body was traumatic for her. She was sobbing when she returned, and unable to hide her emotions as well as Mr. Edwards, she completely broke down when she looked at the concerned faces of those waiting for her. A short while later, Chris's arrival was a great comfort to her, but she had to rely on her husband to describe Chad's condition to him, still being too emotional to do so herself.

Around two p.m., Maggie and her parents left to go to the school so that Maggie could arrange for the substitute a few more days, just in case, and to pick up Car. She wanted to explain things to Car about Chad and why everybody was there, then grab a shower and maybe a few hours sleep. It was agreed that Mrs. Edwards would go next, and then Mr. Edwards.

Sally Marie stayed with them until five o'clock, but before leaving she exchanged phone numbers with everyone, and asked if someone would call her when they heard any news.

Maggie was back by six o'clock, feeling a little better, having showered, eaten, and getting about two hours sleep. When she got there, Mrs. Edwards left to go to Chad's and Cheyenne went to Maggie's, both promising to be back by eleven o'clock. Chris and Savannah stayed, hopeful that Chris would get to see Chad soon.

Maggie dozed off sitting in the chair, but was startled awake, when her phone rang. She quickly answered it before it woke Mr. Edwards, who had drifted off as well. She was surprised to see Mrs. Edwards number on the caller I.D.

"Hello?" she answered quietly.

"Maggie, honey? I'm here at Chad's. I've found something that I really think you need to see."

CHAPTER 50

Perplexed, Maggie hung up after promising to come right over. With a look of confusion on her face, she quietly explained the phone call to Chris and Savannah as she gathered her belongings, hoping they could shed some light on the mystery. Chris and Savannah glanced at each other, both pretty sure about what Chad's mother may have found. But unable to say anything—lest they betray Chad's confidences—they kept quiet and hurried Maggie on her way. Given the circumstances, they felt Maggie had a right to know.

Mrs. Edwards was waiting for her at the door. She quickly explained that, after showering, she had gone to the kitchen to fix herself some soup before lying down, and saw an open book on the counter. Glancing at it out of curiosity, she recognized Chad's handwriting. It was a journal. She remembered he had started keeping one back in high school. Unable to stop herself, she read the entries on that page, and was so completely shocked by what he had written, she skimmed through the rest of the journal. At first she felt uneasy reading his most private thoughts, but what she was seeing was tearing out her heart and she went into protection mode for her son, determined to get answers. Beside herself, she went in search of past journals, sure now, Chad had never stopped keeping them. What she found in a box in Chad's closet, were now stacked on the counter in chronological order. She explained to Maggie that, even though they were personal, she felt they were way too important for her not to see, especially with Chad's condition to consider now.

Maggie was still confused, but took a seat on a stool at the counter and picked up the journal on top. Giving her some privacy, Mrs. Edwards went to lie down. Maggie opened the journal to a page where a book mark had been placed, she assumed by Chad's mom, and she began to read.

April 17, 1998

Tonight I met an angel.

April 18, 1998

She's amazing

April 25, 1998

I can't wait to see her again.

Maggie stopped reading for a moment, and searched her memory. She knew this was about the time she'd met Cole and Chad, but couldn't recall the girl Chad could be talking about. Could this girl be the reason she could never successfully play matchmaker with Chad? If so, who was she, and why had Chad never introduced her to anyone? What happened with them and where is she now? Eager to find out the identity of this "amazing" girl, she continued reading.

The entries over the next several weeks only referred to Chad's concern for Cole not having chosen his major yet, and other issues regarding school. She skimmed over the pages searching for any mention of the girl.

June 26, 1998

I saw her today.

She's more beautiful than I remembered.

July 4, 1998

I've never met anyone like her.

Maggie looked up, remembering that particular Fourth of July, when the group of them had gone tubing and then to Pigeon Forge to watch the fireworks. It *had* to be one of the girls with them that day! It couldn't have been Stephanie or Maresa, they would have told her, but she couldn't remember Chad paying particular attention to anyone. Baffled, she read on.

August 2, 1998

I get to see her pretty often now, and my feelings
grow stronger every time I do.

August 28, 1998

I love her.
I may have lost her.

Oh no, Maggie thought, I wonder what happened? Who the heck is this girl?

September 10, 1998

My best friend has met a special girl.

Maggie smiled, knowing this entry was referring to her. She went on.

September 19, 1998

What's a man to say, What's a man to do,
When he has not the right to say,
Pretty Lady, I love you.

Maggie's heart skipped a beat when she read Chad's reference to this girl as "Pretty Lady". Though she was hesitant to admit it, the fact was, it made her a little jealous to know she wasn't the only one he called "Pretty Lady". She began flipping through the pages, even more desperate now to find out who this girl was.

December 18, 1998

Such an enormous price to pay
for the things I can never say.

April 19, 1999

Tonight I celebrated the anniversary of her coming
into my life,
and Cole celebrated his future.

May 15, 1999

I fight these feelings, they can never be.
I can't let my selfishness hurt the two I love so.

May 25, 1999

Such is my plight, for I love the heart of the man,
Who stole the heart of the woman I love.

More confused than ever, Maggie read the entries again. Her hands were shaking now. Her heart was beating fast. It couldn't be. She tried to concentrate and read the next entry, written on her wedding day.

May 29, 1999

How does one live around the love of his life,
when his love becomes his best friends wife?

A sob escaped her lips as it became clear. It was her! Chad had been in love with her! How could she have not seen it? Her mind racing now, she brushed the tears away, and picking up the journals, she moved to the couch and began to read where she left off.

July 19, 1999

I have sacrificed so little, yet I have received so much,
The radiance of your smile, the warmness of your touch,
I couldn't bear the thought of never hearing your name,
And knowing it would end like this, I would do it all again.

March 23, 2000
Where do I go for relief? Why must I carry this guilt?
My heart remained true to my friends.
If only I could have fallen out of love,
As quickly as I fell in.

August 6, 2000
How can anyone look at a baby, and not believe in God?
What little miracles they are, and this little miracle bears my name.

The tears were flowing freely now, and Maggie began scanning the remaining journals, reading entries at random.

November 6, 2000
Doused by a million tears,
the flame still burns.

August 6, 2001
I couldn't be prouder if Car were my own son.

October 3, 2001
Maggie's trying to fix me up with Shirley. She's really sweet, and beautiful too. Would it be fair to try to love Shirley,
when my heart belongs to Maggie?

June 1, 2002
Shirley is gone to Peru, and she seems happy.
She is a good friend.
I wonder how long Maggie will wait, before she starts again.

So, he had been on to her! She chuckled, but the tears kept coming. She picked up another journal, one more recent.

October 20, 2005

Cole, I know that where you are, you can read my heart
and know my feelings for Maggie. I swear to you my friend, I
never betrayed your trust. I always put you, and your love for
Maggie first. I have so much to say to you. This seems selfish, but
how could you leave us? We all hurt so much. Do you remember
my sinus problem the day after little Chad was born? It was
because I cried all night, Cole. It was from both joy and pain.
He carried my name, but not my blood.
I can't go on right now, Cole.
Please forgive me if I seemed to babble. God, how I miss you.

November 5, 2005

What a cruel twist of fate for me to become a doctor
and not be able to save you, Cole.

December 1, 2005

Dear Lord, There is a song named *Once I Had a Secret Love.*
Parts of it surely apply to me. I fear if people could read my
heart, they would find me as pathetic. Lord, you know how I
struggle with what's right. Please don't find me pathetic.
It's only you that gives me strength.

December 4, 2005

Maggie found gifts she had for Cole, today.
She called me in tears. It kills me to see her hurting so.
I wanted to comfort her, but I couldn't trust myself.

January 12, 2006

I have *got* to stop loving her.

February 25, 2006

Maggie looked stunning tonight. I think she really enjoyed
*Phantom of the Oper*a.
I would devote my life to making her smile
like she did tonight, if only I could.

February 26, 2006

I saw the looks and whispers in church this morning.
Seeing Maggie so happy last night made me drop my guard,
forget. It can't happen again.

March 4, 2006

I have to keep my distance, but I can't function
without knowing if they're okay.

March 31, 2006

Tomorrow's April Fool's Day, and I am the biggest fool of all.
She doesn't need me, she hasn't even called me.

Maggie had to stop reading. She remembered thinking *he* didn't care about *them*, and that was why he hadn't called them. It tore her heart out now, to know how much pain he had been in, and in her ignorance, she had been so selfish! Still berating herself, she recalled things had gotten better, briefly, around Chad's birthday that year, but then got really bad, and she read on hoping to find out what changed.

April 15, 2006

Car asked me to be his new daddy today. God help me,
nothing would make me happier. Chris and I had an
argument tonight. He figured out how I feel about
Maggie and Car, and can't understand why
I don't just tell them.
How can I possibly make him understand?

So, *that* was why Chad had been so aloof for all those months. And Chris had known all this time! Maggie put aside the journal, the rest of the entry unread, and picked up the latest one, wanting to see Chad's most recent thoughts. This journal appeared to start after the New Years Eve kiss, and Chad's subsequent disappearance, prompting her now regrettable phone call, telling him to stay out of their lives. She thought of how painful it must have been for him, and now he was fighting for his life in the hospital. She wiped her eyes, and tried to focus on the words written on the page before her.

January 14, 2007

Car needs me. What a wonderful feeling!

February 1, 2007

Cole, I wish you could have seen Car today, throwing the football. He's definitely a chip off the old block. You would be so proud of your son. He is a treasure. I said I wish you could have seen him, then I realized that maybe you can. Dear God, if Cole can look down and see, please don't let him see that little bit of envy that lies within my heart.

February 27, 2007

Maggie has been amazing at the clinic. I couldn't have done it without her, and wouldn't have wanted anyone else. Today, for her birthday, we only had time for dinner, but I will make it up to her once the clinic is open, and I can figure out how to upstage *Phantom of the Opera*.

March 18, 2007

The clinic opened today, and everywhere I look, I see Maggie. She had a hand in every aspect of it, and everything went smoothly. My only regret is that now that it's finished, I have no excuse to demand so much of her time.

April 3, 2007

After only two weeks, I have more patients than I can handle.
My relationship with Maggie and Car is more than I could ask
for. I am so happy.

April 14, 2007

Foolish wishes fill my head, Lord.
If only one wish would come true.
Just to hear the one I love, Lord,
whisper back "I Love You, Too".

April 15, 2007

Today is a special day. Car is doing a piano solo at school.
I'm so proud of him. I can hardly wait until tonight,
so I can be with them.

Maggie just finished reading the entry Chad obviously wrote yesterday morning, when Mrs. Edwards came out of the bedroom. Maggie looked up as she approached. With tears streaming down her face, she shook her head. "I didn't know," she cried. "I didn't know he felt that way," she said, her voice filled with anguish.

Mrs. Edwards went to Maggie, and pulled her into her arms, cradling her as she cried.

"Neither did I, honey. Neither did I," she said gently, while they cried in each other's arms.

CHAPTER 51

Interrupted by the ringing of a phone, Mrs. Edwards pulled out of the embrace and rushed to answer it. She turned to face Maggie as she said, "Hello? No honey, I was just about to head back. What is it? Has there been any change?" she asked quickly, looking at Maggie who was anxiously trying to read her expression while listening to the one sided conversation.

"Okay...okay...good...all right, I'll be right there...I love you too... I will...bye, honey." She hung up. "The doctor came to tell them Chad is still stable, and they have stopped the medication to keep him unconscious. If he continues to do okay, they'll be taking him off the ventilator some time overnight. He said they let Chris go in to see Chad just before he called.

Maggie stood up. "That's good. That sounds good, right?" she asked hopefully, looking for confirmation.

"It does," she said, smiling, her eyes shimmering with tears. "The doctor said he's still in very serious condition and not out of the woods, but at least he's not gotten any worse. I'm going to head back now," she turned to pick up her purse. "Are you coming?" she asked.

Maggie hesitated. "I'm going to stay here a while, I think. I just skimmed through his journals, and I'd like to read more. I'll be there soon, though. You'll call me if you hear anything more?"

"Right away, I promise. You're sure you're okay?"

Maggie nodded. "I'm fine. I'll be there soon."

Mrs. Edwards left and Maggie returned to the couch, prepared to read each journal all the way through. A little while later Mr. Edwards slipped in. Maggie was so engrossed in the journal she was reading, she didn't even hear him. It wasn't until he emerged from the guest room after sleeping for a few hours, that Maggie realized he was there. Amazed she hadn't heard him come in, and all the time that had passed, she apologized for not greeting him, and asked if there had been any changes with Chad. He told her there was no change, and she asked about Chris getting to see him. He said Chris was pretty shaken up, but was being very optimistic.

She sighed, hesitant to ask, but she had to know. "Did Mrs. Edwards tell you about..." not able to get the words out, she gestured toward the journals, worried about what he would think about Chad's feelings toward her.

He looked at the journals, then back at her, and nodded his head solemnly, which made her heart sink. Clearly he didn't approve.

"I've always known Chad was one smart guy," he said, a grin spreading across his face.

Maggie, not realizing she had been holding her breath until he smiled, sucked in a gulp of air, then she hugged him, grateful for his support. As he got ready to go back to the hospital, she told him she was going to finish up there, then see Car off to school and shower, and be back at the hospital by 8:00 A.M.

When she got back and was stepping into the elevator, she saw Sally Marie who was on her way up with a basket of muffins and cookies for the family, before she had to go to the funeral home. Maggie read in the paper that the funeral was being held tomorrow, and had arranged for flowers to be sent. The family was very touched with Sallie Marie's kindness and concern for Chad, whom she had never even met, especially considering the grief she was going through herself.

Just before Chris and Savannah were going to leave to go to Chad's to shower and get some rest, the doctor came in. He had everyone's immediate attention.

"Shortly after I spoke to you last night, Chad's medication was stopped, and a few hours after that, he was taken off the ventilator. His vital signs have remained stable throughout the night, and he is breathing on his own."

Smiles spread throughout the room as they breathed a sigh of relief.

The doctor hesitated for a moment, his splayed fingertips touching as if making a steeple, before going on. "However, he has not, as yet, shown any signs of regaining consciousness, or responding to verbal commands or stimulus. I must tell you, that while it *is* possible he's still reacting to the medication he was given to keep him unconscious, it is highly unlikely. He should have been showing signs of responding by now. Until he does, it will be very difficult to tell the possibility of, or severity of, any brain damage, because neurological tests are not possible to conduct when the patient is in a coma."

Mrs. Edwards and Savannah each turned into the comfort of their husband's arms, while Sally Marie grasped Maggie and Cheyenne's hands.

"Are you telling us Chad is in a coma?" Mr. Edwards asked apprehensively.

"I want you to be prepared for the distinct possibility. As I said, he should be responding by now."

"Can I see him?" Maggie asked abruptly, bringing the doctors attention to her.

"Your relation to him?" he asked.

She hesitated. "Close friend," she reluctantly admitted.

He shook his head, "At this time only immediate family are allowed access to the patient—"

"But—" she tried to interrupt, to tell him the extenuating circumstances.

The doctor held up his hand stopping her so he could explain, and continued, turning his focus back to Chad's parents.

"If there is no decline in his condition, I have ordered him to be moved to a room where visitation is still limited, but more liberal. We believe some patients are able to hear everything around them and I feel it would be beneficial for Chad to be aware that his family, and close friends," he acknowledged Maggie with a nod, "are here for him. As soon as his move is complete and he is settled, I'll see to it you be allowed to see him." He looked back at Mr. and Mrs. Edwards for confirmation. They both agreed. "I hope to see you shortly then," he said. Every one thanked him as he took his leave.

Around 2:00 p.m., approximately six hours later, a nurse named Gale was on duty, and came to get Maggie at the doctor's request. She informed everyone Chad was still unconscious and unresponsive, before taking Maggie to see him.

On the way back, Maggie tried to brace herself, but she gasped in shock when she stepped into the room and saw his swollen and bruised face. She froze in place. Closing her eyes, she prayed for the strength not to break down, and when she thought she could be strong, tentatively made her way to his side. She lightly touched his hand, afraid she might hurt him. Every inch of him looked discolored or scratched. She pulled in a ragged breath, with tears threatening, in spite of her fighting them back. Softly, she called his name.

"Chad?"

There was no reaction, no sign he knew she was there. She tried to swallow past the lump in her throat, and started again. "Chad? It's me, Maggie. I hope you can hear me. I have something important I have to tell you. Please, *please* don't be upset Chad, but I've read your journals." She hesitated briefly, looking for a flinch, *anything*, then quickly explained. "I know they're personal and you have every right to be mad, but please hear me out. I didn't *know*, Chad. I had no idea. I'm sorry I didn't understand, and I'm sorry about how I reacted when you didn't come around. All I knew was how much I needed you in my life, in *Car's* life. I was afraid of losing you. Don't you see, Chad?" she pleaded. "You have no reason to feel so guilty. There is *no* one Cole would have wanted to take care of us more than you. It's perfect really, because there's no reason for either of us to hide how we feel about Cole! We both loved him very much, and still do, except he's not here now. We have to go on, Chad." She stopped for a moment, searching for any indication that he could hear her. Finding none, she went on. "I know how difficult it was for you when Car asked you to be his new daddy, and I'm sorry for that, but I'm *not* sorry he asked you." Her voice started to break when she began to cry. "So please come back to us Chad. Please come back to *me*." She stood, and leaned over his bed to kiss him lightly. Then she whispered in his ear, "I love you, too."

EPILOGUE

Four Years Later

Maggie and her Uncle Charles just finished having a nice conversation, and he was now ready for a nap, so she took him by the hand and helped him in from the deck to the family room, which had been converted to a bedroom for him. When she heard he was going to have to go into a nursing home, she knew she had to do something. So with the help of her family, she remodeled the family room, because all the bedrooms were upstairs, and turned the formal living room—which never got much use anyway other than her piano lessons—into their new family room.

Uncle Charles had been there for about two months now, and Maggie had taken an extended leave of absence from teaching because taking care of her family was her number one priority. Everything was going smoothly, thanks in part to two of the nurses she had gotten very close to during Cole and Chad's time in intensive care, Elizabeth and Dorothy, who each came by as often as possible to check in on Maggie and her beloved uncle. And at least twice a week, Sally Marie would come by to visit, and to sit with Charles if Maggie had errands, because they enjoyed each other's company so much. They had already become very dear friends to each other.

After making sure Uncle Charles was comfortable, Maggie went to the new family room, which was still a work in progress, and continued her project. She turned on the radio to listen to some music while she worked. She was going through the books in the bookcase, and taking out her old schoolbooks she hadn't looked at in years, to put in the attic and make room for new books. As she pulled a volume out, something fluttered to the floor. She picked it up and smiled in remembrance when she read it.

It was the fortune she had gotten after her first dinner with Cole and Chad. "A Fortune Foresees Your Future...In Your Future, Four C,S

Are Your Fortune." She remembered Cole's translation, and smiled. Suddenly a chill ran up her spine. Just then, the door opened and Car came in, now twelve years old, and quite handsome.

"Mom, look what Dad got for me at the store!" he said, holding up a new football.

She looked from Car to Chad, who had just entered, carrying their two year old daughter, Sydney, who was holding a new doll. She sighed at her obviously futile attempt to make more room.

"We're going to need a bigger house, aren't we?" she asked in admonishment.

Chad just gave her a sheepish smile, shrugged his shoulders, and said innocently, "I love you, Pretty Lady."

Her heart did a flip flop, and her resolve to be firm about the kids getting too many toys, melted. "I love you, too," she said. She looked back down at the fortune she was holding, goose bumps still on her arms, and for the first time, she realized there was no typo after all! It made perfect sense! Four C,S. Cole, Chad, Car, Charles, Sydney. Her family! Her Fortune!

As if on cue, *Angel Eyes* by Jeff Healey came on the radio. It was the song Chad had requested and dedicated to her at their first wedding anniversary celebration for them to dance to and it was very special to both of them. She raised her eyes and met Chad's. Looking at her family and their smiling faces, she was so thankful! She couldn't even imagine what their lives would be like if she hadn't found out the things he hadn't told her!

ACKNOWLEDGMENTS

There are SO many people I need to thank, without whom this would have been much more difficult to come to fruition! First and foremost I need to thank my mother, Ann Edwards, for all of your love, support and encouragement, but most of all for repeatedly being subjected to draft after draft to edit and critique, only to be presented with a new "final draft". Thank you for everything! I love you!

My dear husband Rodney, I could not have done this without you! Thank you for your help with the story line, the characters, the writing, and listening to me read to you endlessly for your opinion! Thank you for writing the two beautiful songs and putting them to music! I thank you for tip toeing around while I was writing, and most of all, I thank you for doing the cooking so that I could devote as much time as possible to the book! You are right up at the top of the list for having faith in me, and giving me the courage to do it! I love you more than you know!

Next I have to thank my sister Maresa Pezzulo and my niece Gabrielle Pezzulo, for subjecting them to the same torture as my mom! I couldn't have done this without all of your help and valuable insights and suggestions! (among a million other things you did to help!) Thank you for believing in me! Love you!

Thank you, Nora Jacome for reading, editing, and offering valuable advice for my first draft. I apologize for putting you through that! It was definitely a "rough" draft! I sincerely appreciate everything you did and your kind words of praise!

What can I say to Linda Wright, Shirley Ortez, Janie Charles, and Nancy Smead, for my jumping the gun and subjecting you to what I thought was the finished product long before it was ready? Well I thank you so much for reading it and telling me that it was good! I hope you will find the real finished product better!

Cathy New Trumbull, you are such an unending source of inspiration and praise! Thank you so much for all of your help in reading the manuscript, the editing process, with photo's for the cover, and all of your encouragement! I can't thank you enough!

Barbie Holbert Marland, you spent so much time carefully editing my book and I thank you from the bottom of my heart! I sincerely appreciate all of your time, advice, words of wisdom, and encouragement!

A big thank you to Randy Clark, the owner of Old College Inn, on Cumberland Avenue, in Knoxville, for your valuable information regarding the background of OCI! I hope this book brings you new customers to try the food that I've heard is great! Best wishes!

I also need to thank Carolyn Jourdan for answering so many of my questions about creating an e-book! I sincerely appreciate you letting me interrupt your busy schedule and for offering your help! I wish you continued success on all of your great books!

Many thanks to Lisa King, and Geri Cox at Colonel Littleton Ltd for answering my emails and going to bat for me! Colonel Littleton, I am so grateful for your permission for the use of the image of your #9 Leather Journal for my title page! It was perfect!

Last but not least, I want to thank our children, grandchildren, and the rest of our family for your love and support, and for giving me ideas for my book from memories of some of your antics over the years! I love you all! Please forgive me if I have overlooked anyone. It was not intentional!

A NOTE FROM VICKY WHEDBEE

Thank you so much for reading *Things He Hadn't Told Her*! If you enjoyed it, please take a moment to leave a review at your favorite online retailer such as Amazon, and please tell a friend about it! Word of mouth is priceless!

I welcome contact from my readers. You can find me on social networking. I wish you many blessings!!

71775828R00202

Made in the USA
Lexington, KY
28 November 2017